I0522481

Joe knew something wasn't right, but knowing it and proving it were two very different things...

Mark paused and Joe heard papers rustling. "Obviously, the Albany Coalition for Families got three million dollars approved during this six-month time frame. The other non-profits got a little more or a little less, with the approved grants spread out so there would not appear to be a pattern. In three of the non-profits, the president or executive director, either died, retired, or left to be with their families during the last six months as well."

"So, Ted's not alone?" Joe asked.

"Not at all," Mark said. "This seems to be a very well planned and coordinated effort to loot non-profits and foundations across the country, Joe."

Joe started to get the picture. Ted Simmons was killed on I-90E, going home to East Greenbush. He fell asleep at the wheel, rolled over several times, and hit an abutment on the road. He never made his retirement. Joe knew that Dan had his suspicions about his father's death. Joe did as well but didn't believe he could prove anything.

However, in light of the other deaths and the mugging of Jim Clark in his own parking lot, it might prove the group's undoing. If this was all true about the Hispanic Management Outreach program, the results from the coroner's office might eventually prove Joe right.

After ten years in the Coast Guard, graduation from the Academy, and receiving his MBA, Joe Traynor takes his first real job at a small nonprofit agency in Albany, New York, working to help impoverished youth. But when he discovers a national rip-off and money-laundering scheme, Joe fears that he might have bitten off more than he can chew, and he's not sure if his education, training, and experience in the Coast Guard—the only other job he's ever had—have fully prepared him for what's now happening. As the bodies begin to pile up, Joe can only hope that he and his friends can stop the gang responsible before any more people are killed…

KUDOS for *Death But No Taxes*

In *Death but No Taxes* by Daniel J. Barrett, Joe Traynor is out of the Coast Guard and working for a foundation in New York. The book is a prequel to the series with Joe in the Coast Guard. Now he is trying to save his foundation from those who would use it for personal gain. The story has a solid plot with lots of twists and turns that keep and hold your interest. I enjoyed the book immensely. It was nice to see where it all started and meet the early characters I'd heard about in the other books. A good read. ~ *Taylor Jones, The Review Team of Taylor Jones & Regan Murphy*

Death but No Taxes by Daniel J. Barrett is a prequel to his Joe Traynor series. The story takes place in new York before Joe starts working for the US Coast Guard as a special investigator. Actually, he's between stints in the service, working for a non-profit organization helping New York's underprivileged youth. But things are not what they seem, and Joe is forced to protect the organization from people who want to use it for illegal purposes. The story is fast-paced and exciting with the extra appeal of seeing familiar characters before the regular series take place. I liked getting to know Joe when he was young and idealistic. An excellent addition to this intriguing series. ~ *Regan Murphy, The Review Team of Taylor Jones & Regan Murphy*

ACKNOWLEDGMENTS

Once again, I would like to thank everyone at Black Opal Books, including Lauri Wellington, Faith, and Jack for their dedication and attention to detail. It is appreciated.

Books by Daniel J. Barrett

Conch Town Girl Series

Death but No Taxes (Prequel)
Conch Town Girl
Can't Sing or Dance
Taking Care of Your Own
Never Say Never

DEATH BUT NO TAXES

Daniel J. Barrett

A Black Opal Books Publication

DEDICATION

I would like to dedicate this book to my wife, Sandy, whom I love dearly, and to my close friend, Peter Stoll, whose death came too soon and he is missed.

CHAPTER 1

It was Wednesday, the day after New Year's, and only a handful of staff members were in the building working. There were no classes for another week, with a new class of thirty youth coming in for job training next week. It was snowing. They expected several more inches to add on to what they had already gotten over the holidays.

It was extremely cold. They were in the heart of winter in upstate New York and there were only seventy-eight days until spring, and only seventy-five days to Saint Patrick's Day, but who was counting?

Joe Traynor saw Ted go down the hall and into Luis's office. Joe wondered what he wanted with him. Ted had been very nervous the last couple of weeks. As president of the Albany Coalition for Families, Ted was always very concerned for the organization he'd started almost thirty years ago. He was less directly involved than he used to be, but he was still very much in charge.

Ted waved to Joe and then went into Luis's office. Joe could hear every word with the door still open. "Luis," Ted asked, "can I meet with you alone for a few minutes, in my office?"

"I'll be right with you," Luis said. As he walked into

Ted's office, he raised an eyebrow. "Ted, what can I do for you?"

"Luis, I would like to fully review where we are with our new grants and where we are going."

Luis frowned. "What's the problem?"

"No problem, Luis. Let's talk about the George Johnson and the Block Foundation grants that we just received," he said. "Two million dollars is more than we ever received at one time, and I won't lie to you, I am very nervous about doing everything we said we would to complete the grants."

"Ted, I am fully committed to seeing these grants through, even if it takes me past my two year commitment," Luis said. "I've lined up all the vendors and colleges we need to train the students and to have them pass their GED test before they actually secure a job. We've already spent two-hundred-fifty thousand dollars in training activities since the George Johnson grant came in, and we're prepared to do the same thing with the Harold Block Charitable Foundation, which is another million-dollar-a-year grant-funded program. If you don't trust me, Ted, I don't know what to tell you. I can always go back to the National Child Welfare Association and start over at a new non-profit somewhere."

There it was, thought Ted. *What you wish for, you may get.* He had better pacify Luis. He couldn't have him walking out now. Ted was between a rock and a hard place, and he had put himself in that position. Now, he knew why Joe was so quiet when all this happened. Ted had better talk to Joe and ask him what he thought about all this. He knew he hadn't been as close to Joe lately as he was before Luis came. Joe was like a son to Ted and one of his own son's best friends. He didn't want to lose Joe, either. Luis's commitment from the national organization was only for two years. Ted had to live with it.

He'd brought Luis in to change the organization and Luis certainly did that. But was it for the better? Maybe Ted was nervous about nothing. His board was thrilled and the community seemed charged up. At this point, he guessed the best thing to do about it was nothing, and that's what he had better do, absolutely nothing.

"No of course not, Luis, no problem. We're well aware of how hard you work, and, as a matter of fact, we knew you haven't even taken one day of vacation since you started in August. We're very pleased with our progress. It's the best in our history," Ted replied. "How about letting us show you our appreciation by giving you a bonus week of vacation and a few thousand dollars in addition, for all you have done. We will even pay the taxes on your bonus so you don't have a problem."

"Okay," Luis said. "Thank you, Ted."

God, that was easy, Luis thought. He would plan a vacation right after the Ettinger grant submission, coming up shortly. Receiving two one-million-dollar grants in a row might have been too much too soon. The family needed the money. He had to see Frank Ramone, anyway. Maybe he would meet him in New York City, and they could discuss how Luis's father felt about this. He also needed to meet with the Hudson Foundation, now that Alicia Torres was fully established there. Then he had to go to Hartford, Connecticut, to see Dave Perez at the Hartford Career Center. Luis was in charge of the entire east coast for his father. He knew he had done a great job of setting up the Albany Coalition for Families to run all the drug trade in Albany as well as loot the organization as soon as the grant money started rolling in. No one there had a clue what was going on. It was like they ran a business in the 1970s instead of 2013. Luis had to make sure that the other non-profits, that he was in charge of, ran as smoothly. If they were not, he would not be very patient and there would be dire consequences for failure.

Dave Perez was not doing well over in Hartford. He might have had the brains for an MBA but he certainly wasn't street smart. He didn't command respect like Luis did. That was his downfall. They handed him the George Johnson Foundation grant proposal to apply for, knowing it was already wired on the inside, and Luis gave him the blueprint. The grant was approved, but for less than half of what they asked for and Dave left a half a million dollars on the table, the idiot. The inside person, selected by those above him, was upset. She was judged on the money passed from her foundation to the non-profit. There were no excuses for failure.

Luis's own vendors were selected and Dave couldn't even sell it to his board or the president of the center in Hartford. *What the hell is his problem? Maybe he needs to be replaced by the next graduate out of the Hispanic Management Outreach program we set up.*

Now, Luis had to do something with Ted Simmons. He'd started to get in the way. *We're going to win the next two grants*, he thought, *because both are already wired. We don't need any more questions on how it will affect the organization.* Luis really didn't care. This was about cash going to his father, the main general of the Mexican Mafia. His father, in jail for life for murder, ran a better organization in prison, than any of the non-profits they selected to infiltrate. For Christ sake, the grants were already wired and promised to their own vendors. They had to move the cash back to the families to pay their bills. His father and the other gang officers were counting on Luis to continue supporting their families. He and the other twenty-nine members had been groomed for this since the day they entered high school. All thirty had clean records and were protected from the streets. They had to be squeaky clean or none of this would have happened. Thirty high school students at the Los Angeles High School were selected for an advanced education, all sons and daughters of the Mexican Mafia members, who were still in jail. They would carry on their work as well-educated second generation highly qualified individuals.

They would run the nation's charities and funders through a complex scheme thought of and carried out in partnership with well-respected professionals throughout the country. Morality was in the eyes of the beholder. Family came first. Their blueprint came directly from the Italian Costa Nostra, the Italian Mafia. The Mexican Mafia was geared up for the twenty-first century. The Italian Mafia was now into legitimate businesses bought and paid for over the years through previous crimes and laundered funds.

Clean cash emerged and became the capital for second and third generations of the same families. They now paid taxes, were community leaders, and served tirelessly on boards for the betterment of their communities. The Mexican Mafia expanded the blueprint and went beyond, becoming members on the inside, who made investment decisions, and were also successful, well-educated, and experienced business people.

Chapter 2

Joe had just gotten home from work, and he was going to meet Mary for dinner later on. They had been going out for the last few months after he came back from Mark's fortieth birthday party, and Joe had finally asked her out. On the ride home, his thoughts had turned to Ted and Luis and what was being planned behind closed doors. Joe now reported to Luis, and before that, to Ted directly. This was his third year at the Coalition and he did quite well before Luis arrived. Joe filed both grants for Luis. He did all the paperwork and prepared all the legal documents required. He was quite impressed with Luis's acumen but there was something bothering Joe that he couldn't put his finger on. He would just have to bide his time and see where it led. Hopefully, everything that Luis promised would come to fruition for the benefit of the impoverished living in the greater Albany community. That was Joe's goal, and he had hoped it was Luis's as well.

It was Tuesday night, it was still snowing, and the roads were not great, but Joe really wanted to see Mary. He had been busy at work and so was she, due to the upturn in accounting paperwork caused by new vendors and scheduling problems as part of the grant process. They were full out workwise, and it would be this way for some time. They never thought there was such a thing as too much money. What a problem to have. Now, the entire staff was not too sure that the increased workload with the same staffing was feasible.

The phone rang and Joe picked it up. "Hello."

"Joe, it's Missy." Missy was Joe's right hand assistant at the Coalition. "I'm sorry that I called you at home but did you see the news tonight?" she asked.

"No, I just got in," Joe said.

"Joe, I hate to tell you this. I am still at the office and a call went through to Doug Jacobs. Ted was killed in a car crash on I-90 only a few miles from his house in East Greenbush," she said. "He was almost home. He was less than 500 feet from the Exit 10 ramp at Miller Road."

He was less than a half a mile from his house off of Miller Road, Joe thought.

"We don't know what happened yet but, evidently, they think he may have fallen asleep at the wheel on the way home. He rolled over several times and his chest was crushed against the steering wheel. That's a really bad stretch of I-90. There have been a ton of accidents there this winter," she said. "His wife called the office as well and she is quite hysterical. Claudia is alone at home, her daughter Susan is away. Dan is on his way to his parent's house."

"Missy, that's just terrible," Joe said. "I probably should go and see Claudia. Thanks for the call. I'll call you later. I put your number into my speed dial." *I had better call Mary. I'm sure Claudia is still at home.* He would call her first and ask Mary to come.

"Mary, it's Joe," he said.

"Are you on your way, Joe? I'm starving," Mary said.

"Mary, Ted was in a very bad car accident on the way home tonight. I'm afraid he died."

"Oh my God," she said. She started to cry.

"I am going to see Claudia. Dan is on the way. Do you want to go with me? I'll pick you up."

"Yes, of course," Mary said.

"If you don't mind, could you make a few sandwiches for the drive? I was going grocery shopping this weekend and I have almost no food here. It will be a long night. Pack an overnight bag if you want. I'll be there in twenty minutes."

He packed a few things and went right up Route 2, straight up the hill across the Hudson River, to Mary's apartment. She met him at the door and they took off for East Greenbush. He knew where Ted lived because he had been there several times. Joe called Dan, Ted's son, and told him they were on their way. Dan said he would meet them at his father's house shortly. Dan and Joe were good friends. They were about the same age. They talked regularly and went out for drinks every few weeks. Previously, they talked a lot about where Joe had been and what he had done before working for Dan's father. Dan told Joe how it was growing up with his father and mother, which was much different from the way Joe grew up in a construction family.

Dan was an attorney in a big firm in Albany. He was just turning thirty. Before he hung up, Dan told Joe that his sister was out of town visiting her husband, Jake's, family. She was twenty-eight years old and had two young children—a girl age three, Olivia, and a newborn son, Josh, only four months old. At least Ted got to see his new grandson over the holidays before he died.

They made it to Ted's house in about forty-five minutes because of the weather. The front porch light was on and a police car was stationed outside. Joe walked to the police car and asked the officer if anyone was with Claudia. He said they were just finishing up the paperwork and his partner was inside explaining to her what her next steps should be, including the funeral home, attorney, and things that would be very pressing very soon. It was good that Dan would be around, especially to handle any legal issues.

Joe told the officer who Mary and he were and asked him if the officer could knock on the door to see if she would like them to come in. The officer took another five minutes to finish his paperwork and then headed up the front stairs to ask. The door reopened almost immediately and Claudia reached out for both Joe and Mary, at the same time. She was a wreck. They held her and told her how sorry they were for her loss.

There were never enough words, or the right words to be said at a time like this. Joe hugged her as he went in the door. "Claudia, I'm so sorry."

Mary did likewise. She asked Claudia if she would like some tea, or coffee, or even a drink.

"Dan's on his way," Claudia said.

"I talked to Dan on the way, in the car," Joe said.

"I tried to call Susan but they were out to dinner," Claudia said. "She's out of town, and she has her cell phone off."

"I'll continue to call her if you want and, after connecting, I will hand you the phone," Joe said.

"Thanks, Joe."

Word of her father's death should come from Claudia not from him, he thought, as hard as that would be for Claudia. Joe knew Susan's husband Jake and, perhaps, he would pick up his cell first. Claudia gave Joe his number and he dialed. Joe finally got through to Jake and handed the phone to Claudia. She went through what happened. There was a pause and evidently Jake told Susan what happened. She was crying when she spoke to her mother. *God, this is awful.*

What they believed happened was that the roads were not only bad but Ted also had sleep apnea, and he wasn't getting any rest, at least not enough to fully function. He was just tested and his C-Pap apnea mask was ordered and on the way, but it was a little too late. *Timing really sucks sometimes.*

"They think he fell asleep at the wheel and—because of the conditions of the road, and going at least sixty miles an hour on I-90—they think he slid and then rolled down the embankment near Exit 10, only a half a mile from his house," Claudia said. "Everyone knows this is a bad stretch of road in the wintertime."

Dan finally arrived and Joe met him at the door. The roads were even worse coming out of downtown Albany. "I got stuck behind a bus for twenty minutes," Dan said. "Finally getting free, I made it to I-787 and then I-90." It was the same route his father took on the way home.

"Dan, I'm very sorry about your Dad," Joe said. "You know how much I respected your father, and you and your family mean a lot to me. Whatever you need, I will be there for you," he said.

"Joe, thank you, that means a lot to me and my family. How's my mother? Not good I suspect," he said.

Joe nodded, and bowed his head. "No, Dan, she's not doing very well. It's so sudden and tragic."

Dan went into the living room and put his arms around his mother and they both wept. "Mom, does Susan know yet?"

"I just got off the phone with her," his mother said. "She and Jake and the kids are coming home first thing in the morning."

∽∾∽

Mary and Joe stayed until eleven p.m. They said their goodbyes and left. Joe took her home and headed to Troy after dropping her off at her apartment. "You should probably come in to work on time tomorrow because I'm sure there will be a big announcement to the staff on what the plans will be to honor Ted."

Joe was sure everyone would attend the wake and funeral, and a reception at the Coalition afterward. On the way out of Ted's home, Dan had taken Joe aside. "Joe, would you oversee all the events surrounding the burial services and reception?"

"Sure, Dan." Joe said. "I would be honored."

Joe spoke to Mary on the way back to her apartment, and she said she would do anything he asked of her. Joe really couldn't believe that this had happened. He remembered the death of his own mother only a few short years ago. When his mother died in 2008, Joe had just resigned from the Coast Guard. He felt empty. Empty, not only because of her death, but also about the time they lost not being together, while he was away at sea. Joe knew she was sick but he just couldn't get home. He was in the intelligence division of the Coast Guard, and what he did was classified. They spoke on the phone as best they could, but it was not often. When his father called to tell him she died, it was the darkest day of his life.

Ted's sudden death felt very bad. He'd had a few health issues, but dying in a major automobile accident, was tragic. Joe had just seen him and talked to him only that day. He'd waved to him in the hall. Now, he would never have the conversation that he needed to have with him about Luis. Joe was upset with Ted because he felt abandoned in favor of Luis, and he never got a chance to talk to him about it.

Joe knew Ted wanted to retire on an up note, and this

was just awful. He was sixty years old and saved all his life for his retirement, which was coming in two more years. He never made it. Joe thought that tomorrow would probably feel even worse because it would affect everyone, including the staff, the board, the community, people in the places where Ted volunteered, his church community, and his own personal friends. Clients at the Coalition probably didn't even know his name and, more than likely, didn't even care. They would be upset because the Coalition would be closed the day of his funeral. The poor always needed the necessities of life, every day, and closing would be a hardship. Still, Ted would be missed. He'd given Joe his first real professional job. Joe would do everything he could to ensure that the following days would give a little peace to Ted's family.

Chapter 3

Joe got to work early again around seven-thirty a.m. No one was there yet, except the people waiting outside for the food bank to open. It was like another day and nothing really happened. Maybe it was a dream. That was short lived. As staff came in, there was a buzz about what happened.

The chairman popped his head into Joe's office. "Where's Luis?"

Joe shook his head. "I don't know. He probably isn't in yet. He said he wanted to have a group meeting with all the building staff and tell them what the board planned concerning Ted's death, so I imagine he will be in soon."

Rumors were that they would take the day off for the funeral and have a reception for everyone afterward at headquarters on Central Avenue in Albany. Satellite offices were to close and the staff was to show up for the reception after the funeral. Emergency counselors and those with direct child supervision would come when they were able, after their duties were completed and replaced by other staff. It was a twenty-four hour a day job, with no let up. Joe had asked the maintenance staff if they would find a black sheet and have it placed over the front door as a sign of respect and mourning. They said they would be honored to because they were friends with Ted as well. Everyone was a friend of Ted Simmons.

The board members came into the large meeting room, and George Fontaine, the chairman, spoke to the assembled staff. "Ladies and gentlemen, as you probable are already aware, our beloved president, Ted Simmons, was killed in a car crash last night. Our prayers go out to his family, friends, and all those who had loved him, over so many years. He will be greatly missed."

Joe turned around and saw that Mary had tears in her eyes as well as countless others in the room.

"I spoke to Ted's wife, Claudia, and his son, Dan, and conveyed my and the boards' condolences," Mr. Fontaine said.

On the way out last night, Dan asked Joe to be a pallbearer and he told him that he would be honored. Even though it was not known around the office, about Mary and Joe going out together, Dan was told by his father, a few nights prior to his death. "Both my mother and father are very pleased for both of you," Dan said. He had known his father very well. "Dad thought the world of you and Mary, and he was a little ashamed that he didn't seek you out more over the last several months. Joe, my father didn't want to upset the apple cart. It was probably one of only a few things my father probably regretted before he died."

"Since this is now Wednesday morning," Mr. Fontaine said, "I was told by the family the wake will be held at the Warner Funeral Home on Washington Avenue in Rensselaer, near the East Greenbush line, on Thursday, from four p.m. to eight p.m. Ted and Claudia were parishioners at the Rensselaer Methodist Church, right down the street on Washington Avenue, only two blocks away. The church funeral service is to be held on Friday morning at ten a.m., with a smaller service at the Albany

Rural Cemetery, only three miles from the Church, off of I-787 north." He swallowed back his tears before continuing. "At two p.m., a reception will be held for family and friends right in this conference room at the Coalition headquarters."

Dan asked Joe to follow up with the caterer, and reception requirements today and make sure everything was ready.

"I'll also be pleased to help in anyway needed," Mary said.

Others also knew that Joe would be running the reception and also offered to help serve guests and cleanup afterward.

Joe conveyed his thanks to the gathered crowd of employees and told them that if anyone needed transportation, they would hire buses so that volunteers, staff, and clients could attend both the wake and funeral. He conveyed that the burial was at the Albany Rural Cemetery and would be a private family affair.

"The buses will leave the Coalition at three-fifteen p.m. for the Wake," Joe told the gathered crowd. "And eight forty-five a.m. on Friday for the funeral, returning immediately after everyone has said their condolences to the family. Everyone is invited to the Coalition reception at two p.m. on Friday afternoon." Joe called the Mayor and City Council members to let them know of the schedule.

✂✄✂

Tonight, Joe had to call Julie, who was finishing up at Brown University, in Providence, Rhode Island. Joe met Julie Chapman when she was in fifth grade in Key Largo, Florida, when he was a nineteen-year-old first-year seaman. He and two other Coasties walked into Key

Largo School, an elementary school in the Monroe County School District, and his life changed. Part of his duties, while assigned to the Islamorada Coast Guard facility, was to participate in Career Day, to recruit and inform young students on the history of the Coast Guard, and serve as a recruitment arm, especially for those who lived for the sea, as was the case in the Keys.

That day, he met Julie Chapman, a ten-year-old girl, who cornered him and asked if she could get a tour of his facility. Come to find out, both her parents died very young, and she lived with her grandmother, Tillie. What started as a small favor became a lifelong friendship. She was the little sister he never had, and Tillie became his surrogate mother while he was in the Keys. From that first encounter, Joe had kept his word and had called Julie every Wednesday night, no matter where he was, if he was near a phone and not in danger. Sometimes, he was in the middle of a large drug interdiction in South Florida and was unable to call. Tonight, he would speak to her for a few minutes, tell her what was going on, and then he would have to cut the call short. She understood, at a very early age, about the calls. He explained to her what he was involved in, and sometimes, he would not be available. He hadn't missed more than a handful of calls ever since. Joe made a point of keeping his word.

⌘⌘⌘

Joe was sure the local paper would have the news of the accident and everyone would have looked in both the newspaper and online for the schedule of services. He asked the tech staff to put all the information on the website. George asked senior management to speak at the funeral and all said they would, including Luis.

After George broke the news about Ted's death to

the gathered staff, Luis cleared his throat. "I have only been here a short time, but I truly admired Ted for giving the organization a new vision for the future, which would ensure his legacy for years to come." He paused, scanned the group. "We will have a plaque dedicated to Ted, with a ceremony in early spring. In Ted's honor, we will also have a portrait of him, to be commissioned, and hung in the boardroom as the first Coalition president."

Everyone clapped politely.

Hell, Luis, it isn't an award ceremony. Joe wondered just how sad Luis really was. He'd seen him arguing with Ted just prior to Ted's leaving that fatal evening. Joe still felt a little ashamed of himself for being mad at Ted for ignoring him. *That's water over the dam now.*

Dan and his mother asked Mary and Joe to be at the wake early so that Joe could introduce the family to some of the people who they didn't know. Because of Joe's increasing contacts with the community over the last two years, and his working with just about everyone in the building and satellite offices, he was fully prepared for the task. Mary would stand with them as well, in case he didn't know some of the employees. She was in the accounting office and met every employee at one time or another. They were at the wake at three-fifteen p.m. They were almost forty-five minutes early and it was the same time that the buses, filled with mourners, had left the Coalition's headquarters.

Hopefully, staff riding the buses could show their respect and be back to the office by five p.m. Many had small children to go home to or had to be at daycare no later than five-thirty p.m. Joe tried to accommodate them. In addition, several senior staff drove some of the board members, volunteers, and senior clients without rides, several who were unable to get on the bus comfortably. A mourning service had to run like clockwork or all that the people remembered was the difficulty they had attending the services. They couldn't be waiting outside for several hours. Joe had seen this many times. However, many attending would be the poor in Albany and they couldn't spend this amount of time in line. The line would move quickly. These mourners would go first at four p.m.

The funeral home had sandwiches and coffee on hand for the family and those who stayed later. Included were the procession drivers for the funeral and the pallbearers. Mary sat with Susan and her husband, Jake, and the kids. Jake took the kids back to Claudia's house and put them to bed. He'd be back at the funeral home in an hour. Jake's mother watched the kids and the house while everyone else was tied up. You heard a lot about break-ins at homes of mourners who were attending services, and no one wanted that to happen to the Simmons family. The local chief of police, in East Greenbush, personally drove by the house, supplemented by his officers, every hour until all the services, including the reception, were completed. Joe thought that was a very nice gesture, and called the chief to thank him personally.

After the buses arrived and those mourners were allowed in first, the line outside the funeral home was starting to fill. It weaved around the building and down the street for almost a block. The mayors from the cities of Albany and Rensselaer, and the supervisor for the town of East Greenbush were escorted to the side door by the funeral director. They wanted the politicians in and out quickly and quietly. Joe stood near Dan and the family, with Mary at his side, and whispered the names of dignitaries coming through the door whom they didn't know, as well as the names of Coalition staff from the other offices.

Mary did the same for Susan while her husband watched the two little children. By eight p.m., everyone was exhausted, including Mary and Joe. It was a long drawn out day. Tomorrow would be even longer.

Mary and Joe left around nine p.m. and went out to have a quick bite at the diner down the road. She stayed at Joe's apartment and they would leave together for the funeral, an hour early, because they had to be at the funeral home for eight a.m. for a short ceremony. The pallbearers had to carry the casket to the funeral car and then on to the church for a ten a.m. service. They got to the funeral home at eight-thirty a.m. for the church service, and Joe went to the funeral director to get a number for his car. He was with the pallbearers and Mary would drive his car in the procession with a few of her friends from the office. She would go directly from the church to the office to help set up the reception. Joe would go directly to the cemetery and get a ride to the office afterward.

After the brief ceremony at the funeral home, they carried the casket and put it into the hearse. They drove silently with the lights on right to the Methodist Church, two blocks away from the funeral home.

The Methodist service was less than an hour long. Several people spoke about Ted and what kind of man he was, and that it was an honor to have known him. The family sat in the front row, and Joe and Mary sat on the opposite side. Luis sat with them, even though he was not a pallbearer or procession driver. He just didn't seem to fit in.

Joe was not sure if it was a cultural thing. It happened to him when his mother died and his girlfriend from Miami at the time, Jennifer Alvarez, couldn't or wouldn't come to Troy for the funeral. Luis really seemed like a fish out of water, the same as Jennifer. Luis was very appropriate, said the right things, did small talk with the board and other senior managers, but he really wasn't a man of the people. He didn't mingle with any of the staff or even the clients who showed up. He spoke to a volunteer or two but was extremely low-key. Joe wondered why. After a while, and he had been there for several months, Joe didn't try to make friends with him anymore. Luis seemed unapproachable, so Joe left it at that. They were polite to each other and worked together for the good of the Coalition, but Joe would really have to think hard and long about staying if Luis decided to stay after his two-year commitment was over.

They finally left the church after the funeral, driving down Washington Street, with the lights on, led by the hearse and the flower car. The funeral procession got on I-787 toward the Albany Rural Cemetery, right along the Hudson River, on the west side of the river. At that point, the funeral procession consisted of only immediate family members, pallbearers, procession drivers, and a few close relatives and family friends, maybe twenty cars in all. Joe remembered Irish-Catholic funerals. A funeral at Saint Augustine's Church took over the entire north end of the small city of Troy. Every Catholic Church had its own designated cemetery, only a short distance away. Smaller churches in Troy shared a cemetery because the upkeep was almost impossible to maintain with rising costs and low perpetual care income. Fees established years ago never kept pace with inflation. Many cemeteries were so shabby that the family members of those interned had to keep the monuments and immediate area free from weeds and litter.

The Albany Rural Cemetery was an entirely different situation. It was a non-denominational cemetery, placed on the National Register of Historic Places in New York State. Incorporated in 1841, the cemetery was a blend of generations of citizens, originally interred in early burying grounds and transferred there. A president of the

United States was joined by five governors, three members of the continental congress, two members of the Philadelphia constitutional convention, thirteen members of the colonial assembly, eight presidential cabinet members, five ambassadors, and many other senators, congressmen, and judges.

Chester A. Arthur, the twenty-first President of the United States from 1881 to 1885, died a year later in November of 1886. Joe hated thinking about Ted's final resting place. *But residing next to what is considered the worst president in history will have to be overlooked today*, he thought and smiled.

Chester A. Arthur was somewhat of a New York City political hack, raised in Albany, who became vice president under James A. Garfield in 1980. Garfield was assassinated the next year. After just half a year as vice president, Chester A. Arthur found himself, unexpectedly, in the White House. He was born in Fairfield, Vermont. *You might know.* Joe's family was born in Vermont as well. He wondered if any of his ancestors knew the worst president in history.

The graveside service ended, the funeral cars slowly left to go back to the funeral home in Rensselaer, and people piled into their cars to go to the Coalition for the reception. Dan asked Joe if he would like a ride in the limousine. Joe gladly accepted. They were all pretty well chilled to the bone. Dan smiled and passed a bottle of bourbon around. His mother smiled for the first time and said cheers to everyone in the vehicle.

"Okay guys," Claudia said. "Let's get this over with, the sooner the better. I'm sorry to be so flippant, Joe." She sighed. "I guess it's my way of dealing with it."

"Claudia, no problem," he said.

"Joe, we're all very grateful for everything that you have done for us and it will be remembered," she said.

"Please tell Mary as well. Ted was very fond of both of you."

"And we of him," he reiterated.

"If it's any consolation," Dan whispered to him, "Ted really thought Luis was an asshole." He smiled. "My father was caught in the middle by the board."

"I know," Joe said. "And I will do everything I can to make his memory carry on at the Coalition,"

"We know you will, Joe," the family said in unison. "It means a lot to us."

They made it to the reception at the Coalition and the limo dropped them off right at the front door. They walked in and there was a reception line of all the dignitaries, officers, board members—and, farther down, the regular people. Dan went right to the back to greet the volunteers, friends, workers, and clients who wanted to greet and thank the family. His mother and sister stayed in line and provided photo ops for the Coalition. A photographer took pictures of everyone at the reception to be used in the spring quarterly report.

Joe saw Luis standing in the corner, talking to George Fontaine, the chairman, and several board members. *Christ, couldn't they wait until the body was cold.* Dan glanced at Joe, while watching Luis, and gave Joe a wink that Joe believed meant *Fuck you, Luis.* He could have been wrong. He didn't think so. Luis was in his glory, telling them everything that had happened, including the new award and the next two grants going in during the next two months.

"Luis, can you meet a few of us here tomorrow?" Joe overheard George say. "We know it's Saturday but we think it's very important to speak with you in private. Around ten a.m."

Luis nodded politely "Sure," he said. "I'll be there."

Dan took Joe aside and wanted to know what the

clandestine Luis and board discussion was all about.

"Dan, my guess is as good as yours," Joe said, "but I think they may offer your father's job to Luis."

"That's bullshit," Dan said, and he was really pissed. "I hope my mother doesn't hear about this. She'll be devastated. They couldn't even wait until they covered him with dirt?" He was really hurt. "They must have planned this while we were at the cemetery."

"Dan, I have my reservations about Luis, and I am making a few very quiet inquiries," Joe said. "Please don't tell anyone, but I'll let you know when I hear anything. I know we've talked about my background, but you don't know what national security clearances I had in the Coast Guard. I don't have those clearances now, but I still have very close friends who do."

Dan nodded.

Joe went back to talk to Mary. It was getting late, around five p.m. and everyone started to leave. Claudia asked them to come back to the house for dinner, and they were honored. They left the house at nine p.m., completely exhausted once again. At least it was Friday night and they could sleep in tomorrow. They went to Mary's apartment and, as soon as their heads hit the pillow, they were sound asleep.

On Monday when Joe got to the office, the photographer that he hired dropped had off the pictures from the reception. Joe started to look at them to see what they could use for the quarterly report and what would be appropriate to give to Ted's family. Perhaps they could put an album together. He would check. He really didn't know if it was appropriate. He would call the funeral director and ask. It might be a valued keepsake for Claudia.

While looking at the pictures, Joe noticed one with Luis. The photographer was taking somebody else's picture but there was Luis with his right foot up on chair. It was taken from less than ten feet away. Luis had his sock down, totally oblivious to the world. He was scratching his ankle in the picture. The next picture, which was only about five feet away, but from a different angle of the couple being photographed, clearly showed Luis with a tattoo on his right ankle. Joe didn't know what it was at first but it was about an inch square, with an orange background and letters in the middle like calligraphy. Spelled with a small "e," a capital "N" or maybe an "M," he wasn't sure. He couldn't really make out the last letter, but it looked like the first small "e." Maybe "eNe" or "eMe" or something like that.

What the hell is that? Is it a hidden tattoo from where he came from? Is it a California thing? Joe was going to enlarge the picture and see if he could recognize it. He wondered if Luis was ever in a gang growing up. Hell, he was the perfect age, growing up in Los Angeles and being of Mexican descent. You just never knew. Joe thought about emailing the enlarged picture to Mark and Jack, his longtime Coast Guard friends. Both were in the clandestine intelligence division, lifers. Joe would see if either one of them could bring the picture up on the FBI database for gang tattoos. *Who knows what they'll find? Wow, could this open a Pandora's box or what?*

Who was Luis Hernandez really? Did anyone know anything about him other than that he was on loan from the national accrediting organization and he was an Ivy-League MBA graduate? Had anyone ever seen a resume or run a check on him for anything? Joe thought that maybe in their haste, blinded by a free highly educated employee sent to them by the accrediting agency, their due diligence may have been lax. For Ted's family's sake, Joe was going to find out. He owed it to Ted.

CHAPTER 4

Joe wasn't sure what George Fontaine said to Luis but he was pretty sure they were meeting on Saturday, the day after the funeral. Joe went to the office early Saturday morning, arriving around seven a.m. to finish the paperwork he didn't have time to complete during the week, due to Ted's death. Around ten a.m., George Fontaine walked in with Sidney Swartz and the Reverend Henry Smallwood, the pastor of the Albany Baptist Church, which was located in the south end of the city. George, Sidney, and Henry were the senior board members of the Albany Coalition for Families and all had served for over twenty-five years. This had been one of Joe's major concerns when he joined the Coalition.

Ted was almost a youngster, at sixty years old, compared to their board members. The average age was around seventy-five years old, and they were only replaced upon their death, which had not occurred to any member in the last five years. Joe saw Luis meet the three of them as they went up to the boardroom on the second floor. Joe didn't want to be nosey but he really wanted to know what was going on. He thought they were going to ask Luis to run the show but he wasn't sure.

Before Luis first came to the Coalition that summer,

after much discussion, Ted had met with the Board to discuss Luis's pending arrival and his potential impact on the organization for the next two years, if not even longer. Ted told the board that the mission wouldn't change, but as Luis had suggested, in private telephone calls with Ted, the Coalition must grow in this economy or fall to the wayside like so many smaller non-profits in the last few years. Luis mentioned that the president of the United States might have suggested that the United States economy was turning around but you wouldn't know that from the job statistics in the Albany Capital Region. He also said the long term unemployed would still remain unemployed, if not retrained. Youth dropping out of school had no chance without job training for the new economy.

Luis also pointed out to Ted, and sent him articles, that the Capital Region prided itself on being "Tech Valley" but that was only true for those companies moving in, bringing their high tech employees with them or they had to recruit new employees from outside the area. Local colleges were trying to catch up but couldn't fill the immediate needs of those new ventures. Thus, the level of poverty was growing, and now included many of the middle class workers who had drifted lower and lower without employment. The housing market was still in disarray and the homes that sold were only those that went into foreclosure and were bought up by the new economy workers. Luis suggested that the Coalition have a major thrust in that direction if it was to thrive and survive. Ted asked Luis if he would mind going to the board meeting, when he arrived. Ted would introduce him and then he could outline his vision.

Upon Luis's arrival, Ted stood. "As the first item on our agenda, I would like to introduce you to our new Vice President, Luis Hernandez. Luis comes to us from the

National Child Welfare Association, and he'll be here for a minimum of two years. He has both a BS and an IVY-league MBA. As Vice President of Operations and Development, I am sure that he will provide us with valuable assistance in restructuring the Albany Coalition into a state-of-the-art agency that we will be all proud of for years to come. Luis, please introduce yourself."

He did.

The board gave Luis a vigorous round of applause. Ted clapped him on the shoulder. "Luis, would you mind saying a few words to our board members and perhaps outline your initial thoughts as to the direction you think our organization should grow and the state of the economy?"

"I would be more than happy to," Luis said.

He went on to speak for about a half an hour on the growth potential of the organization. "Before I came, I did some detailed research on the region, state of the economy, employment opportunities, the Albany Coalition for Families, and other local non-profits. There is only one way to go, and that's to get more jobs for the poor and disenfranchised, especially for a growing Latino population."

The board listened attentively and gave its initial approval to start the grant process, slowly at first and then to review those results to see their impact on the future of the organization.

"Thank you, Luis," Ted had said, "and thank you members of the board for this very productive session and positive direction for our future."

Since that time, Luis could do no wrong. And now, with a third million-dollar grant underway, and a fourth pending, it would only be natural that the board would be enamored with Luis and ask him to fill the job upon Ted's death.

After that first board meeting, after Luis arrived and made his presentation, Ted came into Joe's office and sounded thrilled to death. Joe thought he might have short-timer's disease and might want to ride the wave of enthusiasm right out to retirement in the near future. If Luis were successful, and so far over the last six months he had been, Ted would have reaped the benefit of a nice golden parachute, gotten credit for his vision, gotten a plaque on the wall, and a nice remembrance.

"Joe, I think we found a goldmine in Luis," Ted said. "You can learn a great deal while he is here. Please take direction from him, and we will all share in this organization's success as we move forward."

In two days, Joe's entire career had been turned upside down. Ten years in the Coast Guard allowed Joe to let things roll off of his back. Hopefully this would too.

Now looking back, Joe thought that he would wait and see what happened. He would be helpful, but his bullshit toleration level had just risen from Code Yellow to Orange—Significant to High—status.

Joe nodded. "Ted, I would be happy to assist in any way I can."

"Thanks, Joe." Then Ted hesitated. "By the way, after lunch, Joe, you, me, and Luis will sit down to see how to start the process. We can meet in his office at one p.m."

෴

Immediately after Ted's death, behind the closed boardroom doors, George called the meeting to order. "Luis, the reason we asked you to come here today was to speak to you about possibly succeeding Ted as interim president of the Coalition. As the senior members of the board, we are quite sure that our request will be honored if you so choose to take the position. We know you have a commitment for two years and you have been here for only six months but we feel you are more than qualified to succeed Ted. If you accept, we would like to make an announcement on Monday to our senior management team and then to the troops."

"Gentlemen, I would be honored to become the interim president of the Albany Coalition for Families. However, as of now, I can only commit to the two years through the NCWA. After all, they are paying for my services through the end of the commitment," Luis said.

Sidney cleared his throat. "Luis, we appreciate that fact and we would also like to contribute twenty-five thousand dollars in additional salary to show good faith to you. After all, you raised two million dollars already and you're working on securing more funding as we speak. We found that to be exceptional, and we wanted to reward you."

Henry nodded in agreement. George concurred.

"We are also aware that Ted wanted you to take a vacation and the Coalition would pay you in addition so you could have a good time," George said.

Sidney and Henry seconded that understanding.

"The one thing that I would like is that no public announcement goes out at this time, Luis said. "I don't want to be bothered by any other outside commitments that usually come with the position."

The board members agreed, and they all shook hands.

"I planned to visit my aunt, my mother's sister, who lives in The Bronx," Luis said. "And I planned on doing some sightseeing. I will be leaving early Monday morning right after the announcement and be back the following week."

The board members said they'd take a vote by telephone over the weekend and they would all be there for the announcement Monday morning at ten a.m.

Joe just finished up his paperwork and was about to leave when Luis stopped at his door.

"Joe, I just wanted you to know that the board asked me to fill in as the interim president for the present time and I accepted," Luis said. "The announcement to senior management will be on Monday."

"Congratulations," Joe said. He wondered what Ted thought right about now, looking down.

"I'll be taking a week of vacation right after the announcement to visit my aunt in New York City," Luis said. "She lives in The Bronx and I haven't seen her in many years. She's my mother's sister," he added.

"Great," Joe said. "Have a good time and we'll see you Monday morning at the announcement."

Luis left the building and Joe decided to call Dan.

"Dan, it's Joe. How are your mother and sister?" he asked.

"They're doing much better. They both got some rest and it helped a lot," Dan said,

"Dan, I don't know how to tell you this, but Luis had been asked to fill in as interim president and the announcement will be made Monday by George Fontaine at ten a.m."

"You've got to be shitting me, Joe," Dan said.

"I wish I were, Dan. I would quit right now, but I don't think your father would want me to put my tail between my legs and take off. And there are too many people here who really care about the Coalition."

"I know, Joe. It's appreciated," Dan said.

"Dan, could you see me as soon as possible. There are things I need to discuss with you, and I think the attorney-client privilege would come in handy," Joe said.

Dan chuckled. "Let's meet at the Denny's at Exit 9

on I-90. It seems appropriate since my dad died at the next exit."

"I'll see you in a half an hour," Joe said.

"Okay, I'll finish up with my mother and sister and leave as soon as I can. We have the final paperwork to complete concerning my father's will."

Joe arrived at Denny's in twenty minutes and got a booth at the back of the restaurant. He saw Dan come in the front and waved to him. Dan sauntered through the crowd. "Could you pick a booth far enough back?" he said smiling. He saw that Joe was in a world of his own and smiled. "Earth to Joe, come in please."

Joe laughed. "Dan, where do I begin?"

"Take your time, Joe, I know you are suffering as well," Dan said.

Joe then explained all his concerns about Luis and what he suspected his ankle tattoo meant. He wasn't sure but he had a very good idea that things were not as they appeared. "And that is why I may need you down the road as my attorney," he said.

"Holy shit, Joe," Dan said. "I never knew what you did in the Coast Guard. But if your suspicions are right, how are you going to prove it?" he said.

"Next week, when Luis is gone. I am pulling in all my ten years of Coastie favors, and I have quite a few," Joe said. "I'll ask Mark to touch bases with Paul Phillips of the Miami FBI. He can give him a call and explain our concerns. I'll also ask him to ask Paul to contact the Albany FBI headquarters at the Post Office Building on Broadway in downtown Albany. In case the shit hits the fan, I may need an attorney. I'll need a good one, and that's you, Dan."

"Thanks for the confidence but I am not a trial lawyer. However, I have some friends who are the best in town," Dan said.

"Good, I may need them." Joe smirked. "Dan, the announcement will be made on Monday and those board members really don't have a clue. They seem to think Luis walks on water. The water is polluted, Dan, and I have to prove it—and I will," he said. "I would tell you what I am going to do, but I don't want you to have any knowledge of anything going on for now. Some of our investigation may prove to be a little gray." Joe smiled. "The fun part though is if I could get the FBI and my Homeland Security friends involved, there would be no trial. I'm not sure but I'll bet Luis could be arrested under the Patriot Act for financial terrorism and sent somewhere that he would not enjoy. He wouldn't be going to Club Fed. He should be going to Club Dead."

"Nice," Dan said in his own sarcastic way.

Joe got to the Coalition early on Monday and already the rumor mill was going strong. Senior managers were all in early for a change, and they all ran around and looked busy. They were waiting for the regime change like no one heard anything about anything over the weekend. George, Sidney, and Henry probably ran a telethon over the weekend to the other board members and from there, Joe was sure his Aunt Ellen in West Brattleboro, Vermont, probably heard as well. He was sure everyone was all a "Twitter," and "Facebook" lit up throughout the region.

An assembly was called at ten a.m. and George Fontaine, as chairman, led the meeting. "It's my honor to introduce Luis Hernandez as the new interim president of the Albany Coalition for Families."

At twenty-eight years old, Joe thought. *What a country.*

Joe saw the resentment on the faces of those long-term employees who couldn't believe the entire episode that led up to this, which included Ted's tragic death. At least they observed a minute of silence in Ted's honor, and then it was business as usual. Luis said all the right things and then told the assembled employees that he was taking a week of vacation to visit his aunt in The Bronx.

God, Joe thought, *what a perfect nephew.*

The sincerity just rolled of Luis's tongue and the accolades, to those who rowed together as a team, almost put Joe over the edge. Afterward, everyone asked Joe what he thought because he worked the closest with Luis. Even the board and the senior managers really didn't know what Luis was like. He appeared friendly, but aloof. He seemed extremely bright, which he was, but there was something about his eyes and direct stare that gave Joe a very uneasy feeling. It was like he looked into an abyss. Although Joe could be wrong. Who the hell knew? But Joe would be active this week. Everyone wished Luis an enjoyable and well-deserved vacation. He left the building by ten forty-five a.m., headed for New York City and The Bronx, they were told.

Joe got Luis's signature on a few documents before he left. Luis patted Joe on the back. " Thanks, Joe, for filling in for me for the week."

No one remembered that Joe ran the entire department, started from scratch by him, only a few short years ago. It was not only Luis's department now, but in fact, it was now Luis's entire operation from top to bottom.

The board members lingered after Luis left. They couldn't say enough nice things about how he stepped up and volunteered to run the organization on an interim basis. It was very evident that by this time next year, he would be the permanent new president of the Albany Coalition for Families. Joe had to figure out exactly what was going on as soon as he could. If Luis was legitimate, all the more power to him. If not, he'd pay.

Joe thought about resigning and perhaps working full

time at the Troy Education Consulting Group where he now served on a part time basis. He would have a talk with Johnathon Mills, the executive director. They got along fine, and they benefited from Joe's participation. Joe got reduced rent on his apartment, which was located at the rear of the consulting group's building, right across the street from Russell Sage College. The bar where Joe worked part time, was also right around the corner. Joe had a lot to think about, but he would not say a word until he understood what had happened. He needed a plan.

CHAPTER 5

The Mexican Mafia prison gang, also known as *LaEme*, was formed in the late 1950s in the California Department of Corrections prison system. It started as a street gang in Los Angeles. It was known for its violent acts toward anyone who crossed them. They had, as a priority, ethnic solidarity and controlled drug trafficking in the area. They were primarily comprised of Mexican-Americans. The gang structure consisted of a chain of command whereby instructions from generals were carried out by captains, lieutenants, and street soldiers. Usually, each prison had separate leadership.

To a certain extent, *eMe* members imitated the traditional Italian Mafia and had a structural framework, which identified them as well organized, and a disciplined organization. They were primarily active in the California and the Texas prison systems. They were different from *Mexikanemi* from Texas and were sometimes confused. They were growing in prison systems throughout the United States. Mexicans now dotted every region in the United States, and many wound up in prison systems in every region.

Financial gain was a powerful motive for gang involvement, especially for impoverished youths with poor education and lack of access to decent jobs. The vast sums of money available through the drug trade had increased the size of gangs, both by recruitment and by longer retention of members. They simply lived longer when organized. Only a few adult gang members made the large sums of money. Aware that courts treated juveniles far more leniently than adults, they shielded themselves by using juvenile gang members as everything from lookouts to gang hit men. Drug trafficking made traditional turf battles bloodier by providing the money for sophisticated weaponry, and it created new sources of conflict as rival gangs fought over lucrative drug territories.

The Mexican Mafia gang member families still resided in Los Angeles, spread throughout the city while the fathers were still in prison. All the "officers" residing in prison still had families including wives, girlfriends, and children living in the Los Angeles area. The generals met with their fellow officers and decided that, like the Italian Mafia, it was time for the Mexican Mafia to start moving to legitimate enterprises.

They sat on tons of cash but couldn't use a lot of it in prison. They used it to keep the wars going, as well as the peace, and the bribes necessary that kept that peace. It went all the way up to the top of the food chain, and included bribes to judges, police officials, and many others. Like the Italians, it was time they moved the third generation, the sons and daughters of gang members, into the mainstream. Those gangbangers, back in the '50s and '60's, were now dead, in jail, or retired. The ones still left alive had great difficulty moving money around, especially without legitimate enterprises from which profits and income could be claimed. Also, new ways to launder their cash needed to be implemented. Since Nine/Eleven, with Homeland Security involvement, it was a very difficult to move cash into legitimate businesses, through banks, insurance instruments, bearer bonds, and other methods that had previously worked. The feds were on to all their games, it seemed. Prison monitoring systems, technology, and other Internet-based means cut into their profits.

It was decided that this third generation of Mexican Mafia progeny would change the way they did business. The street soldiers would always remain the same, had to, no feet on the street meant no collections, no cash, and no business. Working with their legitimate—seemingly so—attorneys, bankers, and accountants, they decided to develop a strategic plan to move their sons and daughters into the main stream of American life. They started to legitimize their activities, and moved cash from illegal sources to legitimate businesses. They changed their way of doing business. New opportunities meant they also needed new methods of laundering their funds, used in creating these new legitimate businesses. The children of the Mexican Mafia would, for all practical purposes, appear to be legitimate but they were still the sons and daughters of criminals and continued that way of life. It was in their blood.

The United States Hispanic population was exploding, growing every year. Gang activity could only go so far and like the trade unions, they had outlived their usefulness and had to protect their way of life. It was expected by the 2020 census that the Latino population in the United States would be at least twenty-five percent of the total legal population—not counting the ten million undocumented Hispanics already here. Hispanics were now mainstreamed into the workforce, just like the Irish, the Italians, African-Americans, and other immigrants, who came to these shores for a better life for their families. Better education and a better way of life had not necessarily meant a high moral standard code. It was hard to get out of the Mafia once in.

The Mexican Mafia formulated their own strategies based on the known facts of the Italian Mafia, the Costa Nostra. The generals, who formulated the strategic plan, watched movies, read books, and learned about organizational structures. They became conversant in finance, business, and wanted their children to follow them, the same as any family owned business. However, these fathers, who sat in prison, would not put up with lazy sons and daughters. They watched and read about lazy children, who felt entitled, who lost the family business in a very short time, a business built by the parents over a lifetime, only to see it go bankrupt. Failure was not an option for these children. There were severe consequences for failure, not only for the youth, but also for their families. Then their fathers who were still in prison faced humiliation, and subsequent death.

CHAPTER 6

Joe remembered, like it was yesterday, when Ted Simmons informed him that a brilliant Ivy-league MBA educated graduate would come to work for two years, at no cost to the Albany Coalition for Families. It was summer, hotter than hell for Albany, really humid. The air conditioners were humming loudly, hanging off the window frames, rattling and dripping onto the clients, standing on the sidewalk, smoking, waiting for their turn to meet with counselors. Mothers and their children were waiting at the food bank. As always, it seemed like a sea of humanity. Ted came into Joe's office and told him about a decision that was made by the board the previous night.

All the executive staff was informed and then key personnel like Joe were told. Ted worked on a program with the National Child Welfare Association, their national certifying agency, located in San Diego California. At the time, he just got back from a one-week national meeting and wanted to tell Joe about an opportunity that a small non-profit would only get once in a lifetime. The Albany Coalition for Families was awarded an Ivy-league MBA graduate, with an undergraduate degree, awarded from a world-renowned California university. This individual would work with Ted as a new Vice President for Operations and Development, all paid for by the association for the first two years. After that, if the individual stayed, the Coalition would have to pay his or her salary and benefits, associated for someone at that level. This gift was worth almost $120,000.00 per year, plus benefits—over a quarter million dollars for two years—and all paid by the NCWA. Non-profit salaries couldn't compete with Wall Street MBA ranges but, after their commitment, the individual could move on or move up, if he or she so desired. It was also believed, by everyone related to the program, that the value received from that hire would be worth far more than the dollars paid. The assigned individual could generate millions in funding, due to their financial and grant writing prowess. After all, they were very well educated individuals and Ted felt in awe that they were selected for this national award.

Ted applied on behalf of the Coalition and upon receiving notification that they won, they were assigned Luis Hernandez, a twenty-eight year-old California native, with both a Bachelors and an MBA, with solid credentials and two years' experience working for Children First, a Southern California child welfare agency. This agency took a state-of-the-art approach to children and youth with complex behavioral health challenges. They combined research-based behavioral health services that included evidence-based therapies and psychiatric services. It was a family-centered effort to identify and address the social, and other needs, of the children as well as the whole family. Ted said this was the direction that he wanted to pursue if they were to succeed and thrive during this economic downturn.

With a twelve-million-dollar annual budget and two hundred and fifty employees, the Albany Coalition for Families needed to grow to twenty million dollars to survive and provide the services that New York State agencies would fund. Grants would only take them so far unless they developed a new strategy, utilizing Mr. Hernandez's strengths.

Joe felt good that they were getting the help they needed from the top and he also knew that, with his own institutional research and IT skills, they could grow and thrive. He looked forward to meeting Luis when he arrived at the beginning of August. He was also assigned to show him around the area, make him feel welcome, and assist Human Resources in getting him settled. This really wasn't his bag. Joe was outgoing to a point but he was certainly not a rah-rah personality.

"I'll do the best I can in getting Luis acclimated," Joe said.

He knew that Luis would arrive on Monday, August sixth. He did some investigation into the National Child Welfare Association's Hispanic Management Outreach program. This program was very expensive and funded by a Los Angeles Real Estate Trust that chose to remain nameless. In 1998, the same time Joe was at MIT, the NCWA developed a program that identified talented Latino youth, freshman and sophomores in high school, who were on track to graduate and did very well on national standardized tests.

Those youth received scholarships to college, if they stayed on course, graduated with honors from high school, and met all the standards for early admission. Those kids were going to a California State University for their undergraduate degrees and then onto graduate school for an MBA. Upon graduation after their MBA, They spent two years working at a California-based nonprofit. They were offered opportunities throughout the country to work in the child welfare field. They were to be a litmus test that all children who, received the same advantages as those with wealthier parents, could perform as well as their counterparts throughout the country. The NCWA started with thirty individuals, male and female. Those with high math skills were chosen first, since the program curriculum was financially based, coupled with social welfare, justice, and administration studies as required.

The funder made up all the difference in cost for each student after they applied for resources as an at-risk, poor, minority, first-time-in-the-family-attending-college student. Each of the thirty individuals selected, successfully obtained almost fifty percent of the cost of their education from the State of California for undergraduate degrees. The two-year MBA program was financed seventy-five percent from the funder and twenty-five percent from the university selected. In all, each student with books, tuition, fees, housing, incidentals, and travel back to home on holidays and summers, when not in an summer internship program, cost almost $50,000.00 per year.

The funder was responsible for half the cost for the undergraduate programs and over $150,000.00 each for two years for their graduate work. As part of the student contract, the individuals worked two years in California, and then signed up for an additional two years across the country with various organizations who wanted and needed the infusion of talent and experience. They especially valued talented individuals who experienced the same conditions growing up in poverty as those they served in their various programs. This unknown funder provided almost $250,000.00 for each of the twenty original participants who succeeded. The rest who did not succeed, still were much further ahead than if they were never participants. The value of this program for the Latino community was immeasurable. The value for the country had a payback twenty-fold. The value to the Albany Coalition for Families was immeasurable since it moved this sleepy non-profit into the twenty-first century.

Joe couldn't argue with success, so, he believed they had nothing to lose and everything to gain, if it worked. His own experience with the Latino community was informed by his years living in Miami working for the intelligence division of the Coast Guard. He was fluent in Spanish, trained for years, because he had to intercept tons of communications from drug cartels almost exclusively from South America and Mexico. It certainly helped him to meet his then girlfriend, Jennifer, and helped him in tight social situations on South Beach and in Little Havana when he needed more information.

Joe never spoke Spanish when he came home and he kept it to myself. He did not want to be the Latino liaison for the organization and he knew that would happen in a heartbeat. He wanted to be good at his craft and not be spread too thin in other areas. If he ever went back to Miami it would once again be helpful. When Joe's mother and father visited him in Miami, they were amazed to hear him order a muffler over the phone from Midas in Spanish, in the middle of the city of Miami. It was the capital of Latin America. Joe just called his local credit union, whose offices were in Albany. He now had to press one for English. Now, he could keep up his Spanish when ordering checks by phone.

CHAPTER 7

As soon as Luis left the building, Joe called Dan at his office.

"Dan Simmons, may I help you?" he said.

"Dan, it's Joe," he said. "Luis was made interim president this morning. I just wanted to let you know."

"Son of a bitch," Dan replied.

"I know, I know," Joe said. "All in due time, Dan. I've started the calls to get the ball rolling. I'm using a burner phone I bought earlier this morning from the Troy Plaza, on my way to work. You never know who's listening. Here's my number," he said, reciting it. "By next week, we should have a lot of information. At that point, I'll probably need your services, as my friend, but also as my attorney. Dealing with the government, especially the FBI and Homeland Security, can go several ways, many of them really bad. I think, after Mark and Jack get me the information I want, we could be in good shape. I'm on your side, Dan. You know that."

"I know, Joe. I'd really like to know if he had anything to do with my father's death. I really don't think so, but it's been nagging at me since he died."

"I was thinking the same thing, Dan. But, he was nowhere around and your father, unfortunately did have sleep apnea, and was driving in bad weather. Let me get to work on this, Dan. I'll let you know as soon as anything pops up."

The next call went to Mark at his office in Fort Lauderdale. Mark said he'd be there all week, except for Thursday afternoon because he had a meeting at the COMMSTA Center in Miami. He patched him in to Jack Forest up in "A" School in Yorktown, Virginia, so they could both listen together. Jack was in charge of the Artificial Intelligence Training Program there and would help.

"Hi, guys, can you hear me?" Joe asked. "I'm outside in my car, freezing my ass off."

"Hi, Joe and Mark," said Jack. "I can hear you fine."

"Me, too," said Mark.

"Okay, ready, guys? This is what I need to know this week, ASAP," Joe said. "Mark, go online to the NCWA technology center in San Diego. You need to pull the electronic files of the thirty students who were originally enrolled in Los Angeles High School and NCWA Hispanic Management Outreach program. First, I need their fingerprints. I know they must have them. They couldn't work for a child welfare association or non-profit without it, even as an intern. Jack, I am sending to both you and Mark a photo of a tattoo taken after the funeral reception for Ted. It clearly shows Luis's ankle tattoo. If I'm not mistaken, it looked like a gang tattoo," he said.

"Maybe when Luis was younger he got it, but it is clear and not faded. He is from Los Angeles and it could mean nothing but I bet it means something. Mark, if that's the case, I need you to try to match the fingerprints of the original thirty members to anyone in the California Prison system, only if none of the thirty have a record, which I suspect is the case. If none have a record, my suspicions of a conspiracy may come true, if they do match someone in prison." Something told him that these thirty individuals were intentionally kept under the radar and out of trouble as part of a larger plan. It was just a guess but it made sense.

"Joe," Jack said, "We have been using a new fingerprint technology which isolates genetic information on parenthood with fingerprint swirls that could possibly match both mother and father."

"I only need the father as a match," Joe said.

"If they match, they would be the sons and daughters of gang members in jail," Jack said. "I'll get on it right away." This also fell within his discretion at his Virginia office. "I have cleared it with my commander," he said. "Joe, the commander was on board with whatever we were doing. Oh, that's right, I am the commander," he said, chuckling through the phone.

Joe snorted. "Mark, I need to know where the original program graduates are now doing their two years' service, like Luis is doing here at the Albany Coalition," he said. "I know from reading all the material that some went to non-profits across the country, some went to private foundations, and some stayed at the NCWA. Please be careful so they don't see anyone messing with their data."

"No problem, Joe," Mark said.

"Mark and Jack, if you can split this up, we have to check on vendors that have subcontracted with us for our foundation grant funded training. There are five major vendors that we dealt with and each had received over $100,000.00 in the last several months, under the first two awards that we won."

Joe wanted someone to check these vendors to see if they were vendors to any of the other non-profits, and to see how much they invoiced those non-profits over the last six months. He also wanted the incorporation information to see when they incorporated, and who were the officers in the corporation.

"We need to know the names of the attorneys who drew up the incorporation paperwork as well," he said. "Jack, this would be easier for you if you could check the foundation list that Luis gave me originally, and see who they funded over the last six months. It might be surprising," he said. "I will send the list to you."

Joe was beginning to understand the scope of what this situation entailed. "We can't prove a thing yet, but under the Patriot Act, we don't have to prove the same as in a court of law. If there were financial transactions, not under the RICO Act, but under the Patriot Act, we could move more quickly. I just read that in the United States, the Racketeer Influenced and Corrupt Organizations Act—RICO—is a Federal law that was enacted to give extended penalties in the prosecution of organized criminal acts. Although intended to be used against the Mafia, and others engaged in organized crime, the RICO Act had been used to prosecute all sorts of criminal activity. Under the RICO Act, a person could be charged with racketeering, which included bribery, extortion, illegal drug sales, loan sharking, murder, and prostitution.

The law gave the government the power to criminally prosecute and imprison an organized crime leader even if he or she had never personally committed any of the components of racketeering. This was because he or she was part of a criminal enterprise."

Since Nine/Eleven, Homeland Security had not let up, and they redefined terrorism to include gang activity. Under the Patriot Act, these top gun gang members were being pulled off the street and they wound up at Guantanamo Bay, Cuba, just like those terrorists from the Middle East.

Joe and his team didn't need the RICO Act. They only needed to prove intent under the Patriot Act, and it was a done deal.

"Mark, do you have access to cell phone information, especially if burner phones were used?" Joe asked.

"Burner phones are harder to trace but we could virtually ping anything within one hundred feet of its origination," he said.

"Okay, here is Luis's Coalition cell phone number. I don't think he would be stupid enough to use it to call criminals but you never know," Joe said. "If there were any calls matched to any of the vendors, or what he believed may be the law firm who set up all the corporations, and they also may matched any cell phones associated with the foundations or other non-profits, then they had collusion as the basis for the Patriot Act. We're not taking any chances, so, see if any phones match any of the other pings in the California prison system."

Joe gave him Luis's home address. "Check anywhere around there as well," he said. "Luis said he was going to The Bronx to visit his aunt, his mother's sister. If any cell phones in the New York City area ping, we need a list of those numbers as well. At this point, I can't think of anything else. How about you guys?" he asked. "Guys, as soon as possible please," he requested. "I'm not sure what we were dealing with but if we got some hits, Mark, I needed to speak to Paul Philips in Miami and tell him what's going on. I also looked up the Albany FBI office. Tom Matthews is in charge here. I don't know him. If necessary, we should definitely have Paul call Tom and set up a meeting for us, me and Dan, and whoever comes here from Miami. Thanks, guys, you're the best."

After his call, Joe got out of his car, went back into his office, and completed the third grant already set up in the queue. He completed the budgets, narratives, partnership agreements, and required documentation in order to submit the grant by Friday of this week. Luis already told George Fontaine that he should sign the grant in place of Ted, since Luis was on vacation. George readily agreed, as if he was personally getting a check for a million dollars.

◌◌◌◌

Joe had already figured out that Luis was reluctant to sign any documentation for the other two grants and probably wouldn't have signed this one either. Not signing gave him a way out, in case there was a problem. Not signing meant he had no fiduciary responsibility for the grant. Ted signed the first two and gave him a premature sense of euphoria. Ted wanted the responsibility. He also wanted the praise as well, Joe thought. *Let it go, Joe, let it go. He's dead.* Joe believed that Luis only did a cursory review of the first two grants and really never read either one. Luis told Joe he trusted him to complete all the required tasks. Joe didn't know if Luis even knew how to complete a grant.

As he looked back over the last six months, Joe wondered if Luis had ever done a grant before. When Joe studied Luis's old non-profit in California, he never saw his name mentioned with any funded proposals at all. That was strange, because he had pumped himself up as the grant guru when he got to the Coalition. Joe didn't believe he had done anything. Joe knew Luis took all the credit and went "golly gee wiz" when everyone congratulated him. He didn't say he didn't do anything either. He did thank Joe for his participation but not for Missy and him doing all the work. Joe really wondered about that now. Teamwork was in the eyes of the beholder, an illusion.

Joe only had one way to find out if Luis was on top of what he was doing, when he submitted grants to various foundations on behalf of the Albany Coalition for Families. For the hell of it, Joe left off the Ettinger Foundation question number eight, "Discuss how your organization will fully support this program and continue it after your grant funding ceases." It was pretty much a standard answer that the program would be institutionalized and then funded through the Coalitions annual budget once grant funding ceased. You could also have more grants secured from other foundations and obtain partnerships that would have assisted in the funding. Joe didn't complete this section at all, and he didn't get George's signature on the Memorandum of Agreement, either. He wondered if anyone ever read these grants or would even notice. If the Ettinger Foundation awarded them the grant and did not point out the unanswered questions, Joe would then know something was going on and he would then investigate.

If they came back and asked about the unanswered questions, Joe thought he could always plead that they had a time crunch since Ted died. For his own board, he could say that they had already secured two million dollars, and that it would be hard to meet all the goals required under those two grants alone. He'd thought about doing this for a while. It was not to screw with getting the Albany Coalition for Families needed funding. Joe did not see any impact on the Coalition to date of the two million dollars that was already won. He only saw the money going to a select few vendors with only a few dollars going to their own operation. He thought the funding looked like a pass through with nothing sticking with the Coalition. This would be hard to prove by itself. Joe also thought that he could quit if confronted, but he didn't think it would happen. It was a calculated risk. He sent the grant out to Seattle by FedEx. *I should call Mark now and see how things are moving along.*

"Mark, it's Joe," he said. "I thought it might be time to contact Paul Philips in Miami to let him know that something is going on here in Albany and that I wanted to know how to handle it. What are your thoughts?"

"It couldn't hurt to get him on board quickly," Mark said. "That way he could point us in the right direction in Albany. As I said before, I don't know anybody in the Albany FBI, do you?"

"No, I don't," Joe said. " I looked up the local Albany FBI and there's a Tom Matthews listed as SAC, special agent in charge, of the FBI Albany Office. I hope that helps."

"Okay, I'll let you know what Paul says and he may want to talk to you directly, Joe," Mark said.

"Sounds good."

With that, Joe started to document everything that had happened to date, from the time Luis arrived until now. If he was going to meet anyone from Homeland Security or the FBI, it was better to hand them a document outlining everything that he knew, or at least guessed, had happened to date. It was a start.

CHAPTER 8

As Joe looked out the window onto Central Avenue, right down the street from the New York State Capital building, he started to wonder what a blur the last thirteen years had been. How had he gotten here? Was it just luck? Joe had a lot on his mind with Ted's death and Luis being named interim president. This was Joe's first real job outside of the Coast Guard. He was in his third year here. He was praised for his work ethic and for the money he raised for the Coalition. He'd started with nothing. No department, no staff, and no prospects for funding. Grant research and development was not his background, but he wanted to come home to Troy after years in the Coast Guard, and he was able to transfer everything he learned to this new position.

He started to laugh at himself. He wasn't the only one in the same boat. Downstairs, the head of job placement for the Albany Coalition for Families, a friend of his, actually graduated from the University of Hawaii with a Geology degree. Now he worked with at-risk kids, getting them jobs and changing their lives. Who would have ever thought that was possible?

Joe was a fish out of water but his years of training gave him the confidence that he would get to the bottom of whatever was going on. The Coast Guard certainly helped Joe acquire high level IT and presentation skills but the research and data analysis set him up for what he was doing at the Albany Coalition for Families. That, coupled with his MBA from RPI, meant he could probably stay at the Coalition and compete at the same level as his big city counterparts. The pay wasn't great but if he honed his skills at this small non-profit, he could move to the next level and develop larger grants involving larger non-profit and business partners.

After two years, Joe had started to really understand the world of child welfare. The commitment and requirements were no less challenging than the Coast Guard. There was structure, licensing, training, professional development, new rules and regulations from New York State and the federal government. There were requirements from foundations, commitments of resources, matching funds. This structure was a world he was very unfamiliar with, but non-profits gave people the opportunity to grow and learn but that was also changing as the world changed. There was less funding going to fewer organizations, to serve less people. The poor, according to the Bible would always be with us, but it seemed to be growing by leaps and bounds since the real estate crash of 2007. More and more middle class families fell between the cracks with lost jobs, lost homes, as well as losing their own identities and ways of life. The poor were even poorer if you could imagine. Children growing up in poverty weren't given much of a chance to succeed.

👁️‍🗨️

As Joe shook himself back to the present, he realized that he was now thirty-two years old with a birthday coming up on April sixteenth, closing in on his upcoming thirty-third birthday. He'd spent ten years in the Coast Guard, receiving his BS in Strategic Intelligence and Research from the Coast Guard Academy in New London, Connecticut at age twenty-eight. Many of his liberal arts classes were taken in Florida at Miami Dade Community College, during his enlisted service and then completed science courses at the Academy, off and on. He worked for ten years as a noncom mostly at the Coast Guard COMMSTA communications facility in Miami—with other various clandestine operations and lifesaving events in Haiti and New Orleans. After he got out of the Coast Guard in 2008—he really didn't want to go another eight year and into Officer training—he spent two years at Rensselaer Polytechnic Institute in Troy, receiving his MBA in management in 2010. He started this job at the Coalition the same year, going on three years ago, and he was doing pretty well for a late bloomer. Getting there was quite a different story.

Joe lived in Troy New York just outside of Albany, ten miles north. He'd lived there his whole life before going away to the Massachusetts Institute of Technology, or better known as MIT, and then the Coast Guard. He grew up in Lansingburgh in the north end. He went to St. Augustine's Catholic elementary school and then on to Catholic Central High School, only a few blocks away. He graduated with honors, had high SAT scores, really excelled in math and wound up with a scholarship to MIT in Cambridge, Massachusetts, across the Charles River from Boston. He was raised in a middle class construction family. His mom was very religious, his dad not so much. He started working construction at fourteen years old during the summers and then on weekends during the school year. He got his chauffer's license in an eighteen-wheel dump truck, at sixteen years old. *It really worked well picking up girls*, he thought with a snort of laughter.

He had a good life, good family, good brother, good support, but that all changed at MIT. He just wasn't ready. He got all Cs as a math major but he wanted more than to just sit in class. He was bored to death. At the end of his first semester, he knew he couldn't go on. He was first generation going to college, and he knew he would disappoint his parents but growing up in a construction family, he also knew that he could take care of myself. He could always go back to school.

Growing up two blocks from the Hudson River, his father always had a boat docked at the Veteran's Club on a 123rd Street on the river. They were cleaning up the Hudson now and it looked like it would take forever, but, when he was growing up, everyone thought you could have walked across the Hudson. It was that polluted.

The day after his last exam at MIT, in December 1998, he went to Malden outside of Boston, only a few miles from school, and signed up with the Coast Guard for an eight-year commitment, which turned into ten. He really wasn't interested in Iraq, and all that, but he knew about Desert Storm, and the bombing by radicals around the world. He had just started at MIT in the fall that year, two years before the bombing of the *USS Cole* in Yemen in 2000, and three years before Nine/Eleven, in 2001. By that time, Joe would have been in the middle of the new terror on America.

At the time, he thought joining the Coast Guard could make a difference and little did he know how much. He thought he could continue his education at some point, see America, especially the coast, do some good, and gain some experience. He didn't know the real terror that was coming and that the Coast Guard would be changed with it. Being eighteen and patriotic was kind of a given in his family. At eighteen, you never thought too much about death or anything else for that matter.

Joe woke up very quickly. It was late January 1999, when he went to Cape May, New Jersey, for basic training. He wouldn't be nineteen until April. He was still a teenager. He had just spent Christmas with his parents and his brother Pete—two years older—in Troy, saw his friends, and had some drinks, albeit illegally. Everyone thought he was nuts, but no one was worried because it was the Coast Guard not Iraq or Afghanistan. They wanted to know if they gave waterskiing lessons off the back of the boat. He laughed and told them he would get back to them on that. He arrived at Sexton Hall in Cape May and most of the next few days were spent getting oriented, learning his way around, getting his uniforms, a really short haircut, and filling out nothing but forms for two days. God, he thought he was back at MIT. He started to panic for the first time.

He met his Master Chief Petty Officer, Tom Jones. No, Tom Jones didn't break out in song. He was tough, forty-one years old, a lifer, and he was going to be Joe's mentor, his instructor, coach, guide, and all around pain in the ass. They learned discipline the hard way, how to take orders, and what was expected of them. Every morning the day began the same way with pushups, sit-ups. They ran for miles, and had lots of swimming. He guessed he forgot that the Coast Guard meant not drowning, and he'd swum all his life but never like this. This was not a boat in the Hudson River. He was waterlogged for all eight weeks of basic training. It was mandatory for graduation that you entered the water from a platform, and then safely swim one hundred meters in five minutes without touching the sides or the bottom of the pool. You then had to tread water without a life jacket for an eternity, about ten minutes.

After the physical training, they were exhausted, and then the real fun had begun. A seaman apprentice was the first step and they taught you what you needed, to be seaworthy. They taught academics related to ships, technology and things you would never think about. He was really glad that he was good in math. The easiest way to literally wash out of the Coast Guard was not be able to swim or not understand math. It was essential to everything they did. Toward the end of training, they participated in small arms training, seamanship, firefighting, damage control and the nomenclature they would need to immediately respond to various situations, on board and off. After Joe's final physical exam and then his written exam, he was ready to start his first assignment.

If he'd graduated from MIT on time, his starting salary as an actuary in New York City would have been $125,000.00 per year with bonuses in 2002. His starting pay with the Coast Guard was $15,000.00 with room and board—three hots and a cot. The best thing, though, was he only had to do was what he was told and be brain dead. He guessed he was sadly mistaken. He was now one of 46,000 members of the Coast Guard.

As part of the original recruiting process, Joe had to pass the Armed Services Vocational Aptitude Battery (ASVAB) test and had to get a minimum qualification score of forty-five or higher. Joe thought that this was pretty easy considering a majority of the test was math. He guess they were impressed and told him that he scored the second highest that they had ever seen, since keeping score data online.

The highest score was achieved by a recruit who had just graduated from college before joining the Coast Guard as an officer candidate. This simply meant that upon graduation, he could go for any one of nineteen different enlisted ratings for which he could actually go on and receive a degree from the Coast Guard Academy in his field, during his eight-year enlistment. That was what Joe had hoped for to obtain a degree on the Coast Guard's dime.

Upon completing the eight weeks of basic training, he was promoted to Seaman (E-2). He was told at the recruitment office that if he did well on his tests and basic, a Guaranteed "A" School program would be within his reach, and he did go right from basic training to his "A" School choice of rating as an Intelligence Specialist (IS). With the Coast Guard taking an increasing larger role in homeland security, he would be one of the first defenders of US ports and waterways. At eighteen years old, he was officially ten light years from where he was less than two months ago.

After basic training, he started his career with fourteen weeks of specialized training at the "A" School in Yorktown, Virginia, only a few miles from Newport News and Virginia Beach. Tom Jones followed the team as a new experiment to have continuous training and team continuity. Yorktown was about the same size as Troy, maybe a little bigger at 68,000 residents. The town was famous as the site of surrender of General Cornwallis to General George Washington in 1781, effectively ending the Revolutionary War that came to an end two years later. All this was fine, but Joe found out you could drink at eighteen in Virginia Beach—twenty-one in New York—which was all the history he needed to know. Little did he know all sailors and Coasties were served, if in uniform, regardless of age. His first lesson about the term Coasties came from his Chief, Tom Jones. He had to memorize and recited the following definition of Coastie:

"A Coastie is one who has served actively in the United States Coast Guard, and has been in the thick of action for some time. He or she has done their tour on a ship or lifeboat station, at an MSO doing boardings, been on SAR, or regularly worked AtoN. Desk driving, while an essential support role, did not count. A true Coastie earned the right to be called such because of their experience, training, and uncountable hours and days sacrificed to help others. True Coasties earned that title, not for self-recognition, but by the recognition from others, whose lives have been rescued or had their lives changed as a result of the dedication of the men and women who proudly and without boasting wore their blue uniform."

Hopefully, someday he would be a Coastie, he thought. Just not yet.

CHAPTER 9

Joe remembered that, only a few short years ago when he graduated from RPI in 2010, he wasn't really sure what he wanted to do now that he was back in Troy. He could have moved back to Florida but that left a bad taste in his mouth after all he went through, and the jobs were scarce there. While getting his MBA, he worked at McGuire's bar several nights a week. At the time, he was living off his savings, tips, and had some money left over from his student loans and GI bill checks, which barely kept him afloat. After graduating, he needed full-time employment and benefits. He had benefits through RPI as a full time student. It didn't cover much but at ages twenty-eight and twenty-nine, what did he really need? He needed a doctor's appointment once in a while, a prescription for cold medicine every now and then. It wasn't much. That was now gone after graduation. *Congratulations*, he thought. *I now have a degree from one of the finest technology institutions in the world and yet I am approaching zero savings, zero medical insurance, and zero job.*

He went to the placement office, run out of the Rensselaer Alumni Office on Ninth Street, right across the street from the main campus, next to the old practice football field. Most of the jobs offered were for out of the area, mostly in California and Texas. Florida was shot, and the economy down there was in total disarray, with housing prices falling apart. It was unofficially in the toilet. He was bilingual and could certainly command higher wages for in-demand job skills and language fluency, but he didn't want to go back after just leaving the Coast Guard and a lost love.

After reviewing the job lists at the alumni office, he found an advertisement for a Director of Institutional Research and Grants at the Albany Coalition for Families. It was located on Central Avenue in Albany, only a few blocks from the capital buildings. The employment rate in Albany was stable because so many of its residents worked for New York State government agencies, located in this capital city of Albany. Over a quarter million people in the Albany Capital Region worked for New York State in this region. What did he have to lose? He could do research in his sleep after the Coast Guard and Rensselaer. The alumni office called the Coalition for him and set up an appointment for the following Monday at eleven a.m. It seemed so long ago, now.

He had one week to prepare for his interview. He didn't know much about non-profit organizations or how those organizations compared to for-profit business and even compared to working for local New York State agencies, right down the street from where he would be interviewed. Joe knew a lot of people who worked for New York State government. The pay was fair and the benefits were great, especially if you were married and had kids. He wasn't married, so this was not quite the priority he required. Hell, most people his age were married and had kids. He probably would have been, as well, if it worked out with Jen in Miami. But it didn't, so here he was.

He had plenty of time before the following Monday to do research during the day and still work at the bar at night. He went to the downtown Troy Library and got a library card that gave him access to books, periodicals, magazines, as well as use of the computer for one hour at a time. During this one hour online, he researched everything he could about how non-profits functioned, how the businesses were funded, who they served, and if there were good ones and bad ones.

Reading the newspapers in between, he picked up on the bad ones from the headlines *"New York State Senator from New York City Arrested for Stealing Millions"* from the non-profit he worked for in The Bronx. Evidently, this agency, with only a few million dollars a year in revenue, paid this New York State senator $500,000.00 a year, with a car, and housing. His wife and children also worked full time in various capacities. On the surface this didn't seem right, but it happened and evidently as he read on, it happened a lot.

Joe boned up quickly. He read that, by definition, a non-profit corporation, also known as a 501C3 corporation, must "operated as nearly as possible at cost, on a cost-recovery basis, an organization not seeking profit and which does not disgorge excess income to its members, in the form of dividends or otherwise." In other words the entire mission was not to distribute profits to shareholders, who buy stock in a company, and expect earnings to be generated on their behalf. He also learned that you had to be a legal 501C3 to apply for grants that were to be used for the benefit of those the organization served.

Excess income to one or more individuals would not be tolerated. That seemed reasonable to him. For tax purposes, every non-profit had to file a Form 990. The Form 990 provided the public with financial information about a given organization, and was often the only source of such information. It was also used by government agencies to prevent organizations from abusing their tax-exempt status.

As Joe had continued to read everything he could get his hands on before his interview, he learned that in 2007, the IRS released a new Form 990 that required significant disclosures on corporate governance and boards of directors. These new disclosures were required for all non-profit filers for the 2009 tax year, with more significant reporting requirements for nonprofits with over one million dollars in revenues or two and one half million dollars in assets that included cash, buildings, furniture or tangible things. In addition, certain nonprofits had more comprehensive reporting requirements, such as hospitals and other health care organizations. The Form 990 disclosures did not require, but strongly encouraged, nonprofit boards to adopt a variety of board policies regarding governance practices. These suggestions went beyond normal requirements for non-profits to adopt whistleblower and document retention policies.

Joe guessed that was what took down the senator and his family in The Bronx. The IRS used the Form 990 as an enforcement tool, particularly regarding executive compensation. For example, nonprofits that adopted specific procedures regarding executive compensation were offered "safe harbor" from excessive compensation rules and were less stringent if they had their own rules in place. Joe bet that would happen as well.

During Joe's research, the library was practically empty by three p.m., so the librarian let him go back on the computer. *If the 990 Form was so important, then the Albany Coalition for Families must be listed for 2009.* So, he proceeded to download their form off the web. He paid for copies and took a good look at the data before him. This would be his life in the immediate future if he were lucky enough to interview well. *He wondered if anyone prepared for a job this way? It certainly seemed like the right way to go about it, even though he never had to before.*

He made notes in the margins, line by line. The form was extensive. It was thirty or forty pages in length, for the 2009 year only. He would go back year-by-year if this was not enough information. It was. The Albany Coalition for Families had an outside public CPA accounting firm that audited the books annually and stated for the record that they were in good shape. Joe wondered now how they would stand under the scrutiny of this outside accounting form. The auditors were not due in for another six months.

The Coalition was a legal non-profit 501C3 with an annual budget of twelve million dollars and expenses at a similar level with about three hundred and sixty thousand dollars carried in a bank account to cover any potential deficits. They did not have to worry about making a profit. In fact, they had to worry about spending the funds down annually. This was quite a different concept for Joe. The accounting firm stated that this three percent retention of revenue, or three hundred and sixty thousand dollars, was standard practice. *So far, so good*, he thought at the time.

Next, they owned the building and it was valued at three and a half million dollars with no mortgage. The best thing about non-profits, as he learned through his investigation, was that a 501C3, non-profit organization, did not have to pay any taxes of any kind. They were not subject to corporate income tax, nor sales tax, nor property taxes for city, village, town, or school. They didn't even have to pay for sewer and water fees or garbage pickup. The funds they raised went directly to the operation, every year, except for the required retention of three percent that went right into the bank. They were very solvent.

The next issue was paying their bills. It looked like the Coalition was excellent in paying their monthly operating bills, salary and benefits, and according to the source, the largest downfall for any non-profit, was not paying the Federal and New York State employee withholding taxes, that they collected from their employees, matched by their share, and supposedly sent to the appropriate government agency. In addition, a child welfare agency, like the Albany Coalition for Families, had to be certified and licensed by New York State and governing associations like the National Child Welfare Association (NCWA). New York State agencies requiring licenses included the Health Department, Mental Health Department, Children and Family Services, and the Education Department.

Joe could see why these requirements were necessary in light of the crooked Senator's plight in his agency that went bankrupt. Joe believed that the senator and his family were now headed to jail for a spell. With crooks in mind, he also noticed that from the 990, no one was making large sums of money. Theodore Simmons, the president of the agency, made $135,000.00 a year, which was well within reason for a twelve million dollar operation. Doug Jacobs, the Controller, made $105,000.00, again not excessive. The senior management team salaries, Joe guessed based on longevity and status, were in the $80,000.00 to $110,000.00 range. So, the president was not making significantly more than his senior staff. There were no large bonuses, since the payments couldn't come from the grants because that wasn't allowed.

There was a very significant reason to keep salaries reasonable, Joe found out. Major funders would not give grants to non-profit organizations that did not meet spe-cific standards for paying senior administrators. Each foundation had its own set of rules but overcompensating individuals at the top, to the detriment of those at lower levels, would block many funding opportunities. Joe re-membered reading that Ben & Jerry, the founders them-selves, only allowed themselves to make three times more than the lowest paid employee. They weren't a non-profit organization but a for-profit who donated a signifi-cant percentage of the company's earnings to charitable causes and it was the same concept.

Benefits included health insurance, either single and family coverage plans, Federal Withholding Taxes—Social Security and Medicare, or FICA, New York State Unemployment Insurance, and New York State Disability Insurance—fell in the range of twenty-to-twenty-five percent of their salary, depending on the number of em-ployees' dependents. Joe knew for a fact that RPI's over-head and benefit rate was over sixty percent because they were a national research institution. He worked on a few projects during his tenure for his MBA and he saw their budgets and mentally compared them to the Coalition ar-ray. Those budgets weren't even close.

At the time, before joining, he was impressed that the Coalition was well organized, so it seemed, and had been in existence in Albany for many years. However, he did notice that the average age of the Board was almost sev-enty-five years old. There hadn't been a board member change for the last five years since a gentleman died at age eighty and was replaced by a seventy year old, new to the board. Joe really didn't know what that meant, but he did have a lot of questions based on this and other re-search. The biggest item he picked up in his research of the Coalition, and talking to other non-profits in the area during his one week of investigation, was that the Albany

Coalition for Families that was advertising this Director of Institutional Research and Grants, barely had any grants at all. They mostly had contracts with the State agencies for which they were licensed. They had several key donations from local corporations and individuals. However, they had no foundation or government agency grants in which you had to apply on a competitive basis and be successful against a number of other non-profits, large and small, regional, locally, and nationally.

He guessed that he had a lot to learn quickly, if hired, but he thought he would be more prepared than most knowing that what they really needed was a very good grant writer, with high technology skills, attention to detail, able to meet deadlines, be competitive, and have sound appropriate budgets, that met all the goals and objectives outlined in their Request for Proposals, known as RFPs. *You also had to be able to leap tall buildings at a single bound and change in a telephone booth while hiding your exceedingly large dark glasses in your tights. He might just be qualified,* he laughed to himself at the time.

ღჳღჳ

On that Monday, Joe left a little early to drive around and get the lay of the land and found a decent parking spot on the street. The Albany Coalition for Families was pretty easy to get to, on Central Avenue and they said to bring plenty of quarters. Anyone with quarters could run Albany. Most of the meters were for twelve minutes at twenty-five cents per twelve-minute, with parking up to three hours. He took out fifteen quarters. He was proud of himself and only had to walk one block to their headquarters. He met Ted Simmons's secretary/administrative assistant at the front desk, after the receptionist called up to come and get Joe for his meeting. Ted met him at the door with his Controller, Doug Jacobs, who had been at the Coalition for as long as Ted, for over thirty years.

Joe was glad that he put three hours on the meter. After two and a half hours, he said goodbye to Ted and Doug. They asked very pointed questions concerning his background. They were intrigued as to his Coast Guard service and what he did. Being in the Intelligence Division, he couldn't answer all their questions due to national security issues.

"How did you go from being an MIT dropout to a Coast Guard Academy and RPI graduate in a short decade?" Ted asked Joe.

They wanted to know how he would fit into a non-profit arena, which was much different than that of a for-profit business.

Joe was honest. "I spent all week completely researching, not only the Albany Coalition for Families, but many local and national non-profits as well, to see how they compared. I also researched large and small, local and national foundations to see what they were funding. I feel at this point as qualified on the subject as anyone. I am a very quick learner."

Joe did not believe that they did much research and were simply interviewing candidates to see how they would fit.

All he knew was the Coast Guard since he was eighteen years old and construction with his family prior to that. He said in the interview, "teamwork in the Coast Guard was even more important because your life depended on the teammate next to you. There's a trust that they would be literally watching your back as you broke down doors on a bust."

This was the highlight of Joe's conversation, along with his vast knowledge of the inner workings of non-profit 501C3 organizations, and the interaction with government and foundation funding. It went well actually.

They told him the salary range and benefits, which seemed to be okay at this point in his life at thirty years old. He didn't have any dependents, or a wife, or any assets to speak of and he really didn't need much to start.

"Joe, thank you for coming in," Ted said. "We will get back to you, shortly."

As Joe was answering their questions at the time, it became clear to him that this was a very old organization, with a much older employee age base, as he discovered in his research. Their questions were more of the bland every day variety. There were no new ideas or thoughts. Joe had asked them about their strategic plans, vision of the future, and what they would look like in ten years. They really couldn't articulate where they were going or what they wanted to do. It was almost like they were living in the past, enjoying the fellowship of the organization, and had not expected too much change for the near future. The entire senior management group had less than five years before retirement. He was told the Board was comprised of individuals who had been on their board for twenty years or more. They verified that the average board member's age was in the mid-seventies.

All of these factors led Joe to two conclusions. Number one, it would be a great place to start his non-military career because it looked like everyone of importance would be dead in five to ten years, and or retired. Really. He could make a name for himself, move up quickly through the ranks, and perhaps be the president of the organization within ten years. Or, It could be a boring nightmare for anyone with half a brain. What the hell did he have to lose? He thought. He could stay in the area, keep his opportunities opened for a State job in downtown Albany, or learn the craft of grant writing, on their dime. They could certainly benefit from his experience, and for $50,000.00, plus benefits, they were getting a bargain. *If I'm offered the job, I'll take it. I have nothing to lose.*

He remembered vividly thanking Ted for his time and the interview. He was polite without kissing up. He had no control over the process, so he would just have to wait it out. Mr. Simmons thanked Joe for meeting with them. Doug Jacobs was an accountant totally devoid of personality.

Ted had said as Joe remembered, '*We have a few other candidates but we were very impressed with your thoroughness and honesty. We will call you in a few days after our Board meets, and let you know of our decision.*' The board met. Joe received a call at home, and he was offered the job starting the following Monday. He was officially, gainfully, employed.

Joe had been there for two plus years now and he enjoyed the work, right up until it was no longer fun working under Luis's direction. With Ted's death, he knew he had to do something to right the ship or everything that he had worked for would be undone.

CHAPTER 10

After Luis left the Coalition offices supposedly to go to his aunt's apartment in The Bronx, he immediately called Frank to make sure what time he would be getting to the Waldorf-Astoria in New York City. There was no aunt in The Bronx.

The meeting had gone well back at the Coalition, and Luis was praised for his contributions and graciousness in accepting the interim president position. Everyone seemed okay with it as he looked around the room, after the announcement, as well as during his short acceptance speech. He looked at Joe, first, who seemed to be fine and really didn't have any expression on his face other than the normal "Joe expression."

Joe really didn't say much to him. He was polite but reserved, and Luis thought that was his nature. Joe certainly did most of the work getting the grants in on time. He said he would put Ettinger in this week and have George Fontaine sign the documents.

The less I have to sign the better, Luis thought. *I really don't want my name on anything unless I absolutely have to. Man, they really fell for the visiting the aunt crap, didn't they?* He never gave them her name, address, or phone number. He would not pick up the Coalition cell phone this week. *If it is a true emergency, I will get the message and call them back on my Coalition cell. I won't use my personal phone. It should be untraceable. Hell, it was my mother's phone and address and paid for by Frank.*

Luis was unfamiliar with driving outside the immediate Albany area. Living off Albany Shaker Road, near Memorial Hospital, he took almost all straight highways to the Coalition building. It was less than ten minutes away. He wasn't there to sightsee or make a home. He was there to make money for his father and his *eMe* brothers. Before leaving, he downloaded MapQuest on his own phone and followed the directions to get to Park Avenue in New York City, directly from the office on Central Avenue. It seemed pretty straightforward. He got on I-90 East until 787 South until he hit the New York State Thruway at the Albany Exit 23, and went due south for about 150 miles. He stayed within the speed limit. Even though he was now the interim president for the Coalition, he was still Mexican and could be pulled over for any reason at all. Some of the black gang members that he recruited in Albany told him that "driving while black" was the first reason to be pulled over. "Driving while brown" came in second. Luis did not need the hassle.

After getting off the New York State Thruway, he got on the New Jersey Turnpike for only a few miles and headed toward the Lincoln Tunnel. From there, he meandered for less than two miles, coming out of the Tunnel, to land right in front of the Waldorf-Astoria Hotel, at 301 Park Avenue, in the heart of Manhattan. He was quite proud of himself. He had never been to New York City before. He went to the east coast for his Ivy-league MBA but never went out of the greater Boston area. Valet parking took his car and luggage as he headed to the front desk. The trip took about three hours with one stop at the last exit on the New York State Thruway.

Frank would be flying in to JFK from Los Angeles around two p.m. and they would meet in the bar around four p.m. Luis had a lot to talk to Frank about before meeting his compatriot, Alicia Torres, who was assigned to the Hudson Foundation in New York City. She reported to Luis as far as the family was concerned. Luis, Alicia, and Frank would meet tomorrow at the hotel for breakfast. They would tour the Hudson Foundation and meet their staff, early in the morning, have lunch, and then go back to the hotel in the afternoon.

They also had to meet several gang-affiliated individuals who lived in New York City, and would be recruited to follow him up to Albany to reorganize the local gangs for drug production and sales. The bus station in New York City was a direct shot to the downtown Albany bus station, and across from the Albany Express Motel, that Luis continued to keep on a monthly basis for this purpose.

Frank got in on time, took the JFK shuttle right to the hotel, checked in, showered, and pulled a beer from the minibar before going down to greet Luis. From everything he knew, Luis was the top dog in this enterprise and had done extremely well in becoming the interim president of the Albany Coalition for Families in six months since he arrived. Frank was surprised that Luis pulled the trigger on Ted Simmons, but it was necessary because Ted was asking too many questions. It was actually brilliant to play the sleep apnea card, combining it with crushed up sleeping pills an hour before Ted was ready to go home. Ted was an accident waiting to happen.

Frank walked in to Sir Harry's Bar, named after a famous explorer, at the Waldorf and spotted Luis at the bar. "Hi, Luis. How are you?" he asked.

"Fine Frank, how are you? How was your trip?" Luis replied.

"Great, no problems," Frank said.

"Let's go sit at a table in the back," Luis said.

They picked up their drinks and a bowl of nuts and went to the back, which had booths that were secluded. "How is my father, Frank?" Luis asked.

"Good, Luis," he said.

"Did you get the money to my mother?" Luis asked.

"Yes, all in tens and twenties, about $10,000.00 in all. Is that okay?"

"Yes," Luis said.

They talked for about an hour, went into the dining room, and had steaks for dinner. They stayed until around seven-thirty p.m.

"We will meet Alicia for breakfast and then go to the Hudson Foundation," Frank said. "She's doing great. So far, she's given out almost four million dollars to the last four non-profits, in reverse order, from the foundations where you received funding."

They had set it up so no two non-profits targeted would get funded at the same time. If that happened a few times, it would have raised some eyebrows.

So far, with all the foundations, they had cleared almost twenty million dollars, funneled from the foundations, to the non-profits, to Mexican Mafia owned vendors. No one suspected a thing. Luis would also bet they could also place another thirty Los Angeles high school gang member recruits to backfill the two-year positions that would be coming to a close. The second wave would be graduating shortly and keeping the supply line open to be placed again, after the original group's commitments ended.

However, Luis and two other of the original members were now president, executive director, and interim president of their respective organizations. They thought they should leave them there, at least until they exhausted these foundations' funding resources and then move to new unsuspecting foundations in the next several years. "Unless of course you want to go home," Frank said. "It's up to you, Luis."

"I'll think about it, Frank, and let you know. Right now, we're doing great, and we should get another two million in the next few months from Ettinger, and now the Hudson Foundation, through Alicia."

Frank nodded. "Sounds good, Luis, I'll see you in the morning.

Luis went back to his room, called his mother and a few friends, and talked until eleven p.m. He had a few beers from the mini-bar, just enough of a buzz with dinner drinks to let him sleep peacefully. With his father as general and what he had already accomplished, Luis could be living large by next year. Perhaps, he could go straight and get a job on Wall Street with his credentials, ethnic background, and now one interim presidency under his belt. Even as the interim, at twenty-eight, he could now name his own ticket. His mind drifted, and he thought that he had to meet a girl. Living alone was bullshit. At least pick something up tomorrow night before he left for Hartford. He had needs that were being left unfulfilled. He felt like he was on a presidential campaign. He guessed being the son of someone infamous was just same as being the son of someone famous. He smiled. *Just spell my name right*. Luis Hernandez, general-in-waiting of the Mexican Mafia, never arrested, and never in jail. A true success story. He laughed to himself.

Luis met Frank and Alicia for breakfast in the hotel dining room. He could get used to the elegance for sure. *Sure beats Albany, New York*. Luis went up to Alicia and gave her a kiss on the cheek. Frank did the same.

"Alicia, you look great, how're you doing?" Luis asked.

"Great, Luis, I haven't seen you since last summer," she said.

They got down to business, right after eating, and finished their second cup of coffee. Alicia outlined their itinerary for the day. They would head out to the Hudson Foundation, a short cab ride away. They would meet her staff, and then have lunch with several senior officials from the Hudson Foundation. The president and founder of the foundation, and his family, were away and would not be back for a few weeks. As Alicia told them, it didn't matter, because they had given her and her staff full reign to pick and choose worthy applications. They had to spend down an enormous amount of their assets, for federal tax reasons. She looked at Luis and saw the twinkle in his eyes.

The Hudson Foundation got in trouble a few years ago for building up the fund and not spending much during the down financial cycle. They had to move back to their federal required spending percentage, over the next two years, and most of that, through Alicia, would be going to non-profits where the gang sent their graduates. This was easier than stealing. You asked for the money, you handed in a ten page report for an organization that was over fifty years old, and they gave you a million dollars a pop. *America, what a country.*

Luis didn't really understand the significance of the federal regulated spend-down. Frank and his handpicked analysts deliberately sought out older private foundations, with aging administrators, and aging family members. They did not have the financial expertise to run a foundation in the twenty-first century. They were handpicked because they all had IRS issues with the spend-down. That was why Frank picked the best financial MBA graduates to go to the foundations, other than Luis, so they could quickly ingratiate themselves into the management team and be the financial experts in approving larger grants because of the IRS financial situation. They had to shell it out quicker but were not capable of doing so while meeting all the IRS regulations. Alicia was an expert in this area. Luis would pick up another check for another million dollars in about two months from the Hudson Foundation.

The day went well. They had lunch with the executive, who was not only impressed by their intelligence, motivation, and drive to help the less fortunate, but they were quality, highly desirable minorities, which would also impress any government agency when called upon. It was a marriage made in heaven. After lunch, Alicia went to her office, and Frank and Luis headed back to the hotel for a short meeting. Frank had a five p.m. plane to catch to Los Angeles. The shuttle was leaving at three p.m. and he was packed, checked out, and had his suitcase in his hand.

Frank set up a meeting with the New York City Mexican gang Los Vagos. Their members lived in East Harlem and The Bronx neighborhoods. The gang routinely collected dues, which were used to purchase firearms, aid incarcerated members, or help deported members re-enter the United States illegally. They were very small and needed to hook up with another Mexican gang to expand their operations. They were very familiar with the Mexican Mafia and would meet Luis in East Harlem at seven-thirty p.m. They would pick him up a few blocks from the hotel and drive him to the meeting. As proof of his gang status, he showed them his *eMe* tattoo on his ankle.

Frank would have crapped if he ever saw it. He told Luis time and again—no tattoos. *How the hell would I deal with the Los Vagos, if I didn't have it?* Luis thought. His father and Frank were getting too old for a young man's game. Yes, Jorge, his father, was ruthless, but Frank was nothing but a rich lackey, who was getting too old. Luis thought he could push Frank aside in a few years. After all, he was no gangbanger. He was a God-damn nerd when they recruited him as a boy, and he was still a nerd. Frank didn't even have a grasp of the Mexican dialect anymore. Luis was able to speak to the Los Vagos as if he were their long lost brother. Luis was not from the streets but received his street education from his father's friends who were not in jail. The Los Vagos boys couldn't believe how polished he was. Make no mistake. Luis was very polished, self-assured, and dangerous. They knew it, and respected it. At least it appeared that way. They wanted something and so did Luis.

His discussions in Spanish, with the local leaders—if you could call them that—were successful. Five of the members would meet Luis in Albany and he would put them up in the Albany Express Motel. They would come up by bus at five p.m. the following Tuesday and he would meet them at the hotel door at five-thirty p.m. He would introduce these guys to those he already recruited and were now "students" on the first floor of the Albany Coalition job-training program. He needed to corner the Albany drug trade and then the entire capital region. Prices were so much better upstate than in New York City with cheap drugs on every street corner. *Christ, it's like trying to beat a price at Wal-Mart.* In Albany, you got three times the price, just from all the college kids alone.

Smiling, Luis asked if they knew of anyone who could relieve a little of his tension from his trip. A beautiful Latina smiled at Luis. She took his hand and showed him to a room down the hall. He smiled and said thank you. *Yes, his night was complete.*

They dropped him off near the Waldorf and Luis was on his own for the night. He was going to Hartford early in the morning. It was only ten-thirty p.m. and he was in New York City, so he wondered about calling Alicia for a little appreciation on her part for setting her up in New York City, but he thought better of it. He would hate to have to get rid of her down the road if things didn't go the way he wanted. Sex always got in the way. *Sex in East Harlem should hold me for a while.*

CHAPTER 11

"Hi, Paul, it's Mark Silva, how are you?"

"Great, Mark. Are you going to the Port Intelligence Group meeting next week?"

"Yes, but do you have some time to see me today? I'm in town at the COMMSTA headquarters and I wanted to bounce something off of you if you don't mind," Mark said.

"Well, I'm in my office all day here in North Miami Beach," Paul said.

"Great, I'll swing by in a half hour on my way home to Fort Lauderdale. See you then."

Mark hopped in the car, a straight shot up U.S. 1, the Dixie Highway, to I-95 North, exit 2B, to get to Second Avenue in North Miami Beach. It was only twelve miles from the COMMSTA center. It took close to twenty-five minutes with traffic backed up as usual.

Mark parked close to the building, put a Coast Guard Intelligence Division card in the window over the steering wheel and walked in the front door. He asked for Paul Philips and went through the security check once again. He went up the stairs to Paul's office on the second floor. His office looked like a closet but they all did. The COMMSTA offices were spread out with technology equipment all over the place. He never thought it was spacious until he looked at Paul's office.

"Hi, Paul, hope I'm not late. Traffic was awful as usual," he said.

"No problem, I'm just finishing up a case," Paul said. "What's up? You seemed quite anxious to see me. What's on your mind?"

Mark proceeded to review the information that he brought with him to show Paul. He had the fingerprints matches, the vendor lists, the overlapping corporate officers, and the gang tattoo photograph from Luis' ankle. He explained in detail the NCWA Hispanic Management Outreach program that involved the Los Angeles High School students. He went over in detail all the foundations, and non-profits spread throughout the country, the winning proposals, and the amount of money involved.

"Holy shit, Mark," Paul said. "Can I bring in my boss to sit with us for a few minutes?"

"Sure, the more the merrier," Mark said.

"You're telling me that twenty of the thirty students originally involved in the program were the sons and daughters of Mexican Mafia gang members still in jail?" Paul asked.

Mark nodded. "Yes, quite clearly, and the Mexican Mafia gang insignia that's on Luis Hernandez's ankle, matched the full blown tattoos on the prisoners."

"Wow," Paul said. "Mark, I want you to talk to my boss, Terry Owens. She's the regional director of the FBI headquartered here in Miami. As you know, I'm the SAC of the Miami office. So what you tell us goes directly to the top. Can you bring her up to speed while I make this phone call?"

"Sure," Mark said.

Terry was in her mid-forties and had been in the FBI stationed in Miami for the last ten years. Mark knew her very well from all the meetings and drug interceptions from Miami to Key West that she had been involved in, with him and Joe, and the Coast Guard.

"Sure, I know Joe very well," she said. "I was surprised when he left the service and went back to school. He went to RPI, right?"

"Yes, in addition to his B.S. in Intelligence from the Coast Guard Academy, he got his MBA from Rensselaer, or RPI as he calls it, two years ago, and had been working as the Director for Institutional Research and Grants for this Albany Coalition for Families," he said.

"Great school," she said. "He's from upstate New York, right?"

"Yes, born right there in Troy, near Albany, where RPI is located," he said.

"I'll bet this Luis character doesn't have a clue about Joe, does he?" she asked. "Joe is so unassuming, but he really knows his stuff. We wouldn't even be talking to you two if we didn't know all about both of you."

"Thank you, I appreciate it," Mark said.

Paul came back in and Terry said that it would be a good idea to talk to Tom Matthews up in Albany to give him the lay of the land and give him introductions to Joe and Mark.

"Joe mentioned to me that he looked up the name, Tom Matthews, as the SAC of the Albany FBI office," Mark told them.

"Mark, our stamp of approval is all you will need with Tom," she said. "He is no bull-shitter, and I think he will really appreciate knowing this and doing something about it. Let me get him on the phone now, and explain what's going on." She picked up her phone. "Mark, are you going up there to help Joe?"

She knew, after talking to Mark, that the evidence gathered from Mark, Joe, and from Jack Forest up in Virginia was solid. Mark also told her that Sean O'Neil up in Connecticut, at the Coast Guard Academy, would drive over and back up Joe as well. Terry made the call.

"Tom, how are you?" she asked. "It's Terry Owens in Miami."

"Hi, Terry, boy its been a while since we last spoke. What's it been two or three years?" Tom asked.

"Something like that," she said. Terry then went on to tell Tom exactly what was going on in his own city of Albany.

"Wow, you really are sure about this, huh?" he said.

"Tom, I have Mark Silva right here next to me, and I'll put him on speaker phone," she said. "Joe's in Albany and lives in Troy near Russell Sage College. He said he would meet with you at any time. Call him directly. I'll give you his number. It's a burner phone."

Mark introduced himself over the speakerphone and reconfirmed everything he just told Paul and Terry. He said he would be in Albany as soon as needed, and he would clear it with his boss down here in Miami.

Tom thanked all three of them and hung up the phone.

CHAPTER 12

While waiting for everyone to get back to him, Joe sat in his office and continued to think about how he got there, how he met his girlfriend, Mary, and how he made friends that would last a life time. He finally got up the courage to ask her out after he came back from Florida from Mark Silva's fortieth birthday party. They had been going out for the last several months now, and it was quite clear that he was smitten with her.

Mark and Jack were just two of those he counted as close as brothers. Of course, he and Mark had been inseparable for the most critical ten years of his life. He entered the Coast Guard as a teenager and became a man. It was his military training, discipline, and teamwork that informed all his decisions since the day he joined at eighteen years old.

During his basic training in Cape May and fourteen weeks at Yorktown, he made friends that had remained with him and would for the rest of his life. His group built a trust system and they watched each other's back, even though they were all as different as day and night. In Joe's class, he was the youngest at eighteen—he turned nineteen in late spring of that year—but they all seemed to get along pretty well. They were literally all in the same boat. There were four others in his immediate group that included Mike McGreevy, who came from Seattle, Mark Silva from San Diego, Sean O'Neil from Boston—they came down together since they both signed up in Malden that same day—Jack Forest from Charlestown, South Carolina, and Joe. They went through basic training and Yorktown advanced training together, ate, slept, and breathed the same air. Especially breathing Mark's taco gas expulsions every other night was a thing to behold. They all made it, and they all graduated together.

Mike was a high school dropout, and he worked on the fishing boats in Seattle. At twenty-three years old, he was by far the most experienced sailor among their group. He dropped out of high school at sixteen. He had family problems and banged around for a few years. He went nights to get his GED so that the larger fishing companies—better pay—would let him run a boat out of the Sound. He actually got his boat pilot's license at nineteen, worked for four years, and decided to join the Coast Guard to get ahead. Fishing was fun while young but not so much when you got older and every bone in your body ached and you were tired of cut up hands and permanent chapped lips. He saw his father now and then on the boats that he worked on but didn't speak to him very often. His mother remarried and left for Los Angeles. He got a card now and then on his birthday and Christmas. He didn't reciprocate.

Mark had just turned twenty-seven years old right before he joined the Coast Guard. He was a Latino from San Diego. They learned several pickup lines in Spanish or Spanglish as he called it. Mark was a former gangbanger when he was a kid but loved the sea and when last picked up at twenty-seven years old for aggravated harassment, he decided that a better option was to join the service. Twenty seven year old gangbangers didn't live very long and probably wouldn't make thirty years old.

San Diego had a large Coast Guard presence as well as a large Naval base. He chose the Coast Guard and got the hell out of Dodge ASAP. It was a good thing he went into the Coast Guard. He didn't know it but the Navy wouldn't accept anyone older than twenty-five and the Coast Guard accepted the oldest enlistees at twenty-seven. He thought it was divine intervention at that point. He just made it. No Coast Guard at age twenty-seven meant no life, either. Someone was watching over him and his mother's prayers were answered. She lost her husband but her son would be saved from the streets.

Mark was extremely smart. He was street smart and had terrific entrepreneurial skills through his gangbanging activities and graduated from high school without difficulty. He worked odd jobs and didn't care to share his employment history with his fellow "guardsmen."

His mother and two sisters lived in San Diego. His father was long gone. One thing, he was the most loyal son-of-a-bitch Joe ever saw. Going drinking with him in Virginia Beach was quite the experience. They were lucky the local citizens didn't shoot them. Hitching back to base and making it by midnight was better training for them in logistics, planning, cajoling, and intimidation than they ever learned in the fourteen-week program.

Sean, at twenty-one years old, was six feet four and 220 pounds and was enormous compared to the rest of them. Joe's six-foot frame felt like nothing when he stood behind him. Joe thought Sean had a seven-foot wingspan. He was a full-grown man. He went to Dean Community College outside of Boston, played basketball and got his two-year degree in liberal arts. His marks were okay but not scholarship material and he ran out of money.

He played for the Dean Community College men's

basketball team against the Coast Guard Academy's JV *Bears* team in New London, Connecticut, and he really liked the campus. They told him upon joining the Coast Guard, that if he did well, he could end up completing his degree there. At that time, his marks were just not good enough, just good enough to become a *Coastie*. He still had two years left of eligibility for basketball. *GO BEARS!*

Jack Forest originally grew up in New Jersey, the Cape May area but his family transferred when his dad's company moved to South Carolina. He still had family in Cape May and while in basic, on weekend leave, saw his grandparents on both sides, as they lived their entire lives in Cape May. His aunt and uncle lived a few blocks away, so it was nice. Jack just turned twenty-two years old and wanted to attend Officer's Training School since he just graduated from Rutgers University—New Jersey's State University—at Camden with a BS in computer science. Jack's computer science degree allowed him to pick the Intelligence field and wound up in Joe's training group.

Jack stayed with his grandparents and commuted to Camden from Cape May the first year at Rutgers to re-establish residency in order to pay in-state tuition the following three years, which was less than half for out of state students. He drove eighty-nine miles each way, three days a week, from his grandparents to Camden, from Cape May. He put over 30,000 miles on his 1991 Honda his freshman year. The odometer read 257,678 miles and the car had to last for the next three years while he lived on campus. Camden, New Jersey was ranked as the poorest city in America. He couldn't wait to graduate. The car was on its last legs as he drove into Sexton Hall to start his basic training. He drove all of us to a party at his grandparents' house for the Fourth of July, during their training, and the car died in the driveway. They were all there, Joe, Mike, Mark, Sean, and Jack, giving the last rights, blessing the car with Holy Rolling Rocks, and praying over the only thing Jack actually owned that was worth more than fifty dollars. It only made it by ten bucks. His Uncle Tim gave them a ride back the five miles to the base. They could have walked but they were so shit-faced that they probably would have wound up in Peoria.

It felt like high school graduation, sneaking back into their barracks, rushing to the bathroom, dry heaving, grabbing on to the face of the earth so they wouldn't fall off. The next day's class was very enlightening. Their instructor led them on a quick five-mile run refresher before classes resumed.

"Joe, can I see you for a minute in my office?"

After basic and into his fifth week of the fourteen-week "A" School training at Yorktown, he thought he was doing pretty well, but what the hell did he want to see him for? He never spoke to anyone alone. Joe was nervous.

"Joe, close the door," Chief Jones said. "Are you okay? You look a little pale?"

Normally, Joe joked around when he was nervous, but he really didn't know what was going on or what to expect, so he said, "Yeah, Chief, I'm fine, just fine."

"Look, you're fine. You're doing fine for a nineteen year old, but your sarcasm gets a little bit much, you know? Happy birthday, by the way."

It was now April and Joe had just turned nineteen.

"Give it a rest," Jones said. "But, that's not why I called you in. Look, Mark is not making it in the class-room, and I need you to tutor him."

"Is that all?" Joe asked.

"No, you might have to go against your normal

smart-ass instincts if you are going to help him. We have decided to start breaking up into two-man teams for the rest of the nine weeks," Jones said. "I want you and Mark to be one team, and I mean one team, a tag team. You're not to leave his side for the rest of the training. If it works out, both you and Mark will be assigned to our COMMSTA Communications facility in Miami, after a short stay at headquarters in Portsmouth at the Maritime Intelligence Fusion Center Atlantic. We want you for your brains, Mark for his Latino background and street smarts. However, he might not make it, and if he doesn't, you won't either. No one here passes or fails on his or her own. You have to work closely together to be successful, especially in where you will be sent next."

"Chief, I will do the best I can, but Mark was a gangbanger from San Diego. I can't understand him half the time. He goes in and out of English and Spanish so much, I don't recognize complete sentences," Joe said. "He's twenty-seven years old, and I just turned nineteen."

The chief sighed. "Joe, this is not a request. It's an order. Do you know what an order is, Joe?"

"Well, since you explained it to me in English, I am certain that I will be able to follow your order explicitly, Chief," Joe said.

"Good idea," Jones said. "And by the way, you better learn to speak street lingo as quickly as you can by the time you land in Miami. Do you think the intercepted message from the Columbians, are explicitly in English, Joe?" He smiled.

Joe smiled too. He got it. He wasn't just thinking of Mark, he was thinking of him as well.

It was amazing how smart you were at nineteen and how dumb you could be at thirty-two. *Must be a gene or something.*

Master Chief Petty Officer Jones told him that book

smarts would catch the bad guys but street smarts would keep him alive. "You are dismissed, Joe," he said. "Please tell Mark that I want to see him,"

Joe saw Mark walking down the hall. "Mark, the chief wants to see you right away," he said. "Boy is he pissed at you. What the hell did you do wrong, now?"

"Screw you, Joe," Mark said.

At least Joe thought that was what he said, but he wasn't really sure. He was sure the chief would be right on top of that, speaking street lingo, and all.

Yeah, right. Joe sat back in his chair. It was like yesterday, but it was in fact thirteen years ago, almost to the day. He decided to call Mark and Jack now that they were on his mind. This Luis situation got to him, and he needed to talk about it.

CHAPTER 13

It was Wednesday morning and Luis checked out of the hotel at eight a.m. He had the doorman get his car and put his luggage in. He felt like a million dollars and gave the doorman a fifty-dollar bill. *What the hell. I'm worth it.*

He was now headed toward Hartford to visit Dave Perez. He'd get something to eat on the way, after he got out of New York City. The later it got, the more congested it was in New York. He'd already downloaded driving directions from MapQuest onto his phone. He headed toward Bruckner Boulevard and merged onto I-278 East on the Bruckner Expressway toward the Throgs Neck Bridge headed toward New England. The Bruckner Expressway became I-95N toward the Hutchinson Parkway North and then merged onto I-95N. From there, he took Exit 6 crossing into Connecticut toward New Haven. He saw the signs for the Coast Guard Academy but thought nothing of it. He then headed to CT-15 North toward East Hartford where he was staying at the East Hartford Econo-Lodge on Main Street. The trip was about one hundred and fifteen miles, give or take. It took about two and half hours with a quick stop for breakfast.

The EconoLodge was only minutes from downtown

and the Hartford Career Center, also on Main Street. It was only a few doors down from the Hartford City Hall. Luis wanted his meetings there to be at this obscure out-of-the-way motel, especially because he was unsure how to handle Dave Perez. He didn't want to show up at the Career Center and have anyone, including Dave, connect the dots of what he was doing there. At $59.95 per night it was a bargain compared to the Waldorf-Astoria. He could have stayed five nights for the price of one night at the Waldorf. *One night here is enough,* he hoped.

Luis met Dave for dinner at Roma's down the street. Dave grew up with Luis on the same street in Los Angeles. He was in the same class and had the same degrees. Make no mistake. Dave was no Luis. His father was a low ranking officer in the Mexican Mafia and was in the same prison as Luis's father. Dave was worried because he knew that if he screwed up, it would have dire consequences for his father. There were no excuses after what they paid to get Dave his graduate degree. They carried his mother over the same thirteen-year period. Dave had brains and like they say if you have an IVY-League MBA you were still called "sir," regardless of where you graduated in your class. It showed. Luis was in the top ten in his class and Dave was near the bottom. The nice thing was, it didn't say that on his diploma. If it did, a lot of people would be extremely pissed off if the degree showed what they actually accomplished.

Luis quickly reviewed Dave's status since he got to Hartford. They'd handed him three grants already, and, after Dave got through with them, they were so bad that the Hartford Career Center only got two funded at half the amount requested. The graduates of Luis's program, placed at the three foundations, were actually embarrassed when they got the application from Dave on behalf of his non-profit.

All three, after much clandestine conversation on their cells at night, successfully convinced the other members of two of the approving committees for each foundation, to fund less, not cut them out completely, and not hold it against these poor young people because the applications were flawed. The third one actually rejected the application and told the organization to get a better grant writer and resubmit. At that point, Luis realized that if Joe Traynor was not good at his job, and if Missy didn't help package the proposals properly, he would be screwed as well. He decided to keep that fact to himself and give Dave a bashing instead.

"Uh, Dave, we handed you three million dollars on a platter, and you could only come up with two for a half million dollars each, and actually received a turn down from the other one," Luis said. "Do you know how embarrassing that is for our people working there, trying to get us funded? We have a quota to get money to our own vendors and to turn the funds into legitimate cash to feed our own families, Dave. Do you get that Dave?"

Supposedly equal in the project, Dave knew he would never be equal to Luis, and he was now putting his family in jeopardy.

"Dave, you had better win the next million dollar grant, or you will be replaced. Do you know what I mean, Dave?" Luis asked. "Do you know what replaced means, Dave? It means your entire family will be replaced, Dave. Do you get my drift?"

At this point, Dave was very nervous. He was humbled and apologetic and actually saw Jesus on the highway, as if he had spoken to him personally—at least it seemed that way. After four years of college and two years at graduate school, Dave actually forgot that he was a lackey to the Mexican Mafia. There was no turning back. His family would be dead. Ten of the original thirty members brought in to do this found out the hard way when they screwed up and were sent home. They were immediately replaced and he would be too. He got Luis's point—replaced meant dead.

"What are we going to do about this, Dave," Luis asked. Answering his own question, he continued. "You're going to do exactly what I tell you to do, Dave."

"Okay," Dave said sheepishly.

"I'm sending you our proposals from the Coalition, and you are to change what needs to be changed to make it Hartford proposals and send those proposals to the next three foundations on your list. We'll revisit the ones you screwed up at a later date and then reapply," Luis said.

"Yes, Luis, I will do exactly as you ask," Dave said.

"I'm leaving in the morning," Luis replied. "I need to meet your local connections to see how you set up the drug trade. Have you started laundering their money through the Career Center? That's the next step, Dave."

Luis was going to meet with the local gang members who were affiliated with the Mexican Mafia. The MS13—Mara Salvatrucha—was an El Salvadorian/Central American nationalities gang that originated in Southern California and claimed allegiance to the Mexican Mafia. They were organized into "cliques" and were considered one of the most violent gangs in the world. They have a small presence inside Connecticut prisons and could be found in most of the major cities in Fairfield County in Connecticut, and in the greater Hartford area.

Dave must have been considered a lightweight college-boy to these hardened criminals. Luis met with their leader, showed him his tattoo, and explained who his father was, the general of all generals of the Mexican Mafia. Luis looked him in the eye and may not have scared him, but he certainly made his point. Quietly, Jason Figueroa, their leader, wanted to know who placed Dave in charge. He wanted to know if he was their "Fredo" from *The Godfather*, the incompetent brother. Luis chuckled and told him that things would change if Dave didn't straighten up, and he meant now. Jason got the point. Luis also invited him to see his operation at the Albany Coalition for Families and how he was taking over the city of Albany. Jason was impressed. Luis told him directly if anything happened to Dave or if anyone moved in on his operation, there would be an out and out war with the real leaders of the Mexican Mafia, meaning he and his father and all those who reported to them.

Jason and his fellow gangbangers were recruited in Hartford jails and from the streets of Hartford and this was easy, since close to fifty percent of the Hartford population was Hispanic and growing. Sixty percent of the Hispanic population was from the Caribbean, specifically from Puerto Rico. The rest was split evenly between Mexico, Central American, and South America. Massachusetts and Connecticut have become the haven for illegal immigration outside of Florida, Texas and California. These states were extremely liberal and bent over backwards for these illegal families.

Even New York was thinking about giving illegal aliens driver licenses as picture IDs. In Hartford alone, the Hispanic population has grown to almost 55,000 out of a total Hartford population of 125,000. The poverty rate was over thirty percent and the median age was thirty years, which meant more and more young Hispanic children were coming to Hartford to live and get a free education and social services. *My God, with those statistics, how the hell could Dave lose any grants, let alone three that were wired to him? He had to be an educated idiot with no common sense, whatsoever. Too bad they don't teach that class in college.*

It was the only thing that made sense. After his conversation with Jason, Luis didn't believe that Dave was long for this world. He would have to discuss it with Frank and, in turn, his father, when Frank saw him in prison, during his father's next "complaint." Frank could only see Luis's father if a formal complaint had been filed concerning violation of his rights. That was when they discussed Mexican Mafia business, in code, in prison.

Luis met Dave for breakfast Thursday morning and they had a very guarded conversation on Dave's attention to detail. Dave couldn't run. Where would he go? What would happen to his father in prison? What would happen to his mother, an illegal immigrant herself? Send her back to Mexico, where? Hell, her entire family, legal and un-documented, were in Los Angeles. Dave was screwed everywhere he looked. *Sometimes just holding on to the face of the earth may be enough,* Dave thought. Before going home, Luis followed Dave to the Hartford Career Center just to see what it looked like. It was early and no one was around. He stopped for a second and called Frank. He wasn't in so Luis left a message. He pulled out from in front of the building and was on his way home.

Luis left East Hartford around ten a.m. to head back to Albany. It was about the same distance to New York City, 110 miles away and about two hours with a stop. He headed west to I-84, merging on to I-91 North to Spring-field Massachusetts, and then connected to the Mass Pike. He was about an hour and a half from Albany. He stopped at a Mass Pike rest stop. He had a burger and fries. He hit the bathroom, got gas and was on his way home. He was meeting his new friends from East Harlem that night and his own recruits to discuss the state-of-the-state of their Albany operation.

Luis made it home early a little after twelve-thirty p.m., unpacked at his condo, and took a nap. He got up at three p.m. and had a conversation with Frank about the Hartford Career Center debacle with Dave in charge.

"Look, Frank, I know Dave's father and my father were tight," Luis said. "Do they know what a clown he is?" he asked. "When the local gang leader Jason Figueroa calls him 'Fredo' to me, it was embarrassing. Call him if you don't believe me. Yes, Frank, call him and see what he thought of me, but if you do call him, just remember you'll be on my shit list." *How's that for asserting myself?*

"Luis, that was uncalled for. I flew to New York to meet you and asked you what you needed. Didn't I?"

"Uh, Frank, I believe that was your job. If you would like to hit the streets with me for the first time and actually see what was going on, it would be a revelation," Luis said. "Remember, after my father's gone, who do you think will be in charge?"

"Okay," Frank said.

Back in Albany, Luis met everyone after dark at the motel, reviewed his operation with his guys, for an hour. He gave every member $1,000.00 in cash, $10,000.00 in cash in total. He told them to only call him on his private cell number. There was to be no office visits upstairs, and no direct calls to the Coalition. He wanted no part of anyone knowing that he had anything to do with these guys. They were to do their job, and they would get their cut.

The East Harlem guys could hop on the bus for New York City and be back every Sunday night for their weekly meeting and money split. The California boys were to stay in low profile, and if not, their money train would end and they would be bussed back to Los Angeles, and not to a friendly reception. Luis learned the Mexican Mafia's methods of intimidation and used those methods frequently.

Luis spent the rest of the week at home, after meeting the boys down at the Albany Express Motel. He was now catching up, talking to his mother, shopping, eating out, and picking up a few new girls at the lounge on Henry Johnson Boulevard that catered to Latinas. He was feeling his oats and knew that someday everyone would report to him.

Maybe I'll move to Mexico and live on the Coast, right on the water. Could be a good life. A few more years of this and everyone will have it made, thanks to me and, to a lesser degree, the other members of the Hispanic Management Outreach program.

CHAPTER 14

Before Luis's arrival at the Albany Coalition for Families, Joe's staff of one, Missy Cahill, and he had been doing pretty well, winning small grants to cover programs. They set up Facebook to get online donations to meet the needs of all they served. They really needed to change their approach and started looking at new ways to fund programs. They spent hours researching state and federal government grants as well as local and national foundations.

In two short years, they had developed a clearinghouse and a data bank to have facts and figures available at their fingertips to write proposals quickly and meet deadlines that were never met previously. That was why they never won a grant before Joe arrived. They could not meet deadlines and in fact did not know how to meet deadlines. Not having the staff didn't mean not producing results. They had to build a library of proposals and facts that they could cut and paste and meet very strict guidelines.

They had to train their Coalition peers to look for contracts that they could produce within literally a minute's notice. Joe couldn't really remember taking much of a vacation over the last two years. Deadlines meant everything. No excuses, no crying in baseball or meeting deadlines.

Grant writing, the real task at hand was a combination of many skills. Good writing skills, budgeting skills, knowing the cost of things to put in the grant to get funded was exceptionally important. Many grants had been underfunded so that the organization actually lost money when meeting all the goals and objectives put into the proposal, required by the funder. The research was easy for Joe. He had all the technology skills he needed to seek out opportunities and then presented those to senior management.

The problem was not even in writing the proposal and winning, but in actually getting management approval to even start obtaining new projects funded like job training for youth, GED programs in partnership with the local community college, mentoring of high school students, fatherhood programs and healthy lives initiatives. At this point, Joe was not a Director of Institutional Research or Director of Grants, but a champion for change. Not only did he have to sell it to the funders, he had to sell it to his own people first. At times, it was exhausting. Finally, they caught on that they had to change or go under. At the time, little did Joe know that he had already greased the wheels of change for Luis's arrival.

There was less funding for old programs. The funding left was attached to cutting costs and introducing new programs to put people back to work. The leading cause of the problems the Coalition addressed on a daily basis was simply the issue of multigenerational poverty and how it ruined the lives within families through every generation.

❦

When Joe first started at the Albany Coalition for

Families, they had no outside grant funding at all. They received a few bequests upon the death of a donor and a few checks here and there to keep them going. They relied mainly on government contracts that were drying up fast. The challenge of obtaining a half million dollars per year, consistently, was daunting at best. They were very good in meeting the health, mental health, social, and personal needs of their clients, but they were not spectacular or even better than anyone else. They simply had served a need for about thirty years of caring for the poor in both the city of Albany and Albany County. They took their cue from both City and County Social Service Department officials. They were funded for parent education programs and they received vouchers for providing service to individuals. The growth was not in developing new programs, but simply serving more people for the same things, over and over. Convincing this management group and even the Board of Directors that change was going to come, was like trying to turn around the Queen Mary ocean liner. *Slowly, but surely.*

A major issue and challenge was that there was no strategic plan for the new "Development Office." To whom were they going to submit grants to, for what reason, and did they have the ability to actually do everything they said they would accomplish during the funded period? Joe had no idea.

Joe developed a matrix of what they already received in funding from all sources. What made up the Coalition's twelve million dollar budget? In fact, ninety-five percent came from the State of New York Offices of Health, Mental Health, Children and Family Services and local school districts. The other five percent came from individual donations, small outside contracts, and only a limited grant program of less than one hundred thousand dollars per year, which was actually just a donation in disguise. That money came from local banks, the community foundation, other local businesses, and sponsorship for their annual banquet that catered to the rich, in hope for a large check at the end. They were basically begging.

He started subscribing to national foundation websites to see what was available. It was like pulling teeth to get the $500.00 annual subscription fee. Do you really need this, why? *Yes, we really need this because you know less about grants than I do, and I know nothing,* he thought at the time. He then isolated New York State contracts from those government departments that already funded them in smaller venues. Joe spoke on the phone to government officials and met them every other day, trying to find out what was available, but especially what they wanted funded, not what the Coalition had to offer. The Coalition never acted as a vendor attempting to please a customer before. It was unheard of in the child welfare field. The days of "if you build it, they will come" were over.

It was easier to get funding when they met the State's goals and provided the service they needed. That was not as hard to sell as he thought because it made sense. If the Coalition offered mentoring, the New York State Office of Families would provide them with $1,500.00 per parent for up to thirty parents, who had children who were believed to be abused, as evidenced through their interactions with their New York State counselors. For the first time, the Coalition received $45,000.00 for this one time program, which was now offered every year, paid by New York State. This served as Joe's government model. He then went to work on meeting with local foundations and found that if funded one year, they might skip the following year and give it to someone else. They thought all non-profits did the same thing. They don't, they never have, and he had to prove their case. He did this by finding out beforehand what their hot buttons were every year, and then matched their need to Coalition programs, which were priced accordingly and fairly.

The MBA and Joe's Coast Guard experienced informed his decision-making but in fact working in construction informed everything he did. In construction you provided the exact product that the customer needed, at a fair price, with higher quality than anyone else, delivered on time, and you win. Rensselaer Polytechnic Institute called that a technology-transfer of ideas. So much for the *highfalutin*, Joe called it simply common sense.

Joe and Missy always investigated the request for proposal—the grant application questions to be answered—before applying to see if they could get funded, who the competition would be, how many grants were funded for the round, where the funding would take place geographically, and did they actually have a chance to win. The chance to win carried the day. If there were six national grants, Albany, New York probably would not get funded unless their program was new, innovative, cost effective, better than anyone else in the country, and met all the funders' objectives and provided better measurable results. Also, did they have the experience that showed that they were capable of doing all that was required? None of these questions were easy. They looked at the chances of actually winning New York State grants, Federal grants, local foundations, and national foundations. Then, if they believed that they qualified, they needed partners that they never had before, like equal partners with other foundations to get bigger grants, partnerships with school districts, and local colleges. All those partnerships had to be established before they ever submitted an application to be funded.

Mathematically, the chances for getting funded for New York State grants was over sixty percent, since they were in the Capital of New York State and their clients had high poverty and great need. Local grants had a probability of fifty/fifty. Federal grants were in the low thirty percent, and the hardest to receive funding from was national foundations coming in less than twenty percent. Therefore for the first year, Joe concentrated on New York State government grants, and partnerships with local school districts. As they grew, he took more chances on the lower hanging foundation fruit. He brought in new money, developed new programs, and became noticed for the very first time in many cases by local government officials, and especially the community. The Chamber gave the Coalition a plaque as most innovative nonprofit of the year. It was a very proud moment for all of them.

This worked wonders for Joe's social life. At thirty-two, he might just as well be a Monk in Vermont singing Gregorian chants and making cheesecake. His only social outlet was tending bar on the weekends at McGuire's, near the Sage campus in downtown Troy. He owed $22,000.00 when he graduated from Rensselaer and the $400.00 a month student loan continues to kill him. He got it down below $10,000.00, now, with two years to go. At least bartending helped pay his loan and he got to drink for free, just enough not to get drunk and close up at two a.m. He got a few dates out of it—not much, but okay.

All that Joe and Missy had done on behalf of the Coalition, now looked like child's play, compared to Luis's efforts over the last six months. Joe brought in a million dollars in two plus years and Luis brought in two million dollars in six months, with another two million in the hopper and pending. Joe looked like a piker compared to

Luis. Joe knew what he built from scratch for this organization. That was why he felt so bad and saw Ted Simmons drift away from him over the last six months. Before Ted's death, Joe wanted to sit down with him and review what they had done before Luis arrived. Joe knew how hard it was to raise millions of dollars. He did not say anything about Luis's efforts but, since he filed all the projects, he knew what was involved.

The last six months of funding came too easily and he was very concerned about what was happening. He didn't see the same results that he had seen when he raised funds, working hand in hand with Missy, the board and their fellow staff members. He saw young adults receive their GED's and obtain jobs directly as a result of their team intervention. No staff was now involved in the grant writing process. It was Luis directing Joe to send in one grant after the other. He may have had a plan but never shared it with him or anyone else.

Joe walked downstairs to the training facility many times and never saw a soul. He shook his head and now was putting the pieces together. What appeared to be happening on the surface was not, in fact, happening to Joe's satisfaction. He needed to construct a timeline of events, funding, dollars spent, and results, to see if it was just his opinion or if it was fact. Nothing happened here at the Coalition, but they sure spent a lot of money.

CHAPTER 15

On Monday, Luis got to the office around nine a.m. He never got there earlier. It would have been bad form for him to have to mingle with the staff every morning over coffee. *How was your weekend? How are you*? He could skip that easily.

He saw Joe in the hallway. "Hi, Joe. Can you meet at eleven a.m. and bring me up to date on what was going on?"

"Sure, Luis," Joe said. "See you then."

Luis started to feel like the interim president as long as it didn't interfere with what he needed to do. After seeing Luis in the hallway, Joe went to his office for the next two hours to finish more paperwork for the Hudson Foundation. He could hardly stay on top of it. Luis didn't seem to know or care what was involved in the processes required by each funder.

⁊⊃⊱⊃

Joe's mind wandered back to the day last summer when Ted Simmons, smiling from ear to ear, walked in to his office with Luis Hernandez.

At the time, Ted had said, "Joe, I would like you to

meet Luis, who is starting today as our new Vice Present for Operations and Development."

The Coalition's old vice president just retired and the board left the position open, hoping that it would be filled with Luis, after learning about the Hispanic Management Outreach program at the NCWA.

"Luis will be reporting directly to me as a member of the senior management team," Ted said.

"Nice to meet you," Joe said.

"You will eventually be reporting to Luis after he gets settled," Ted said, "and, in the meantime, you will still work directly with me on grants." He turned to Luis. "Joe has been here for two years and has done a remarkable job. We never had any grants of any significance, let alone pledges on Facebook, until Joe got here. Not bad, considering this is his first job in the private sector since high school."

"Where were you before, Joe?" Luis asked,

"I took a long route to get here." Joe smiled. "I went into the Coast Guard at eighteen, spent ten years, got my degree from the Coast Guard Academy and just completed my MBA before starting at the Coalition."

Luis smiled back. "That's a hell of a route."

"Yes, I look forward to working with you after you get settled," Joe said.

"Luis, Joe offered to show you around," Ted said, "get you settled and help acclimate you to our area."

I offered, huh? Joe thought.

Ted clapped Joe on the shoulder. "He grew up in Troy, just up the road, and knows the area better than almost anybody."

"Where are you staying?" Joe asked Luis.

"Well, I just got in last night from California and I booked a room down on Broadway near the bus terminal. It's the Albany Express Motel," Luis said. "It seems very convenient for now. I can walk up the hill to Central Avenue and it would probably do me good."

"If you want, I can drive you back down when you're ready to head out," Joe said.

"Thanks, Joe. That's great. I'll take you up on it. Can we leave around four p.m. this afternoon? That is, if you don't mind, Ted."

"No problem," said Ted. "We are glad to have you on board. Whatever you need to make you feel more comfortable and fit in, we'd be glad to do so."

"Thanks," Luis said.

"Ted, do you want me to show him around today for a while before we leave?" asked Joe.

"Not today, Joe, I'll bring him around to the rest of the staff and then he can meet you at the lobby by four p.m."

"Great, nice meeting you Luis, I'll see you at four," Joe said. *And off to the races.*

At the time, Joe remembered that Luis seemed okay, a little reserved, and it was to be expected. Joe was also a little reserved when he first started. It was Joe's first job and he wanted to make a good impression. *That's probably all that's going on,* he thought at the time. Now, it was a different story. Joe thought he got a good read on Luis and would move accordingly, now that he was interim president.

When Joe had shaken his hand last summer and looked him in the eyes, he noticed a darkness that he could not figure out. At the time, he thought it must have been him. Joe also was probably a little pissed and jealous as well but didn't think so at the time. Now that he looked back, that was exactly how he felt. But who could have blamed Ted at that time for getting free help. He also hoped that Ted wouldn't underestimate his skills now that he had Luis. With Ted's death, that went away quickly, especially since Dan, Ted's son, was a close friend and would help Joe with his investigation and any legal issues that could arise. He thought at the time that things would be very different, but didn't think it would be this different now.

Joe remembered calling Mark and got his read. Mark thought that maybe he was a little jealous at the time but really didn't blame him. Mark wanted him back in Florida as his partner in the investigation department for the Coast Guard. He knew that Joe could come back anytime he wanted.

Joe remembered that, at the time Luis arrived, no matter what, he decided he would show Luis the ropes and drive him around the area. He still had his staff of one, Missy, but wondered if that would change as well when put under Luis's supervision. *Time would tell*, he guessed.

Joe met Luis in the lobby that day and they walked out together to Joe's car that hot summer evening. Joe asked him if he wanted to go to dinner. He said he could wait in the car until he went back to the motel and cleaned up.

"Thank you, I had a long day," Luis said, "and I just want a sub and a couple of beers."

They stopped at Subway and Stewarts and got Luis his dinner and liquid refreshment. Luis thanked Joe and said he looked forward to seeing him the next day and if they had time, they should go over the Coalition's current grants and those in the hopper and any other ideas they might have for the year. Joe said goodbye and took a left back onto I-787, and drove home to Troy.

Joe remembered Ted patting Luis on the back and he felt like he was being treated like a peon. Missy noticed it as well and said something quietly to Joe. She wanted to know if she should update her resume. Joe assured her that it would be unnecessary, even though he felt the same way at the time.

Joe was puzzled, at the time, on what he should and shouldn't say to Luis. Maybe it was just him. He thought he would wait until he got the lay of the land from Luis before he started spilling his guts. He's glad he did, now. He really didn't know if he was there for the long run or just to fulfill his obligation. Hell, he didn't know anyone here and he was 2,500 miles from home. *Does he have a girlfriend?* Joe didn't know if he was married or single. He read his bio. Joe said to himself, at the time, tomorrow was a new day. Little did he know, at the time, what was coming.

℘℘℘

The two hours came quickly on Luis's first day back from vacation, and Joe went into Luis office, which used to be Ted's. That was hard getting used to. Joe went over the submission of the Ettinger grant that he sent in while Luis was away on vacation. He called the foundation and they told him that this year they would notify the winners as soon as they receive a submission that they deemed responsive to their needs. He also worked on the Hudson Foundation grant for the exact same thing. Luis quickly told Joe that the Ettinger Foundation of Seattle just called him and told him at ten a.m. that morning that they had secured an additional million dollars, each year for three years, for career development for Albany at-risk youth. He wanted to wait until Monday to make the announcement with the board of directors.

"Congratulations, Joe, for a job well done by both you and Missy," Luis said.

Luis finally admitted to himself that Joe, even though he didn't like him or trust him, was very good at his job.

They now could provide training for jobs for over 400 youth per year but Joe didn't have a clue how that would be possible with the limited space downstairs. He would ask Luis eventually about the requirements for space as they kept assigning more youth to job programs. *Ground Hog Day, here we come.*

Nothing else of importance was pending so Joe told Luis that he met with various state agencies that week for pending grants for the fall. There was in fact a grant season. The federal year ran from October first to September thirtieth of the following year. New York State education grants tended to go from July first to June thirtieth of the next year. National foundations had cycles that reflected their own internal mission and usually had due dates four times a year at the beginning of each quarter. Grants were really tough to keep track of from year to year. Most grants overlapped the Coalition's own fiscal year of January first to December thirty-first. That meant that grant funded programs, and contracts, overlapped year to year, falling into one year and then another, while Joe had to keep track of both. He also had to keep track of budgets for the departments, funded by the grants, and made sure that those grants reflected actual monthly expenses and billed accordingly.

He spent a ton of time with accounting. That was how he met Mary. She worked on every grant they produced.

Mary told Joe that, in the case of multiple year grants, it was damn near impossible to keep track of what fiscal year each grant fell into. They also had to make sure that when one grant ended, another started right up so there was no lapse in service or payments to vendors and needed to keep their own Coalition employees flush. It was tough laying people off because a new grant didn't get funded when an old grant expired.

That was what Joe was dealing with on top of managing all of these new Luis' career grants.

After work, Joe met Dan at his office only a few blocks away down State Street, at the foot of Capital Hill in Albany. Joe called him around three p.m. and told him it was important, very important to meet.

"What's up, Joe?" Dan asked.

Joe went through everything he knew at this point. He also explained the significance of leaving out a very important question in the request for proposal for the Ettinger Foundation. "Dan, I even left off the required signature. Luis never read it. He was away, and George Fontaine doesn't have a clue. However, in less than a week, this grant was fully funded for $1,000,000.00 per year, for three consecutive years, without answering the most important question left off the narrative. They never read it at the foundation, and they seemed to push it through at record speed." He shook his head. "Dan, something's not right."

The information Joe requested from his friends Mark and Jack would be coming in soon and, hopefully, confirming his belief that there was a conspiracy going on in huge proportions across the country. This Albany Coalition for Families was just the tip of the iceberg, but it was the tip that would tumble Luis and his friends.

CHAPTER 16

The Mexican Mafia, *LaEme,* worked with their legitimate—seemingly so—attorneys, bankers, and accountants and decided, as a first phase of a strategic plan, to legitimize their illegal activities. They needed to move their children into the main stream of American society, in the eyes of the public, through education, good jobs, and a place at the table for business opportunities. Gang membership was down. Those in prison were pretty much there for the duration, and, since Nine/Eleven, Homeland Security was not letting up and redefining terrorism to include gang activity. Under the Patriot Act, these top gun gang bangers were being pulled off the street and wound up in rendition to Cuba, just like those terrorists from the Middle East. They were lumped together and the generals needed a new direction.

Jorge Hernandez, age fifty-two, had been in the Duel Vocational Institute in Tracy, California for the last fifteen years, with a life sentence, on a conviction of first degree murder. He was second generation Mexican Mafia, and over the last several years, had moved up in the organization as the managing general at this facility. Since all gang activities were managed within prison walls in California, it was almost like being at corporate headquarters. Jorge's attorney, Frank Ramone, of the law firm Smith, Finkle and Ramone LLC, had come to the prison to supposedly discuss his ongoing court petitions for various disagreements inside including his ongoing appeal. Jorge would petition over the smallest slight, simply to get his attorney in front of him so he could discuss gang business from the inside. This law firm was considered a premier firm in the Los Angeles area. Like the Italian Mafia, on the East Coast, the Mexican Mafia could afford to pay the best attorneys in California. The fees charged for services, more than justified a partner showing up to visit a client in prison.

"Good morning, Jorge. How are you?" Frank asked.

Across the table, Jorge was chained arms and legs to the table and the floor, the price that Jorge paid to get his attorney in front of him. "I'm fine, Frank. How's my appeal going?"

This was code for a conversation that would take place with a normal litany of terms that the guards, who no doubt were listening, would only have thought to be normal conversation. Frank was told by Jorge to update him on the laundering scheme. After all, Frank just met with Luis in New York City and Jorge wanted to know how he was doing. In code, Frank told him that Luis was well, was doing great, and was on plan. He let it go for now. Jorge didn't know that Frank hated Luis and Luis hated Frank. Frank needed time to turn Luis around. Luis had no access to Jorge without Frank's intervention.

Frank, as president of the Glendale Real Estate Trust LLC, financed the gang's Section-Eight apartment complex in Glendale for five million dollars over fifteen years. The property with one hundred apartments, was fully paid for, and, managed by the attorney firm through its senior partner, Frank Ramone. The apartment complex was valued at $100,000.00 per apartment for a total of ten million dollars. To ensure that the loan went through, the Real Estate Trust LLC collateralized the Section-Eight voucher payments, which were then sent directly into a lockbox depository, set up by the savings and loan, so that the government payments could only be used to pay down the mortgage.

Both Jorge and Frank knew that the Glendale Savings and Loan Association saw this as a very good investment. It was fully secured by an asset twice as large as the one-hundred-percent fully secured loan. This loan was approved and a check for five million dollars, from the legitimate Real Estate Trust LLC run by Frank, was used to start an Endowment for the new Hispanic Management Outreach program at the National Child Welfare Association, NCWA, in San Diego for the benefit of thirty high school students at Los Angeles High School. Luis was one of the first students approved for the program.

Jorge remembered asking Frank at the time how Luis was doing. He was doing very well and was in the top five in his class in high school, taking all college prep courses. Back then just like now Jorge insisted on telling Luis "no tattoos" or any indication of the life they led.

This was also code which told Luis, both then and now, to watch his rear end, and do not get involved in the business of the streets. Luis learned the ins and outs, outside the eyes of the world. Frank funneled thousands of dollars in cash every month to every family member of those gang officers and soldiers in prison. Obviously, the generals and other upper officers were well taken care of, and all the other gang member families were given a stipend as long as the gang member stayed in line. It was how they kept order and how orders were never questioned.

Frank was really pissed at Luis after meeting him in New York City. Here he was, now a partner in one of the biggest law firms in Los Angeles and had to listen to that punk who thought he knew everything because his father was the general of all generals. Frank started young and would have been dead without the Mexican Mafia helping out him and his family as he grew up on the streets of Los Angeles, living next door to Jorge and his family,

Little Frankie Ramone, age twelve, lived on the same block, actually next door to Jorge. He knew he wanted be a lawyer someday. Frankie was the Mexican Mafia's first project twenty-four years ago. Now, at forty-six years old, Frank Ramone was a senior partner at Smith, Finkle, and Ramone LLC, a proven law firm in Los Angeles, with a lot of political clout. The gang protected Frankie all the way through middle and high school, with a "do not touch" label. They paid his way through Cal Tech, and then on to law school. He was, at twelve years old, small and nerdish, the perfect combination. Frank was heavily recruited by several major law firms in Los Angeles. The gang thought that Smith, Finkle LLC would be ideal for him. He was the first Hispanic lawyer for the group, specialized in real estate, and was an example for the Hispanic community on how you could rise above poverty and pulled yourself up by your own bootstraps and became successful. No one ever knew that the gang spent over a million dollars on little Frankie Ramone and his family. They more than got their money back. *Screw Luis, he thought.*

After seven years, Frank was invited to be a partner and the cash contribution for partnership was $600,000.00. On the up and up, he went to the Glendale Savings and Loan and took out a fifteen-year loan, secured by his partnership agreement. Cash was given to Frank directly by the gang to pay the monthly installments. In time, Frank moved to Glendale, became a pillar of this community, and was asked to sit on the Board of

Trustees for this savings and loan. A savings and loan association was owned by its depositors. So, there was never a shareholder inquiry or stockholder meeting to contend with. It was pretty much run by the internal Board.

When Frank brought the five million dollar loan opportunity to his own Glendale Savings and Loan, he abstained from the voting, since he was president of the company who asked for the loan, wink-wink. The savings and loan was too small to carry a loan of that size, with their debt and asset structure they could only approve two million dollars. They packaged the loan and sold it to the Los Angeles Life Insurance Company, through its investment department. This placed the loan even at further arms' length so there was no question of legality and possible contact to the real owners of the loan. It was divided into so many sub-loans that no cursory audit would ever pick up any collusion. Jorge was very pleased with Frank, his involvement with the gang, and he knew that the future of the Mexican Mafia would be secured through this endowment effort.

The generals, including Jorge Hernandez, and their associated captains and lieutenants, decided that this new strategic direction would now include as a start the establishment of this special fund to identify high academic achieving sons and daughters of the Mexican Mafia as third generation members that would continue pursuing legitimate enterprises with laundered illegal funds. This program followed the same principles for buoying up Frank Ramone so many years ago.

The program identified these youth and followed them through high school, to college, and on to graduate school, as they became the supposed legitimate members of the upper class based on educational attainment, and recognition of their mental abilities, as a front to their real intentions later on to continue gang activities. As they knew, most of the Mexican Mafia officials could teach a college course in entrepreneurship and business. Their children were extremely smart, but no one had the foresight to move them into the legitimate economy. The Italian Mafia was not just a role model for illegal activity, but also, became their model into respectability, as well as their entry into the legitimate business world.

The gang attorneys, bankers, and accountants previously did exhaustive costly research on opportunities to move their illegal funds to a legitimate operation. They would donate a large amount of cash, once laundered, through one or more of their large emerging legal enterprises, to a non-profit national accrediting council. They decided on the Glendale Real Estate Trust and used this as the vehicle to start the process. It would be a legitimate tax deduction for the front businesses, already established in the city of Los Angeles, against any Trust earnings. They had worked on the legitimization of their organization for a while, but never had a total plan. This would be the start of a strategy for another era.

It took a while, but their research finally focused on the National Child Welfare Association "NCWA," located in San Diego, California. The NCWA was a premier national child welfare association that certified non-profit organizations across the country as to standards and quality assurance that would meet local, state, and Federal regulatory requirements. They were the watchdog organization and certifying entity for their member organizations. The gang wanted the Association close to them but outside Los Angeles for authenticity and legitimacy reasons. As soon as identified, the mortgage was immediately secured for the endowment, and no time was wasted.

The front group presenting the endowment opportunity to the Association, funded fully by the gang, included many very prominent professionals in Los Angeles, including the law firm of Smith, Finkle and Ramone, LLC. They met with the NCWA in San Diego. The presentation was for the development of this well researched and funded Hispanic Management Outreach program, under the banner of the National Child Welfare Association. The NCWA would receive the five million dollar endowment that would come from the Glendale Real Estate Trust. However, the donors were to remain anonymous even though to the world they were legitimate, that would fully fund this program. They did not want the publicity or a focus on their activities. The NCWA gladly complied.

A combined group consisting of NCWA members would manage the endowment with a majority of membership handpicked through the representative group for the anonymous donor. The NCWA would receive annual compensation of five hundred thousand dollars per year for their efforts. The endowment could only be forfeited if the Association merged or closed.

The first group of youth selected came from Los Angeles Senior High School. Thirty students, selected through a screening process, were selected. The process was based on pre-SAT scores, standardized tests, and the applicants, boys and girls both, had to be of a minimum of fifty percent Mexican descent. The papers were signed. The program began that fall. Recruitment started during the summer prior to classes beginning. The thirty students selected, with bribes to school officials from the gang members, and other well places sources, included thirty very smart young men and women, all Mexican Mafia gang member children.

The high school itself was selected because that was where the families resided. The children already went to school there. Selecting them was not an issue because these individuals were already being groomed as third-generation members, heading to legitimacy. They each knew the score, kept their noses clean, and all graduated with honors. Each of the thirty was very smart and did well on their own. They all could have gone legitimate but that wasn't really the point. Los Angeles High School with a student population of over 2,000 was eighty percent Hispanic—1,600—and eighty percent socio-economically disadvantaged as well. If your parent was in jail, you were deemed economically disadvantaged. It was the perfect center for choosing "legitimate" Mexican kids for higher education opportunities.

The point was for these thirty participants to be as clean as the driven snow while they were fully supported by the gang, who protected them on the streets, in the schools, and there was no question that if anyone screwed with anyone of them, there would be severe consequences. It was well understood. It was the Mexican Mafias main identity of intimidation. Each "student" had an invisible mark or a halo over each of his or her head. *Do not touch.*

The program worked like a champ. The NCWA didn't have a clue to what they bought into. They were enjoying their five hundred thousand dollars administrative fee every year. The kids had summer internships during their sophomore, junior, and senior years, in San Diego all at the NCWA and each had a paid mentor, a paid clean-cut family member, keeping a close eye on them while they were away.

They did very meaningful work while at the Association. The Association was happy and bragged about this national outreach program that they developed for their Association members. These kids were bright just differently motivated, unknown to the Association.

All thirty participants graduated on time with honors

and then they applied to the same colleges and universities, all part of the California University system. Once they applied, they received scholarships based on merit, ethnicity, and poverty. The endowment picked up all the difference in tuition, room and board, and living expenses including trips back home. Not all of these students who started had completed their first college degree. Of the thirty, five dropped out and went back to the barrio from which they came. They were in for dire consequences from the Mafia family member who had to explain to their general "why?" Some were replaced, never to be seen again, entire families.

Of the twenty-five left, twenty went on to an IVY-league MBA degree and/or whatever degree they needed to land at a non-profit agency or foundation throughout the country. The other five came home and started to work in the legitimate family grown businesses, assuring their legitimacy. The stories were heartwarming to the rest of the members. They accomplished this first and later it was proven to be very rewarding in the long run. The remaining twenty completed their Masters level work, and completed internships at both national foundations and non-profits in Southern California. Upon graduation, each of the twenty spent two years at another Southern California non-profit before the NCWA offered their services to non-profit members across the country.

Luis Hernandez was one of the original thirty applicants approved for the program. He was a son of the general of generals, who was in the California penal system for life. At fifteen, at Los Angeles High School, Luis was kept out of gang activities, had no tattoos. None of the approved thirty did. Luis sat in on gang business for educational purposes. He assisted at a low level in the planning of gang activities, was taught everything he need to know to be street smart without getting into the street. As a third generation on his way to big things, he knew no other life. He studied hard, had no reservations about what was coming, and make no mistake, he was a lifer. A "made-man" in the Mexican Mafia at eighteen.

His initiation, like the other thirty, had to do with mental challenges not making his bones by killing someone. He had to remain clean and presentable at all times. He was akin to the Russian gymnast brought to Moscow at age eight to start his sports training for the Summer Olympics, ten years later. He was the boy who joined the Catholic seminary at age sixteen to become a priest, knowing no other way of life. The only difference was that he was surrounded and watched by family members unlike the seminarian and Olympic star who left home and family forever. Luis was the family jewel.

Upon completion of the master's degree, ten graduates went to non-profits, eight went to national foundations, and two worked at the NCWA in high-level positions. This assured that the five million dollar endowment was only touched by those related to the gang. The ten non-profit candidates like Luis, who went to the Albany Coalition for Families, wound up in Bethlehem, Pennsylvania at the Children's Action Network, Cornerstone Family and Children in Tyler Texas, the Gary Community Coalition in Gary, Indiana, Great Lakes Parents and Children in Racine, Wisconsin, Northwest Families in Hillsboro, Oregon, The Council for Children in Boca Raton, Florida, Renton Family Services in Renton, Washington, the Gilbert Action Network in Gilbert, Arizona, and the Hartford Career Center, Hartford Connecticut.

The other eight, who went to work in large national private foundations, went to the George Johnson Foundation in San Francisco, the Harold Block Charitable Foundation in Houston, The Ettinger Foundation in Seattle, The Hudson Foundation in New York City, Bremmer

Family Foundation in Las Vegas, the King Family Foundation in Beaumont Texas, The Parker Foundation in Miami, and CYC Corporate Foundation in Boston. All of these foundations served families and children at risk throughout the country, and specialized in job placements for minority youth and education. All were privately funded and all had IRS tax issues and had to increase their annual giving to get back in good graces with the IRS.

When Luis gave the names of the foundations to Joe to start the application process, he told him, after Joe asked, that the foundations were picked after much research. He told him, during his internships at the association that he was to identify national foundations that would fund programs across the country specifically for teens and young adults to get jobs in high tech areas. That was partial true, but not the real reason. Luis, although the son of a Mexican Mafia general, was also heavily involved in the administration of the roll out of the Hispanic Management Outreach program that wound up at the NCWA in San Diego.

His priority for picking both the non-profits and the foundations had only a few key criteria. Number one: they were spread out and of a certain size—ten to fifteen million dollars in annual budgets—and number two: the organizations needed an influx of minority employees and had been criticized in the past and couldn't win grants from Foundations that required the employee mix to reflect a minority community that they served.

Another major criteria included complacency, with no real growth in several years, and an aging senior staff and aging board. This would mean that offered the opportunity for a well-educated free IVY-league MBA graduate, they would hop on the opportunity, thinking funding would soon follow, especially, when backed by their own accrediting association. The Foundations were picked for pretty much the same reasons. Family-owned foundations, older family members in their seventies and eighties who were tired of the responsibility and the chance to bring in new blood for the twenty-first century, especially minorities since that was who they were funding.

The NCWA was a breeze. Hardly any association would turn down a five million dollar endowment established, and advertised with their name on it and to get a five hundred thousand dollar annual fee to manage thirty kids and pass through their scholarship fees, was a godsend. They thought they died and went to heaven. So now the base would be built to accomplish everything the Mexican Mafia would need, would have zero visibility, and have white, highly respectable professionals in charge, with legitimate companies funding the project. And, they were even allowed to keep the name of the donor anonymous. Great.

It was just a matter of time before the Mexican Mafia really began to produce income with new and improved laundering opportunities.

This was a legitimate chance to turn five million dollars into a billion dollar enterprise if done right, and when moved from Foundation to non-profit, to non-descript vendors, by the time it was done, there would be no trail whatsoever. It was brilliant.

The process had to take place and be established during the first two years of inception so that the next wave of Los Angeles High School students, all gang member children, could then move into those jobs. The final twenty would move into the companies set up with foundation funds flowing to the unsuspecting non-profit companies. The management team at all the locations, including the NCWA, would be noticeably well educated, impeccably credentialed, third and fourth generation Hispanic upper

middle class citizens. No one would ever suspect anything. It was the perfect plan.

CHAPTER 17

Luis had been at the Albany Coalition for Families since the middle of the summer, almost six months since the day he arrived. As soon as Luis started, after Ted's introduction, Joe knew things were going to be much different. He just had that feeling. Joe always got to work early around seven a.m., parked his car, and got his coffee and two donuts at the Dunkin Donuts on the corner. Thank God for Dunkin Donuts. Day in and day out, Joe got the same order. He never had time or the inclination to cook his breakfast or make his lunch. He hardly had time to breath in the morning, get out of bed, shower, have one cup of coffee and then head out before I-787 became a parking lot going into downtown Albany.

He knew they were not New York City or Boston but at eight a.m., there must be at least 100,000 people driving along I-90 and I-787, the center of New York State and government offices. By ten a.m. you could walk down the middle of the highway and not see a car. Traffic, once again, became unbearable at four p.m., when state workers started heading north, out of the city toward home.

He tried to catch up on his work before everyone got in. He have two grants due by that Friday, and it was now

Tuesday and he had not gotten his answers back from program staff to complete the narrative and budgets, and they needed it approved by the end of that week. Every day felt like the movie *Groundhog Day*. He thought he did the same grant over and over and over again. He could hear Cher singing *"Then put your little hand in mine." God, he was going nuts!* Same answers, same information just piled higher and deeper depending on the size of the grant. These two grants due that week were for $100,000.00 each to serve local dropouts, to get their GED, and hopefully a job at the local grocery chain. Little did he know at the time that these two grants were miniscule in relationship with what was to come under Luis's leadership. He thought later that maybe Luis was right. It was easier to secure a million dollar grant than two individual one hundred thousand dollar grants.

The paperwork for major grants was the same as for smaller ones. The budgets just had bigger numbers. The grants were not long or intricate and the applications were to two local foundations that have funded them previously. However, like everyone else they wanted something unique, interesting and could be submitted in fewer than ten pages of narrative and a one-page budget. He had to write thirty pages and then cut it to ten pages to meet their required information. *No problem.* On that day, it was getting close to nine a.m. and he had to spend most of the morning with Ted and Luis to decide what they wanted to tackle after these two grants went in. These two grants were a major priority for Joe since their board members were close friends to several board members on both of the local foundations.

Luis was already sitting at the conference table and looked like he had been there for a while. He had two empty coffee cups and what was left of a half-eaten donut. *At least we agree on nutrition,* Joe thought at the time. They didn't agree on much else.

"Joe, will you fully review what you had worked on the last year and give a synopsis of where we are going?" Luis had said.

Joe realized at the time that Luis had an agenda but he didn't quite know what it was.

Back then, Joe had wished that he had a little notice beforehand of what was to be discussed, but as he suspected, this was not Luis's plan. *Do your very best*, he thought. From memory, Joe took both Ted and Luis through what they had submitted over the last year, what got funded, what didn't, what would be resubmitted after looking at the reviewer notes, and then they would decide if they could actually accomplish what they intended and what they wanted to do as a non-profit organization. Everything that Joe had submitted since he had been there met the mission statement of the organization. The board had insisted on that from the start. In total, they had already raised almost $1,000,000.00 since Joe got there, only going into their third year of developing proposals for submission.

"Luis, we are being noticed," Joe had said at the time, "and we are now getting a seat at the table for government agency meetings, school districts, and local foundation presentations that we have never been invited in to participate in, before."

Usually, from everything Joe read, it took a good solid three years of progressive marketing and building fundable programs before things started to click. He was also sure that if he'd had the background and knowledge coming in, that they could have won more. They were paying Joe $50,000.00 a year, plus benefits, and for the amount of time he had been there, he had accomplished quite a bit as he developed a reputation for success outside the Coalition. He got the feeling that Luis would never be satisfied. It was just a hunch. Joe had no direct knowledge of anything pending but Luis was only twenty-eight years old and wanted to make a name for himself over the next two years. *And here we go*, Joe thought at the time.

Then, after Joe's presentation, Luis finally spoke. All he did for two hours was to listen to what Joe had to say. But Joe played it close to the vest. He really wanted to see Luis's plans and agenda and a timetable for programs over the next two years.

"Joe, you've done an excellent job here," Luis had said. "Hopefully, in addition to what you started, which is very good, we will set the groundwork to really take off and grow the Albany Coalition for Families. I know it may seem premature, but I believe we can really get some national attention and find some national foundations to help us move in the direction that will help us become self-sustaining in the long run. I believe we will be successful and do enough to attract attention to change the way child and family welfare agencies operate and we will become a model for replication nationally."

Well, there it is, Joe thought. *We did "very good,"* he heard, *not great.*

"That sounds great, Luis."

"I believe we can move in that direction with careful planning," Ted had said. "We want to get our collective feet wet first and then try a few different things that include the development of a plan so we're all on the same page."

Joe didn't think they needed a full-blown strategic plan, but they needed a real carefully developed operating plan this year, especially with money tight and their funding from government agencies drying up. Luis sat there passively with a slight smile on his face. Joe couldn't read the meaning of that hardly noticeable grin at the time, but now after he spoke to Mark and the boys earlier, he knew he should be doubly careful on what he would say or do.

As Joe thought about it now, he knew that his first impressions were always the best. His first impressions of Luis were not flattering. *It's funny but I'm not all that much older than Luis*. He was twenty-eight and Joe was thirty-two, but he had a lot of hands-on experience in the Coast Guard and he definitely thought he was more mature than Luis because he had been on his own for so long.

Joe had similar academic qualifications but Luis did have the backing of the national association. Luis was very bright but he certainly didn't have the experience. *Let's see how this all unfolds*. Being buried in books wasn't the same as working at it every day. Luis had spent two years in California and at the National Child Welfare Association in high school for summer internships. Joe was sure that he wouldn't be here if he wasn't capable. At the time he had to trust the Board that things would work out.

Now, with Ted gone, and the Board falling all over Luis, Joe was not enamored by what he saw from Luis on an every-day basis. He was not a team player. He was aloof, and somewhat condescending. He definitely thought he was the brightest one in the room.

All Joe had, that he brought every day to the Coalition, was his reputation and hard work. Coming from a blue-collar family, and trying to live to a certain code, informed by all his experiences, is what got Joe up every day. He had always given a full day's work for a full day's pay. He never lied, cheated, or stole in his life. However, he was becoming very reluctant to put himself in a position that he would not be able to win. He was a movie buff and he always tried to memorize a lot of lines, just for fun and bar conversation. It was really good for cheesy pickups. But as Robert DeNero said in *Ronan*, "Never go into a room that you haven't been in before." *Words to live by, Bob.*

Ted had been a friend and a mentor, but everything changed after July. He got Joe his first start when he really needed it. Joe would never say anything against the man, especially now that Ted was dead and Dan was a very close friend. Joe respected the entire family and would never do anything to dishonor Ted's memory. That was why he went to Dan only days ago to tell him what he had suspected from the first few months since Luis arrived. Joe sincerely hoped that Ted's hiring of Luis wouldn't eventually seem like a joy ride in a stolen car with Ted's reputation left holding the bag as his legacy.

Chapter 18

Joe always was thankful for the training he got in the Coast Guard. He was also very thankful for the friends he met when he was eighteen, and still had now, at thirty-two. Mark Silva was like a brother to him. In fact, Joe was probably closer to Mark than to Pete, his own brother. Pete always sided with their father, no matter what the circumstances. Joe always thought Pete resented him because he was better at sports and was much better academically as well. There was no question that after high school, Pete would work full time for his father. There was also no question that Joe would not. He was headed for better things with a full scholarship to MIT. It was a surprise that he took a right turn after the first semester of his freshman year and headed to the Coast Guard. Everyone knew that Joe was extremely smart and would wind up on his feet wherever he landed. No one was ever sure about Pete.

Looking back, Joe's fourteen-week training program gave him the basics he needed to succeed for the next ten years in the Coast Guard and beyond, as he was finding out now. Mark probably saved his life on more than one occasion with his Spanglish lessons every other waking moment. The guttural sounds Joe began to know and love were like learning Shakespeare for the first time. "To be or not to be" was not quite as intuitive as "put a cap in your ass, mofo."

Learning from Mark was almost like learning math from the nun, Sister Edward Mary, who taught Joe in his third-grade classroom. They went over the times tables every day, twenty times a day, for the entire year. Even to this day, he still shook like a leaf when he saw an older nun on the street in her full veiled glory. Sister must have been at least seventy years old when she taught him. He couldn't stand her by the end of the year, but, by God, if they had *Jeopardy* for times tables, he was there. Joe's memory or recall, as it was now known, was unbelievable, and it really helped him understand math differently and that's why he was such a quick study. *What goes around comes around*, he guessed.

Mark and he were together for almost a full ten years both through boot camp to their assignment together at the COMMSTA communications facility in Miami (his last two were at the Academy, off and on, online and during the summer). Joe and Mark were inseparable teammates and they both spoke Spanish fluently, only thanks to Mark. Being together those last nine weeks at Yorktown, improved Joe's Spanish vocabulary, words he never spoke before, a duel language. Mark and he were joined at the hip. Their other starter-team mates went on to other things but they always tried their best to stay in contact with Mark and Joe, knowing they were never far apart.

Jack Forest moved on to officer's training his second year. Sean wound up at the Coast Guard Academy in New London during his fourth year. Mike's first love was the sea and wound up as a boatswain mate and master seaman, serving on a Coastal Patrol Boat out of San Diego. His vessel, the *Haddock*, was an eighty-seven-footer with one officer and ten enlisted men. She—boats were she, except for Russia, where boats were he—had a top speed of twenty-six knots, 2,860 horsepower engine, two fifty-caliber machine guns, and a number of smaller arms. She was commissioned after a 5,000 nautical mile voyage from Louisiana. Since Haddock's arrival to the west coast, she had actively patrolled from the United States and Mexico borders to Los Angeles, and offshore up to 200 nautical miles. Her primary missions included search and rescue, homeland security and law enforcement. Mike was second on this vessel and he had seen plenty of duty chasing drug boats, illegal immigrants, and other internal homeland security issues, none of which he could discuss.

Mark met Mike when he went home to San Diego to visit his mother and sisters, since Mike was now stationed there. Mike kept updated on his boot camp friends. Both Mark and Mike have a strong loyalty and sense of responsibility for their mutual friends, including Joe. They had their backs.

Joe finished up after ten years as a master chief petty officer—E9—a non-commissioned officer, the same rank as Tom Jones. It was as far as he was going to go without becoming an officer. Joe's history, his own internal structure, was blue collar all the way and this was where it ended for him. He didn't want to become a lifer in the Coast Guard. He wanted more. He wanted out. He figured out that the thing he was the best at in the Coast Guard was insubordination. He was able to piss people off within ten seconds. It was a gift that he had learned to use wisely. In spite of this gift, as a final hurrah, he got his Bachelors of Science in Strategic Intelligence as a reward for his service doing specials ops at the COMMSTA facility in Miami all those years. Even after coming home, Joe and Mark, and the boys, tried to always stay in touch the best they could. They were family as much as any real family, and in many ways, they were even closer.

∽∾∽

Joe came home with his Bachelor of Science and could speak Spanish fluently, not just classroom textbook Spanish but real Latino street lingo. He never told anyone his secret. He also received eighteen credits with a minor in Spanish but continued to keep that to himself. There were no transcripts in the Coast Guard due to national security for Joe's job. *Thank God.*

What he learned over the years in communications, analysis, operations, planning, data retrieval, computer technology, and clandestine work had served him well, even now, and especially now with his sights set on Luis. Hopefully, Joe would know when someone was bullshitting him, in two languages—actually three, including Spanglish—who to trust, tell-signs learned in poker games during down time, and other street-smart skills. Mad math skills helped, but the other attributes trumped math.

He knew but could not prove yet that Luis had another agenda. He also thought Luis had something to do with Ted's death, but that was probably never going to be proven.

Joe also learned other various skills from Mark: how to strip a car; open a door in under one minute; how to hide valuables; surveillance, the real kind; and how to know when trouble was coming. Having an idea that the bullets were flying beforehand helped your self-preservation instinct. How to pick up Latino girls was actually very helpful. It was not the language. It was the attitude and exact wording, the gestures, different from his own in upstate New York. That made all the difference in the world. No one expected it of him, and they were quite surprised.

Their chief, Tom Jones, didn't teach them to kick them in the balls and run. "These colors never run," he'd said.

The kick them in the balls, a special lesson plan, was provided by Mark. He was a good friend to have, and a bad enemy to make. Mark quoted regularly from The Attila the Hun School of Management handbook that stated, "Only Make an Enemy on Purpose." They learned that lesson well. Evidently it was in the gangbangers' collection of persuasion and management techniques. It was quite effective.

Jumping into the deep end of the pool without a life-jacket at eighteen, literally and physically, really helped Joe figure out who he was, what he wanted to be, and how he needed to act. The things he could do, would do, and learned not to do, gave him his moral compass. It was the same, but a very different view, the flip side view from his Catholic education and upbringing. Being trained for peace meant being trained for war. The war on cartels was just as dangerous as those who experienced daily terror in the Middle East and Afghanistan.

Thinking about it, Joe loved his older brother, Pete, but his experiences and Joe's were so far apart, it took him a long time to recognize Pete's good traits and ignore his provincial look on life. Pete worked with his father and would until the day his father died. His life would suffer so much more than Joe's because of that intractable tie, when their father died or even retired. Pete would then have to stand on his own. Joe has done that since he turned eighteen.

Joe remembered that he was scared entering the service. Afraid no. Joe wasn't afraid standing up to older kids at One Hundred Twelfth Street Park in the Burgh. Joe got his ass kicked many times, but never backed down. Joe told one kid when he was twelve, and the older boy was fourteen, that he would have to kill him before he would stop. He did not want to go home with a black eye and cuts without a win, or at least getting in a few good punches. In the midst of some very dangerous situations, he still remembered the look on that kid's face. He knew how serious Joe was, even at twelve. Joe couldn't joke his way out of that, couldn't really do it now. Still tried, still didn't work. Joe's father always told him to stand up to a bully. If you hit him hard enough, and often enough, he wouldn't bother him anymore. Bullies are usually cowards and almost always will back down. Joe would carry that to his grave.

CHAPTER 19

Luis had to go back to the Albany Express Motel on Broadway, at the foot of State Street. He had to meet again with his own California crew and the just-recruited Orange Street Boys. Orange Street was just two blocks east and down the hill from the Albany Coalition for Families. Other gangs in Albany included the Crips and the Bloods but the Orange Street Boys were not affiliated with either gang and could be recruited easier by just showing them the money.

When Luis asked them what they did, one of the OSB said, "We do all kinds of stuff but mostly make money selling drugs. We do pack guns, but that's only for protection in case something jumped off."

They all wanted the lifestyle, the money, the partying, the girls, and no one giving them shit anymore. It was hard to break away.

"We're tired of being poor," one of them said.

Luis had his work cut out for him, especially now that in addition to his own California crew, he had to please his new friends from the South Bronx and the OSB. They even told Luis that they didn't even sit out on their front stoops anymore. That was how they got recruited as sixteen-year-olds living in the south end.

Drive-by shootings in the south and north end sections of Albany were becoming a common occurrence. Most of the OSB members were friends growing up and joined because they wanted to be just like everyone else. They all were trying to make as much as they could so they could get out of Albany, and head to the City, New York City. The dropout rate in Albany was over fifty percent at Albany High School, not as alarming as it sounded since all the inner city school districts had the same situation. Out of 10,000 students in the district, Albany High graduated 135 students last year. There should have been at least 500.

Luis had set up operations on the first floor of the Albany Coalition building, in the Career Center, where supposedly all the job training was taking place as part of these new grants. Every day, Luis went down and spoke to Jim Clark, the director for the center. Luis was not pleased with Jim's attitude toward the youth that Luis was recruiting. No longer were they being fingerprinted or even have a sheet pulled on the individuals to see if they had a record. Jim used to do a lot of sporadic drug testing. Luis told him since the funds were coming from private foundations that they didn't have to do that anymore. Just last year, Jim secured a grant, through Joe Traynor, that was supported by government funds. Although the grant was finished, and it was for only one year, Jim had used the same selection process, drug testing, and accountability practices to recruit young at-risk Albany kids.

Luis knew that eventually, Jim Clark had to go. He also knew that Jim and Joe were pretty good friends. Luis couldn't have him killed in a roll-over accident, like Ted, but he needed to get him out of the way. In the next class, Luis had recruited five Orange Street Boys to become students to earn their GED and get jobs. Luis couldn't have cared less, but he needed them to show up every day and have them act as Luis's eyes and ears. Five out of fifty would not really amount to anything suspicious. It would look like the Coalition was reaching down to train the poorest of the poor, and help those by giving them a second chance. The week before, Luis had discussed with Joe the possibility of developing proposals to the United States Juvenile Justice division to give job skills to youth coming out of incarceration. Joe was in favor of such training but the supervision would eat up all the grant money, and they needed special counseling, social services, housing, and child support that the Coalition was incapable of providing. Luis told Joe that they could do all those things under the private foundation funding. Joe was reticent, but there was nothing he could have said or done. It looked like Luis was on a mission.

Luis beckoned to the Orange Street Boys. "I'll look favorably on a mugging of one, Jim Clark, as he walks to his car, in the dark, down the hill."

Jim always stayed past six p.m. just to make sure that all the students had their lesson plans and all were out the door by the time he left. He was a creature of habit and everyone knew it.

⌘

Joe and Jim got together for lunch on several days during the week, just to talk about what was going on, what was working, what was not. Joe could tell that Jim was holding back when Joe asked him several direct questions. Joe knew that Jim was not happy with the current non-restrictions for participation. There were no pulled records, no drug testing, no TABE testing to see where they were academically. It was becoming a job mill, and Jim could not keep up with the internships and job placements they needed. He knew there weren't 400 job internships in the entire City of Albany. He was not allowed to hire any new direct counselors or job placement staff. He was told that the subcontractor vendors took care of all that. Jim was simply reduced to a building manager.

Luis only cared that the building was heated, the lights turned on, and that the doors were opened in the morning and locked at night. Joe saw the frustration on Jim's face but Joe certainly could not tell him of his suspicions about Luis and what he believed was happening.

Jim left right on the button at six p.m. He locked up. He was the last one to leave from the first floor. Joe was still on the third floor, in his office, completing, once again, another grant. The Hudson Foundation was due soon. Jim walked around the corner to lower Lark Street. The Coalition had a small parking lot in the back. He looked up and saw that several of the spotlights in the lot were blown out—or a rock had taken them out. Vandalism everywhere was on the rise. The economy may be back, but not on these streets in the city of Albany. There was still a recession going on here, and the poverty rate was skyrocketing right around the corner in Arbor Hill.

As Jim, hit his key fob to open the driver's side door, he noticed two guys coming up quickly from his front. He never saw the guy behind him with the tire iron. He went down hard. They continued to kick him in the head. They emptied his pockets, took his wallet and his watch. What the hell did they want with a fifty-dollar Timex watch, he thought later on. He never knew what hit him. A short time later, the Central Avenue bus stopped on the corner and left off its passengers. An older African-American woman got off the bus, and saw Jim on the ground as she walked by. She didn't have a cell phone but she went to the corner Dunkin Donuts and told the workers that someone had been mugged and to call an ambulance and the police.

Lower Lark Street was less than two miles from Albany Medical Center. The ambulance came quickly and they took Jim to the hospital. He had no identification on him, so they thought he may have been homeless but he was dressed normally, and they noticed that a key ring on the ground next to Jim. They pressed the button on the key fob and the doors opened and the dome light came on. They took down the license plate number and gave it to the policeman who had just arrived. Almost immediately, they found out that the car belonged to Jim Clark.

The police called his house and got a hold of his wife, Marie. Their oldest son, Tony, was there and together they rushed out of their Colonie home and headed to the emergency room. On their way to the hospital, Marie called Jim's office but no one answered. She immediately called again and got the directory for Joe. She was transferred to his office as he headed out the door. He wasn't going to answer the phone but he thought it might be Mary. They had a date later for dinner.

"Joe, Jim just got mugged in the parking lot. Marie said when Joe answered. "We are on our way to Albany Med."

Joe had spoken to Marie many times over the last several years and knew her voice immediately.

"Marie, I'll meet you at the Albany Medical Center Emergency Room." Joe called Mary, told her what had happened. "Can you meet me there?" From there, they would go to Wolf Road and have dinner, if it wasn't too late.

"I'll meet you there as soon as I can," Mary said.

Jim was in critical condition. He had a fractured skull, contusions, and multiple lacerations around the face and neck. Marie was in tears as Joe walked into the emergency room door. A police officer was with Marie and her son, Tony. The older woman, who saw Jim in the parking lot, was long gone. They didn't believe she saw the incident but they would go door to door down Lark Street just in case. If she came from the bus, she obviously lived in the area. They also knew it was rather difficult to identify anyone in the hood, especially if you were an older woman. Word would have gotten out that she was a snitch. At least she'd saved his life. Jim was breathing, although very shallowly, but the doctor who saw him in the ER said that he would make it. Jim's other vital signs were good but obviously they didn't know what to expect, if and when he woke up.

Mary came in shortly after and headed toward Marie. She too was a good friend of Jim and met Marie through Joe.

"Marie, Jim is in our prayers and he will be mentioned at Mass this weekend," Mary said.

Everyone was Catholic, so, everyone knew what that meant. Joe had to admit that growing up Catholic presented a whole lot of different views. Although the Capital Region was changing, and less people were going to Mass regularly, or to church at all, almost fifty percent of the region's population identified itself as Catholic, in one form or another. The Catholic faith was still the largest in the country with over eighty million people identified as such. The second largest religion was non-practicing Catholics with over forty million and growing, coming from the now practicing.

Hell, he thought, *Luis is probably Catholic, being Mexican, even though he came from California.* Most Hispanics identified themselves as Catholic. There wasn't much Joe and Mary could do at this point. He would tell Luis in the morning what was going on. They needed someone at the helm downstairs to continue the work under the grants. Joe could volunteer but that would rapidly put him behind schedule for the Hudson Foundation and others in the hopper. *Talk about a blur.*

CHAPTER 20

Both Joe and Mary were parked in the emergency room lot, adjacent to the double doors. There was only a thirty-minute limit for parking and then the car had to me moved. They were there for about forty-five minutes but they didn't see any meter maids at seven p.m. They were lucky. Hundred dollar fines were levied if ticketed. Mary followed Joe, meandering toward Central Avenue West and headed toward Colonie Center and Wolf Road. They would be there in fifteen minutes, traffic permitting.

As he drove on, Joe thought back to when he first met Mary. She worked in the accounting department, under Doug Jacobs. He had been reluctant to get into another relationship with anyone, especially after breaking up with Jennifer Alvarez, who was his girlfriend when he was stationed in Miami. Joe had been at the Coalition going on two years when he met Mary. He thought that, as soon as he saw her, he liked Mary Lynch, very much. She was very pretty, very bright, had a good figure, and seemed to get along fine with everyone. She was new and started in early May, the previous year. Joe really didn't want to hit on her at work, but where the hell could he meet women at thirty-two years old, in bars or at work?

"Christian Singles" and the Internet really were not his style. When Jennifer left him at the door in Miami, he knew then, like he knew now, that it would be difficult getting over her. He tried but he was not there yet. *Someday, hopefully.*

Mary seemed to be a very nice girl. She was five years younger than him at twenty-seven. She got married young at nineteen, as he found out through the grapevine. It didn't last and she got an annulment. Being Catholic, it was kind of important. It was to Joe's mother, anyway. Now that she was gone, it made it easier in the religion department.

After thinking about both Jennifer Alvarez and Mary Lynch, he wondered how two people could be so different and how attracted he was to both of them, or at least was attracted to Jen, at one time. There wasn't really much of an age difference. Jen just turned thirty and Mary was almost twenty-eight. Jen was still drop dead gorgeous in that exotic sort of way. She had deep dark eyes that glimmered. She was only five foot three inches tall but she was the epitome of a Hispanic woman in full bloom. She was, he guessed you would call it, voluptuous. Eyes turned everywhere she went and she knew it. She was not only well built in all the right places, but she was in great shape as well. She worked out every day and it showed. Jen's hair was to her shoulders and was getting lighter every day due to science. But, at that time, he had loved her either way. He thought, dark hair or light, she carried it well.

Mary was tall and slender, but the word elegant came to mind. In high heals, she was almost as tall as Joe was, at six feet. She was around five feet nine inches tall in her stocking feet. Both Jen and Mary were quite beautiful in their own way. Mary was not glamorous, like Jen, but she had a slow beauty that you didn't notice at first. She had auburn hair, cut short at the neck, and she had the most beautiful blue eyes he had ever seen. If possible, they were bluer than Joe's. The Irish were known for this characteristic. Cuban versus Irish and both were okay in Joe's book. Ten years spent in Miami informed that decision.

As far as temperament, Jennifer and Mary were as different as night and day. Jennifer was explosive by nature. It was in her Cuban blood. You could not imagine anyone more passionate about everything. However, her passion and stubbornness, as well as her family, broke them up. Every day was a different challenge. Nothing was, as it seemed. Everything was challenged on a daily basis to the point that he didn't want to go home. Beauty only carries the day for so long.

On the other hand, He didn't know Mary that well before they started dating. They had only worked together since May of last year. What he did know about her and their interactions together told him a lot. She was extremely bright and so was Jen. Jen was a nurse and Mary was an accountant, a CPA, or Certified Public Accountant. On the other hand being an accountant worked for Mary. She was quiet and thoughtful and fun to be with, not on a date, as of then, but he enjoyed her company. She listened as he spoke, and tried to help him with his grants in any way she could, even before Luis arrived. She was very private while Jen was very open and in your face. The word "demure" came to mind with Mary, not with Jen.

Both were well educated and it showed. Both were extremely competent. Someone told Joe, while he was in the Coast Guard, that he didn't suffer fools well. He had been well aware about his lack of patience and his temper for some time and he tried to improve in one area, while attempting to control the other. It didn't always work out.

Jen liked to fight. He couldn't because he didn't want to get mad and say something he would regret. He did, though, and he believed that Jen never forgave him, even after apologizing a million times. You could only apologize for so long. He blurted out something about her parents being a pain in the ass, in the heat of the moment, and he believed that he also said she was becoming her father.

୧୬୧

Joe was about a block or two from Colonie Center, west of Albany, and started to chuckle about an incident at home that made Joe laugh every time he thought about it. It was about having dinner at home with his mother and father and brother when he was only sixteen. The subject was about passing the potatoes. That didn't work out either. He smiled again. Some memories, although embarrassing, were actually quite funny in the long run. Joe had temporarily lost his mind and asked his mother to pass the "fucking potatoes."

That was what happened when you started working young, with adult men, construction men with limited formal education, but filled with street smarts, who lunched in bars like Walsh's Grill on upper Congress Street in Troy. Normal routine: two beers, maybe three, and lunch eaten in twenty minutes. Steak dinner on Thursday was three dollars a plate. He went home that night, when he was sixteen, after he worked all day with the guys. Dad was on his estimating jobs routine that day. While having dinner, Joe must have had a brain fart or lost his mind completely. He still, even today, could not believe that he asked his mother to pass the "fucking potatoes."

As soon as the words left his mouth, he thought he

saw Jesus. He looked at his brother and father. He was going to blame them for leading him down this path to hell. The looks he got back said they would kill him if he blamed them.

He still remembered saying, "Mom, I really don't know how to tell you how sorry I am. It will never happen again."

And, it never did. She looked at his father at the time, with a small movement to her upper lip. You couldn't tell if she was pissed or laughing. She smiled at Joe and let it go.

She had said, "I accept your apology, Joe, and don't let it happen again."

To this day, Joe was very careful about what he said and to whom he said it. Not all the time, it did slip out now and then, but hopefully, when it did, in the future, it would be with friends not business associates.

Joe told Jen that story, but she didn't seem to have that "good" sense of Irish humor. Actually, Mary did and she laughs at herself more than anything else. She laughed like hell when he told her the story about the "potatoes" after going out for a while. Being self-effacing was a very admirable trait in dealing with others. He really thought that was what he likes better about Mary than anything. The rest was just a bonus. He thought that Jen would never be happy until she got out from under her parents' collective thumbs, or as Joe called it at the time, "meddling." How could he be attracted to two so extremely different women and personalities?

Mary had a few boyfriends, nothing special, no kids, and no big issues, really a nice woman. They talked now and then and seemed to hit if off well enough. He meandered down to accounting now and then to get copies of invoices and salary information for his grants and they talked. He thought he had better do something about it before it was too late. He just didn't want to be a stalker. He guessed now that if he asked her out, and she liked him, then it was not stalking, even though it felt like it to him. As he looked back, he was an idiot for not asking her out sooner. He waited until he got back from Florida to ask her to lunch and she told him it was about time. *All that worrying for nothing.* They had been together ever since.

CHAPTER 21

On his way to work the next morning, Joe called Marie Clark on her cell phone number. She had been at Albany Medical Center all night. Tony went home to pack her a few things and was headed back to the hospital.

"Joe, Jim is still in a coma but he's breathing normally without any equipment," Marie said. "The doctor said it was just a matter of time before he woke up. Evidently, the damage to his head and face was not enough to put him into extreme critical care."

He wasn't upgraded but the doctors were not as worried about Jim's condition, once they took their cranial pressure tests, and other vital measurements. However, when he came out, and they were sure he would, they were not sure how badly his mental condition would be.

"The doctor believes Jim will be okay," she continued, "but will need many months of therapy and rest to be back to normal."

"We're so happy that he will make it, Marie," Joe said.

"Luis showed up around midnight after the police got a hold of him and told him what had happened in his own parking lot."

Luis never let on that the Orange Street Boys already called him after the beating to let him know that he owed them a big favor, and a lot of money. They told him that they were almost seen by an old black lady getting off the bus, walking down the street near the parking lot. They just barely jumped over the short fence that surrounded the parking lot and ran down the back alley, parallel to Lark Street. They wanted to know if Luis wanted them to find the old lady and silence her. They said that would be $5,000.00 more on top of the $10,000.00 he already owed them for the beat down.

"Let it go because I don't want it to escalate," Luis said. "If you're worried, you can take care of it your-selves but I'm not going to pay you." He really didn't care one way or the other.

Joe was usually the first one at the office, but today, Luis met him at the front door. "Joe, the police notified me last night about the incident and I've already been to the hospital to see how Jim was doing."

"I've already spoken to Marie on the way in this morning," said Joe.

Luis asked him to meet him on the first floor after he settled in. Joe went to his office, dropped off his bag, and headed to the bathroom to gather his thoughts. He was not sure if there was any relationship with Jim's incident and everything else that was going on, but he would keep that to himself until Mark and Jack got back to him with his requested information.

Joe walked into the Career Center and met Luis in Jim's office. Luis spoke first.

"Joe, I'm very sorry about what happened to your friend Jim. He's a great guy, and I sincerely hope that he will get better and be able to come back to work with us. In the meantime, we need to stay on top of all our grants and especially on the daily operations. We can't let anything go, or we won't get any more grant funding or even be able to perform the programs that are under way. So, I'll run the Career Center, myself, until Jim gets back. If you can help run the administrative offices and cover upstairs, that would help a lot. I don't want to hire anyone to take Jim's place because that would be unfair. We can do this, Joe."

Joe was very quiet during Luis's speech. After he was done, Joe nodded. "Luis, I'll be glad to cover upstairs and make sure that all the administrative offices are running smoothly."

Maybe this was what he had planned all along. What better way to oversee everything that Joe thought Luis was doing than to do it from the first floor Career Center. He could keep an eye on everything moving in and out. Joe knew that Luis didn't like paperwork, meeting and greeting, or anything else to do with the administration of the organization.

"Do you have time right now?" Luis asked. "I want to go over everything that we are involved in, including all your grants and where we stand with those in the hopper."

"Sure," Joe said. He then started reviewing everything they had done and what they were working on so that Luis could prioritize their time.

 જ芝જ

Joe remembered their first conversation in Ted's office, when Luis joined the organization during the summer of last year. After lunch that day, Luis and Joe met in Ted's office and they started to outline potential grant opportunities to expand their programs at the Albany Coalition for Families. What Luis wanted to do was fully expand job opportunities for young adults who dropped out of school, youth who didn't have a GED nor had any job training or certifications that could lead to good paying positions. At the time, Luis outlined what he did in California for the previous two years while he was interning at *Children First*, a non-profit in Los Angeles, serving youth.

"We fully expanded programs to attract low-income youth by providing them with a GED, job training, internships, and certifications in construction and energy efficiency. Over the two years, we placed almost three hundred youth in basic starting positions with employers in their immediate area, where the agency was located."

At that time, he asked Joe to do a survey of businesses in the Central Avenue area in Albany, which was a corridor for the region. Joe knew that Central Avenue was not Los Angeles or even southern California but he did as requested.

In the surrounding area, and on Central Avenue in Albany, there were numerous car dealerships, regional chain grocery stores, national pharmacies, and New York State offices only a few steps from the Coalition's front steps. Joe said to Luis, " we already had placed some youth in internships with these state agencies but we don't have a strategic plan to do so on a larger scale."

Luis immediately wanted to develop questionnaires for these businesses to see if there was support. Joe was to drop everything to start this process. In addition, he was to continue to write grants across local and state agencies as well as from foundations that have funded them in the past. Joe still needed to continue to successfully fund $500,000.00 per year as he had done the previous two years, in addition to this new venture. Joe agreed to start this ambitious plan of attack. Joe was not adverse to hard work and at the time, and still continued to think that it was a good idea. Joe still thought it was the proper approach to help the poor inner city youth of Albany

Luis had told Ted that he had already started the process of researching national foundations that provided funding for jobs for at risk youth and their families. He did this while in California, at *Children First*, and gave Ted the list of foundations for which they could develop applications, on a staggered basis, so that they would submit one national foundation application after another over the next two years during Luis's stay at the Coalition. Luis said he would help develop the proposals and the submissions but Joe was to take the lead.

"I'll make this a priority," Ted had said at the time.

Over what? Joe wondered.

Luis had given Joe a list of eight national foundations and the priorities for submission. Those foundations included the George Johnson Foundation in San Francisco, the Harold Block Charitable Foundation in Houston, The Ettinger Foundation in Seattle, The Hudson Foundation in New York City, Bremmer Family Foundation in Las Vegas, the King Family Foundation in Beaumont TX, The Parker Foundation, Miami, and CYC Corporate Foundation in Boston.

All of these foundations served families and children at risk throughout the country, and specialized in job placements for minority youth and education. He wanted Joe to start in the above order he gave him, filing one after the other as soon as practical. What was nice about filing grants with national foundations was, that if and when these grants were successfully funded, they would fund your program almost immediately, if you were successful in your application process. You didn't have to wait like with New York State or the Federal government grants, where due dates, starting and ending, were prescribed around their annual fiscal calendar, not yours.

This parallel timetable for grants created problems.

The Coalition's legal year was January 1st to December thirty-first of the following year. The Federal year for budgeting purposes started October 1st and ran to September thirtieth of the following year. Thus, there was a lot of overlap between years, and they had to budget these funds over a two-year cycle not just one. Grants were very complicated. Foundations were less so stringent.

Joe had asked Luis how he knew about these specific foundations, especially spread across the United States. He said that while as an intern at the association, in San Diego, for his summers before college, and all through his four years during college, he was charged with researching Foundations that awarded funding, not just to one identified community, but across the country.

Specifically, they were interested in job training for at-risk kids and young adults, late teens and early twenties, who dropped out of school, had no GED, no training whatsoever, and limited personal skills acquired in everyday life. He researched over two hundred foundations and Luis was sure that the ones he identified would provide them with the best opportunity.

As a test case, during his two years after his MBA at *Children First*, he wrote several smaller development grants to those foundations to see if they would pay for his non-profit to go into the job training business. Even though *Children First* was specifically aimed at children, age's birth through eighteen, programs didn't work well if the children's parents weren't working. Therefore, every youth program, adopted and funded, had a parent education and job-training component, if the parents were teens to early twenties. The older the parents were, the less likely the children would succeed.

The cycle of poverty was well defined and researched. Luis said he won three grants for $25,000.00, each to hire a consultant, in the young adult job training field and got the State of California's Labor Department to match the funding. That was how he developed his theories and strategic planning methodology. He felt that the Albany Coalition for Families was a perfect fit for these funded resources.

Joe certainly couldn't argue with the logic of that. Actually, that was very clever and very insightful. He thought he could learn a lot from Luis at the time. He asked Luis if he had copies of those funded programs and he said he really could not share *Children First* proprietary information. Joe was surprised, mainly because kids in poverty all over the country were basically the same. They had the same needs, same set of circumstances, and the same family situations. He let it go. He wondered why he wouldn't share, because he's here now. They were across the country and the Coalition was not even competing for children's programs. *They're targeting young adults*, he thought.

After his explanation, he told Joe that each application, after a quick review of the Foundations list that he had given to Joe, was in the range of $750,000.00 to a million dollars each, per year per request, and each had a minimum of a three-year commitment. This was not chump change. If they won any of these grants, it would move them in the right direction and help pay for their growing overhead costs, especially employee benefits, which rose at a rate of almost fifteen percent a year. They would develop strategies to recruit and place two hundred youth per year, ages seventeen to twenty-five, in jobs after they gave them the education and training required by local businesses that Luis would recruit. In addition, Joe told Luis that he had four grants, ranging from $50,000.00 to $100,000.00 each, which were renewals from the previous year and he had promised the New

York State agencies that they would be in on time.

"Luis, it would look bad if we didn't comply," Joe said.

Luis agreed. Joe would complete these grants first. He would hand the grants to Missy for signatures and copies, and then have her deliver to the agencies, located only a few blocks down the hill at the New York State Capital office building.

Finally, they reviewed the grants Luis wanted funded, starting with the George Johnson Foundation. It was approved in November, about two months after they filed their first grant. Ted received a call from their headquarters in San Francisco.

The foundation's executive director, John Swanson, called. "Congratulations, Ted. The Albany Coalition for Families is one of only a few proposals to be fully funded for a million dollars per year each year for three years. The Coalition was in the top three of the proposals received out of over a hundred applications throughout the country."

Ted was asked to fly out to San Francisco at the time for the presentation of a huge check by the Foundation to the Coalition. Joe remembered that Ted was beside himself with excitement. Never before had anyone the size of the Albany Coalition for Families, within the Greater Capital Region, received a grant of that magnitude. The only requirements were a few budget adjustments. The maximum indirect overhead for administration was capped at ten percent not the eleven percent that they requested. The difference could be moved to supplies. The $10,000.00 addition to that line item bought them the bilingual media and advertisement that they wanted but could not afford.

This first major grant definitely assisted them in recruiting a growing Latino population, residing in the

South end of Albany. Ted was also requested to bring their Controller, Doug Jacobs, George Fontaine, the Chairman of the Board, and Luis as the Vice President for Operations and Development. They had left by the end of that week. Joe was not included.

Ted had made the announcement at the end of that day that they were notified of their winning. He gathered the senior staff members and board members that he had called almost immediately after hanging up from the Foundation's Executive Director. Ted called the meeting for four p.m. in their largest classroom and then spoke, grinning from ear to ear.

"Today, the Albany Coalition for Families has moved in a new direction. I wish to announce that our first grant proposal to the George Johnson Foundation in San Francisco was funded to the tune of one million dollars per year, each year for the next three years," Ted said.

Everyone went nuts! He continued, "I really don't know how to thank Luis for all the work he did on this and through his vision, we have just been awarded the largest grant in our history."

This announcement was followed by a standing ovation for Luis. He smiled. "Thank you very much. Our work is not done. I want to personally thank Joe and Missy for a job well done."

Joe and Missy smiled. Mary Lynch looked at Joe and smiled too. At the time, he figured that she understood that they all benefited from the long hours. *I'll be a son of a bitch*, he thought. *Luis really knows his stuff.* Joe wished he could have gone to San Francisco as well.

"Pizzas are on me," said Ted as he continued to grin. His retirement and legacy would be assured.

After continuing their review of where they stood now in February, they realized that they had already spent almost half this year's funds for the Johnson Foundation, and would bill every month for the rest of the requested amount. That was true of the other approved grants as well. The Block and Ettinger foundation grants were approved and they would follow the same funding pattern and operational structure. Invoices had already gone out on the Block Foundation, and the executive director for Ettinger had just sent them a check for the initial phase of their project. It was a check for $200,000.00. National foundations usually sent money to award winners to help jump-start their projects that were approved. Most foundations gave twenty percent to start. The Coalition was told to bill for the funding immediately upon approval.

ↄ〜ↄ

Joe was completing the Hudson Foundation application. He got the required signatures on all the cover sheets and attachments. He included their Federal required annual 990 form and all the signatures for the memorandums of agreements with the subcontractor vendors.

"Missy, please make the required six copies and the original and would you send it out return receipt requested?" he said.

Joe also made several copies for the Coalition, and kept it on his Mac for review and to keep the updated information for future grants coming up. Since the grants were very much the same, Joe figured that the questions and answers would be as well.

They weren't recreating the wheel. Basically, all foundation grants were similar and the same information was usually required. The difference between the largest and smallest applications was usually in the budget preparation and the partners required to sign up and share in various program elements. The local community college would supply the GED instructor. The Workforce Investment Board staff would help with the soft skills, resume preparation, and how to dress for success classes.

Joe really didn't know what they were signing up for.

As his father said, '*Always accept the check, you can always return it.*' Words to live by.

It really can't be this easy, Joe thought at the time and still did. He worked too hard, day and night, to raise a million dollars in two to three years, and Luis raised two million already with another million just approved. Not in total but every year, staggered every three years. This twelve million dollar annual budgeted non-profit organization just increased its annual budget by three million dollars, and it was growing with each application sent in. How could they possibly handle all this? As he looked around the first floor, in his meeting with Luis, he didn't see ten people come in the door and it was already nine a.m. How was that possible? The vendors teaching the curriculum were not even there yet.

After Johnson, they won The Harold Block Charitable Foundation from Houston next, then The Ettinger Foundation from Seattle. The Hudson Foundation in New York City was being sent in now. After that, there was no end in sight. The rest would roll out accordingly. Luis said that these grants were also selected because they gave a quick response to submitted applications. New York State and Federal grants didn't answer for six to nine months.

That was a long time to wait to get funded. They needed money now so this was a really good idea. That was why Joe was backfilling with his continued Federal and New York State grant funded programs to serve as a stopgap measure so there would be no interruption in funding due to timing of requests. There was a continuous grant cycle, that if followed correctly, they could write Federal and New York State and local foundation grants every day, forever. They probably wouldn't need those grants after a while if these Luis inspired foundation grants continued. As he told Luis, his game plan, in the meantime, was to continue to develop smaller local proposals. Joe's grant writing skills started getting better, and he felt more confident in the entire grant process. It really didn't matter, large or small, every grant seemed to be the same, over and over like in the movie, *Ground Hog Day*.

CHAPTER 22

Joe was anxious to learn what Mark and Jack were able to find out about Luis and all the other questions he had surrounding Luis's arrival in Albany that hot summer day. It was around eight p.m., and Joe had just gotten home from the office. He hadn't spent time at home for quite a while. There was just too much work and too much on his mind. He and Mary hadn't gone out for a week or so. She was as swamped as he was. She'd just finished up the year-end book for the Coalition. She prepared the new federal 990 form and filed all the non-profit tax reports required, and she was exhausted.

Joe stopped at Mr. Subb and got a large Italian mixed sub with hot peppers, extra onions, light oil and provolone cheese, extra meat as well. He had a six-pack left of his favorite beer, Sam Adams Oktoberfest. Just as he sat down, the phone rang. It was Mark. It reminded him to call Julie over in Providence. He was so deep in thought all week that he forgot to call her. It was only the fourth time he didn't call her on a Wednesday night at seven p.m., in almost thirteen years. He had to call Tillie, Julie's grandmother, as well, down in Key Largo. He was going to plan a week's vacation as soon as Julie graduated from Brown University with her masters in fine arts.

"Hi, Mark, what's up?" Joe said.

"We got your information, Joe. It was pretty much what you thought."

Joe then dialed up Jack up in Virginia and they had a three-way call. Jack and Mark matched up the names of the original thirty high school students at the NCWA. It was sheer genius how they got their fingerprints from the association. Like any association, they were required to fingerprint staff and volunteers, regardless if they were full time, part time, or even interns. Jack believed the new fingerprinting technique would work and a match could be made with the fathers in prison. It was great having friends in high and low places. Joe only needed the father to match.

"I went into his federal database and found a match to twenty of the thirty individuals students, whose fathers were in the California penal system," Jack said. "Of the twenty in prison that matched the youth, I also found that each sported a gang tattoo of the Mexican Mafia."

"So, most of these students were planted in the NCWA Hispanic Management Outreach program by the Mexican Mafia," Joe stated.

It was that obvious to all three of them. They had been doing this for a long time so they knew they weren't wrong. Joe would bet that the other ten students, with more investigation, would prove likewise.

"Among the twenty identified, I found a match to a Jorge Hernandez, a known general in the Mexican Mafia," Jack said. "Jorge is fifty-two years old and in the California prison system for murder. He is Luis's father. It looks like Luis is a front for the Mexican Mafia."

This new DNA information was not a coincidence. There were no coincidences in the intelligence field. Everything was thoroughly checked out even if it was only used to eliminate suspects or to not indict. Mark and Jack got the information from the NCWA technology center on where the twenty identified youth went after their internships.

Mark cleared his throat. "They all went to California state colleges and universities for their undergraduate degrees and all twenty graduated with an Ivy-League MBA or related master's degree. They all wound up working for either a non-profit organization, throughout the country, or for a private foundation serving youth in obtaining jobs in technical areas throughout the country. We drilled down into the foundation database, which was not for public consumption and found out that over twenty million dollars had already gone to the non-profit organizations in the last six months, where the Hispanic Management Outreach program graduates wound up for their two-year stint. This is definitely not a coincidence."

Mark paused and Joe heard papers rustling. "Obviously, the Albany Coalition for Families got three million dollars approved during this six-month time frame. The other non-profits got a little more or a little less, with the approved grants spread out so there wouldn't appear to be a pattern. In three of the non-profits, the president or executive director, either died, retired, or left to be with their families during the last six months as well."

"So, Ted's not alone?" asked Joe.

"Not at all," said Mark. "This seems to be a very well planned and coordinated effort to loot non-profits and foundations across the country, Joe."

Joe started to get the picture. Ted Simmons was killed on I-90E, going home to East Greenbush. He fell asleep at the wheel, rolled over several times, and hit an abutment on the road. He never made his retirement. Joe knew that Dan had his suspicions about his father's death. Joe did as well but didn't believe he could prove anything. However, in light of the other deaths and the mugging of Jim Clark in his own parking lot, it might prove Luis's undoing. If this was all true about the Hispanic Management Outreach program, the results from the coroner's office might eventually prove Joe right.

ℭ∽ℭ∽

While Luis was on vacation, Joe had decided to pull all the invoices related to the first two grants funded to the Albany Coalition for Families by the private foundations.

Joe stopped in to see Mary. "Can you pull the five vendors that had in excess of one hundred thousand dollars in invoices, for only a six-month period, and send them to Jack and Mark?"

"Sure," Mary said. "But, I need to do this quietly since Doug's looking over my shoulder. He would be the first to tell Luis what we're doing."

Joe knew that he was not to be involved in the day-to-day operations. Luis took care of operations by himself, and only by himself. Joe had to be very careful about being noticed in the accounting department. One night previously, he explained to Mary his suspicions about Luis and Ted, and she helped him without any questions. Joe hoped that his relationship with Mary didn't bite her in the rear end.

She was extremely bright and she immediately got the information he asked for and passed it on to Jack and Mark. He knew that if Doug Jacobs found out, he would immediately tell Luis what he found. Doug Jacobs was a "kiss up" of the first degree. He would be Joe's first choice to get booted if this came down like Joe suspected. A controller is the watchdog for the organization. He didn't play that role. He seemed to have short-timers disease. He was coasting toward retirement like where a great many non-profit administrators seemed to be head-ed.

"Not only are other non-profits funded by the same foundations, but, we also know where the graduates wound up," Jack said. "In addition, each non-profit used the same vendors across the country. This was also not a coincidence. The graduates were placed in the founda-tions and the non-profits and the foundations appeared to be funding the same organizations. They were staggered in their timing but they were all there."

Joe had access through Mark and Jack's computers. They went in to each site, both foundations and non-profits and got what they needed. They were trained to not leave a footprint wherever they were. Joe had the same training, even if he was a little rusty. It was like rid-ing a bike.

To appear above board, the Coalition had several small invoices for the local community college GED pro-gram, a few lunches, outreach programs and other associ-ated requirements for certification. However, the bulk of the invoice money, over five hundred thousand dollars at the Coalition alone, went to five vendors, approved by Luis, with only his approval. Those five vendors kept ap-pearing over and over at the other non-profits who were also funded by the same private foundations. Joe guessed that the Coalition was not "the best" application as im-plied by the foundation staff. They were one of the most wired as he could certainly now tell. He could prove a conspiracy but not yet under the RICO Act. He needed other evidence but he didn't need that kind of evidence for the Patriot Act. This would be the next step. It was slow but well worth undertaking if Joe, Mark, and Jack were right.

Joe suspected that was what was happening on the first floor of their facility, the Career Center. It was really bothering him now that Luis would be there full time, downstairs in the Career Center. If Joe was right, taking out Jim Clark was a blessing for Luis, and made his life that much easier. If he did that, Joe knew that he would be next in line. Joe was the only one who worked closely with Luis. Luis never got his hands dirty or ever interacted with anyone in the office. If someone knew too much, Joe knew it would have been him. He needed to get this under control soon, or he could be the next victim. The board, the controller, all the vice presidents, none of them even suspected a thing.

Joe knew the Albany Coalition for Families, like a majority of non-profit organizations in the Country, was undermanaged, passed by in their ability to serve those most in need, and woefully left behind using technology. Their management skills were thirty years behind the times. Their systems were unable to manage an influx of three million dollars in increased revenue within these six months. They didn't have the ability to audit or even analyze what was going out the building. They were unable to grasp what Luis had ingeniously cooked up to loot them. *All the others in this conspiracy are in the same boat.*

Joe figured out that the number of youth sitting downstairs in training rooms could not possibly be the number required to meet all the goals and objectives of the three just funded grants. There should be almost three hundred young adults being trained today. The first floor Career Center could not possibly handle half of that and yet the invoices paid to the vendors reflected the training for three hundred youth. Joe would not confront Luis with this. It was too early. When he had everything in place, Luis would be in for the shock of his life. Joe owed that to everyone who worked hard for the Coalition, every day. The clients deserved it as well.

If Joe counted fifty students in the Career Center, at any one time, it would have been a lot. The first two grants should have had one hundred and fifty youth each, participating every day in some form of training or other. That's where most of the money was supposed to go to kids for stipends or pay training partners for education and certification programs. There should have been at least a total of two hundred young adults running around the first floor for the first two winning grants, just to start. A while ago, he asked Luis this question and he always said most of them were off site in internships with other businesses in the area. He let it go because it was none of his business, at the time. Joe really learned a lesson, that when you wrote a grant, and got funded and then allowed others, outside your organization, do the training without any auditing or questioning, get another job. The real world caught up with you pretty quickly.

Jack also did a corporate search for incorporation papers, names of officers, company addresses, locations of their corporate headquarters, and any other information he could get. Although all five vendors were set up all over the country, all five had the same accounting firm and law firm in Los Angeles, who set up the original paperwork. The president of all five vendors was Frank Ramone of the law firm Smith, Finkle, and Ramone LLC of Los Angeles, California. Corporate headquarters for all five were located at the same building as the law firm, very convenient.

Joe and the guys tried to find out who the anonymous source of the original funding was that gave the five million dollars to the NCWA in San Diego. They also gave them five hundred thousand dollar annually to continue to operate the program. It was expected that there would be over one hundred students going through this Hispanic Management Outreach program, if all went well, over the next few years. The invoice from the NCWA for five hundred thousand dollars annually went to a corporation in Los Angeles that was also set up by the same law firm of Smith, Finkle, and Ramone LLC. They were busy little beavers. Joe was sure they were earning their fees, a lot of fees. Enough to turn a blind eye? Perhaps.

The cell phone investigation hit pay dirt as well. Luis didn't use the Coalition cell phone. After much investigation, the guys found out that Luis used a cell phone that had his mother's address associated with the billing. That was fine, but it was paid for by the Smith, Finkle, and Ramone LLC law firm, with a note to the attention of Frank Ramone. The California cell phone pinged not in The Bronx but at the Waldorf Astoria at 301 Park Avenue in Manhattan. Interesting. Another cell phone pinged as well at the Waldorf and it was assigned to Frank Ramone, paid through his law firm. Another ping came from the Hudson Foundation and at the Waldorf. Joe guessed there was a meeting at the Waldorf with Luis, Frank, and someone from the foundation. They were looking further into that cell phone records as well. It pinged again in East Harlem. What was he doing in East Harlem? There was no aunt in The Bronx. Joe knew that now.

Another coincidence happened. Luis must have taken his non-existent aunt to East Hartford, Connecticut, and stayed at the EconoLodge at 490 Main Street. He also must have taken her to the Hartford Career Center or to City Hall at either 546 or 548 Main Street in Hartford. A cell phone paid for by the NCWA in the name of Dave Perez, and assigned to this center, also pinged. They had enough pings to play that Ukrainian Christmas favorite "Carol of the Bells"—ding-ding a ling, ding-ding a ling. Next came some numbers back and forth from the foundations, the NCWA, and several non-profits, all coming from the NCWA Hispanic Management Outreach program graduates.

"I'm available and I'll come up to Albany from Florida for a few days to help you, behind the scenes, after I contact Paul Philips at the Miami FBI," Mark said to Joe. "I'll get Paul to set up a meeting in Albany with the local FBI."

He'd already told Louise that Joe needed him, that he was Joe's brother, and that he was going. She was not easily fooled. She heard Mark speak to the FBI in Miami earlier in the week, when he thought she was not listening. She had been. She now told him to be careful.

Joe had been doing his research, after he came home from the Coalition, from the front offices of the Troy Education Consulting Group, where he worked part time during the week. He had a key and had complete access to all their computers and technology, and Internet access which was substantial. When Mark came up, he would pick him up at the Albany Airport and then he would pick up Mary and return to his apartment in Troy. Dan Simmons would meet them there as well. May as well have his attorney there to help him as well. He needed to protect Mary if and when they were ready to act.

Mark had never met Mary before. He followed Joe's love life with Jennifer Alvarez while he was in Florida. Mark hoped that Mary was better suited to Joe than Jen had been. Only Mark, and a very select few others, knew Joe's complex makeup. He appeared to be very easy going and laid back, but underneath that exterior, Mark knew Joe's capabilities. They had saved each other's lives a few times, and this would be another.

ɷɷ

When they eventually met, Joe would set up a chart

with the non-profits listed in the left column and the foundations on the top row. With the information they retrieved, Joe would place the dollar amount awarded in each box related to the Foundation making the award. They would then place the graduates/intern into each box that showed the connection to the original student names. He would put the dates of funding received, the dates the president and or executive directors died or left, and then would place the vendors in each appropriate box. They would put the dollar amount each vendor received in invoice payments, over the last six-month period. It would be either a remarkable coincidence or they might just find the most sophisticated money laundering scheme in America. It would be like inventing the pet rock and the hula-hoop all at once. It was never conceived before. They also placed the names of the attorney and accountant, which showed up in every case, under all the vendors, all the foundations, all the non-profits, and at the national accrediting agency that started the entire conspiracy.

Frank Ramone was president of every vendor and president of the realty company that donated the original five million dollars to the NCWA and paid the annual fees. Frank was also the managing partner in the law firm of Smith, Finkle, and Ramone, LLC. That, coupled with the DNA fingerprinting which came back and grouped at least twenty students to twenty fathers in the California Penal System. Each father in prison had Mexican Mafia tattoos on their bodies. This, no doubt, gave a very interesting picture. The tattoos were exactly like the one that Luis had on his ankle.

"Having the placement of the graduates in both the identified non-profits and private national foundations was also interesting in that the foundations funded the same non-profits and at the same time, the same non-profits used the same vendors," Joe said. "All were connected to the Mexican Mafia."

Jack nodded. "The transfer of funds from the foundations to the non-profits to the identified Mexican Mafia gang reached over twenty million dollars in less than six months, according to Joe's calculations based on the vendor invoices."

Joe knew that he had more grants in the hopper for the Ettinger Foundation—just sent out and won in just one week's time—and now the just submitted Hudson Foundation, and, low and behold, they were also identified with having NCWA graduates on the staffs of those foundations.

Luis's Mexican Mafia tattoo was probably all they really needed and they could check the others when everything went down, and then see if the other graduates had the same identifying mark somewhere discreetly placed on their bodies. Joe couldn't believe they would be that stupid. Luis seemed to be immune to normal behavior, regardless of his education. It might have been the brightest-person-in-the-room syndrome as well.

Luis reminded Joe of another case study at Rensselaer Polytechnic Institute, whereby the father worked very hard for forty years to build a food distribution business only to have the son piss it way in less than five years. The professor called it, not kindly, "The Idiot Son Syndrome." The son dropped out of college—just the opposite in Luis's case but the same attitude—and went to work for the father with his limited experience and education.

Eventually the son started to tell his father what to do and would not listen to his father. The father wanted his son to be successful and didn't want to interfere with his son's growth because he would eventually take over the business and fund his retirement that he worked so hard to achieve. The son thought he was important, decided that he was in charge and had built the business himself, and that his father was a dinosaur, who couldn't get out of his own way. The son expanded the business without any plans and pissed off his customers. Within five years, the son went through several million dollars, leaving the business worthless, and with no retirement income for his parents. It finally went bankrupt and the son blamed the father. This seemed to be Luis's forte. Thinking everyone else was stupid was truly a mistake. Overestimating one's own strengths was an even bigger mistake.

Joe couldn't understand how Luis himself could think he could run a twelve million dollar non-profit at age twenty-eight. Yes, he was educated but had limited experience and did not have the worldliness needed to interact with all levels of people and personalities. Joe thought he, himself, would be hard pressed at only thirty-two, even with his own education, experience, and ability to face responsibility under trying circumstances. *What was the board of the Coalition thinking? What was Ted thinking at the time?*

All of the information that was gathered, coupled with the DNA fingerprint samples, told a story that would never have been believed. It was incredible that third generation Hispanic youth, with premier degrees from first-rate colleges and Ivy-league MBAs, would be criminals, just like their fathers.

Joe called Sean in Boston, where he was home on leave.

"Can you come over and bring your side arm just in case, as soon as you can," Joe asked.

"I'll drive over as soon as I can. When do you plan to do the takedown?" Sean asked.

"Soon. As soon as we can set it up with the FBI in Albany, we're going in. It sounds like they want to do a national takedown as well. It has to be well planned and coordinated for it work."

"I hear you. I'm coming," said Sean.

Mark would also be bringing his firearm. Joe had to get one. Jack was on hold, in case they needed more tech information. Mike, now in San Diego, said he would take care of the NCWA, if needed. He notified his commander and they would receive confirmation from the San Diego FBI and Homeland Security folks as well. Mike was assigned less than three miles from the Association's headquarters. He would be on hold until Joe formulated a plan that included the FBI, and Homeland Security. Joe found out through Jack that there were two graduates still working at the NCWA to make sure the program continued. Mike was on call and he was told by his commander that he could have as many Coast Guard officers as required to do search, seizure, and arrests where appropriate. It was close enough to the Coast Guard base to make it a Coast Guard case.

CHAPTER 23

Joe hadn't had a vacation in almost a year. After the Ettinger grant came through, he mentioned it to Luis. "Fine, take a week off," Luis said.

Mark was turning forty years old and Joe was asked by Louise, Mark's wife, to attend a big birthday bash at the Hard Rock Café in Fort Lauderdale, in celebration. Louise worked there and set everything up. She said that Mark knew nothing about it. Joe mentioned to Louise what was potentially going to go down in Albany, very shortly, and Mark would be coming up to help. Louise knew this and told Joe that it wouldn't interfere.

So Joe headed to Fort Lauderdale for a week. He called Julie in Providence but she was tied up with classes and wouldn't be back this year for winter recess in Key Largo. He called Tillie, Julie's grandmother, and told her about the party but she couldn't drive that far, especially in her old Ford Escort. Joe said that during that week, he would come down to visit her and stay overnight and then head back to Fort Lauderdale, where he would be staying with Mark and his family. Tillie was like his second mother, especially after his own mother died of breast cancer. They were Joe's second family and meant as much to him as his own father and brother.

Joe had enough work to choke a horse, and he didn't think he could afford to take the time off, but he took a week off, anyway. The work was getting to him. They owed him three weeks' vacation that he had to take or lose. Luis was getting to him, and Joe had that situation on his mind. He wanted to get together with Mary when he got back. He was afraid, at the time, that he would never get a second chance to ask her out if he didn't do as soon as he got back.

☙❧

Everything was set for that weekend for Mark's fortieth birthday party. Tom Jones was coming. That was great. Mark would be pleased, especially since he didn't know a thing, they all believed. Tom, now in his mid-fifties, retired a number of years ago and they tracked him down to Orlando. It was only a few hours from Orlando to Fort Lauderdale, down I-95 South. Louise booked him a room so there would be no question that he would come. The rest of the gang got a discount as well. Joe booked his flight through Southwest and got a great deal. Mark didn't have a clue that they were coming. Everyone, but Mark, was going to meet at the Hard Rock. Louise got an employee discount for the catered affair and had about thirty people coming to the party, which included Mark's mother and two sisters from San Diego.

He'd be shocked when he opened the door. He had no clue. Joe smiled. He finally got a chance to break Luis's ass. It snowed yesterday. Not even mid-winter yet. It was going to be a long way to spring. Joe took a direct flight on Southwest at six thirty-five a.m., from Albany to Fort Lauderdale. He arrived at nine-fifty a.m., which gave him most of the rest of the day before the party at seven-thirty p.m. He took a taxi to the Hard Rock Hotel. He'd flew in on the day of the party because he knew that he would probably have run into Mark somewhere, with his luck. Hollywood, where the Seminole Hard Rock Hotel and Casino was located, was only a few miles from Mark's home and work. As you looked out the plane as they descended, they could see the Seminole complex to the right as they landed at the Fort Lauderdale International Airport. Names were deceiving. Just like Albany, where you can fly to Montreal, in Fort Lauderdale you can fly to Bermuda, making both flights "international." Joe guessed that this was Airport Marketing 101.

Joe also liked the fact that, unlike Albany, where you can drive anywhere in twenty minutes in the greater Capital Region, if you bus, it would take you all day to get from one end to the other within the region. Fort Lauderdale was on the South Florida Regional Transportation Authority Tri-rail system. For five dollars you could get on every twenty minutes at Fort Lauderdale and go all the way to the Miami International Airport, over thirty miles away, in less than an hour and a half. It would also drop you right downtown near South Beach.

Mark had it made as far as his living location from home to work. He lived in a condo community in Dania Beach, near the ocean, and was stationed near Fort Lauderdale, just up the road in Broward County Park on North Ocean Drive. It was a stone's throw from Fort Lauderdale. His "cover" office was there but he was actually stationed at COMMSTA—The Coast Guard Communications Facility on SW One Hundred Seventeenth Avenue—in Miami. He only went there for Intelligence department meetings and worked from the Dania Beach station. He took the Florida Turnpike two days a week, and it was about thirty miles, which can be twenty-five minutes or two hours depending on the traffic. It was known as the world's largest parking lot.

It brought back a lot of memories for Joe.

When Mark and Joe graduated from the fourteen-week intelligence-training program, they actually went to the Maritime Intelligence Fusion Center Atlantic in Portsmouth, Virginia to complete their training. This was in the Coast Guard Fifth District, and the center for intelligence—other than Washington DC—for the Atlantic Coast. From there, they transferred to the COMMSTA Coast Guard Communications facility in Miami, right off the Florida Turnpike and the Tamiami Trail, making it convenient, if there was such a thing in Miami, to all locations. It was only a few miles from Joe's apartment over on NW Seventh Street. This was where Joe shared his life with Jen when they were living together in Miami.

He was there for a week so he thought he should use the time constructively. After the party, maybe Sunday, He would take the Tri-rail down to the Miami International Airport and walk over to see his old apartment, where Jen still lived. He had not talked to her or emailed her in a while. She hadn't spoken to him at all since he came back to Troy, other than being polite on the phone when he called. She never returned his emails.

He checked in at the Hard Rock around noon. They let him in early because of Louise's discount and being a friend of an employee. He got his key and went to the tenth floor, room 1010. It was quite beautiful. Louise must have really gone to bat for them. The view was beautiful. He could see the whole complex and the surrounding area. The pool was right down below his window. He unpacked and changed into his bathing suit. He grabbed his sandals, T-shirt, and a towel. He put his key in his shoe. He figured he could eat lunch by the pool, have a beer, and then go see if anyone else checked in. Louise wasn't scheduled to work until five p.m. so she didn't upset the applecart by coming in early. She could do what she needed when she got there, almost two hours before the party. It was Mark's birthday and she still had to work that night. It would all work out.

Louise said she could take her dinner early and for Mark and the kids to be there by seven-thirty p.m. in the restaurant. She told Mark that she made reservations for the back room so they could be alone with the kids. Louise could do or say almost anything with a straight face. Anyone would believe just about anything she said. She was so convincing that she could be breaking your ass and you almost felt like it was a compliment coming off her lips. Joe toweled off, went back to his room for a shower and then decided to explore the Casino. He vowed not to spend more than $100.00 gambling. He was lousy at it and he didn't see the fun, really. Hell, he lived thirty miles from the Saratoga Thoroughbred Racetrack in upstate New York, and his friends at McGuire's were lucky if they could drag him there once a year during August. Their slogan *The August place to be* didn't really resonate with Joe.

He went downstairs to the front desk and asked if Mike, Sean, Jack or Tom had checked in yet and they said no. It was only one p.m. Tom wasn't much of a party guy. If he left Orlando at noon, he probably wouldn't even be there any earlier than three-thirty or four p.m. He knew Mike was coming the farthest from San Diego and he believed he made arrangements to meet Mark's mother, Ana Silva and Mark's two sisters, another Jen and Maria. *God, Jen must be like Mary in Spanish.*

So what do I do? He wanted to start dating Mary in Albany, when he got back from the trip. He wanted to settle things with Jen before he got seriously involved with anyone else at that point. He knew it was over with Jen, but he wanted to do it right. He really hoped for the best. If nothing worked out, at least he tried to make it right.

Sean was coming from New London Connecticut, probably on a Coast Guard transport. The Coast Guard didn't pay very much as it was. For him to take shore leave meant this was really important to him. The same went for all the guys. Jack was still stationed at the "A" School in Yorktown, Virginia in charge of the Artificial Intelligence Training Program. He was the directing officer in artificial intelligence and advanced computer theory and analysis. All required to figure logistics for clandestine classified intelligence across the gamut of illegal and terrorist activities. Joe, Mark and Jack had been on the phone frequently about Luis and they might take a few minutes after the party or the next day to figure out logistics. None of the three had seen each other in person in some time.

It's funny what popped into your head when daydreaming. The advanced strategic planning, logistics and analysis brought Joe back to his time at Rensselaer. At Rensselaer they studied the Poisson distribution in Advanced Statistical Analysis for Scientists and Engineers. Why he needed this for an MBA was beyond him, but evidently it helped the nerds gain an MBA, and the nontechnical MBA students, like him, gain a perspective on how really Goddamn hard RPI was to get through. Joe chuckled to himself. A Poisson distribution was a probability distribution, which arose when counting the number of occurrences of a rare event in a long series of trials. One of Joe's final exam questions was answer the question—If six boats came into the dock at three p.m., what was the maximum number of boats that could arrive at any given time—using the Poisson distribution methodology. *No kidding.*

Learning grade-management at an early age, and

having somewhat of a photographic memory, really was the process he used to get by. He memorized the Poisson distribution formula as well as many other formulas, worked around the question, and rewrote the entire formula verbatim, putting an equal sign and nine. He was wrong. It was eleven. He wouldn't know the correct answer if it hit him on his nose. However, since at RPI an "A" was curved down to a sixty on a scale of one hundred. He got eight out of ten points because of his most thoroughly documented formula. It was a thing of beauty. These were the things he remembered. Wouldn't count for much but great in the retelling around two a.m. at McGuire's.

All the guys were in by five p.m. Joe called all their rooms and met them at five-thirty p.m. in the lounge for drinks. Mike came in with Ana Silva, Mark's mother, and Mark's two sisters, Jen and Maria, followed by Tom, Sean, and Jack. The girls were in their early thirties and gorgeous.

Maria Fernandez was married to Bill and had one daughter, Cristina. Bill was an accountant for the City of San Diego and they lived close to her Mom. There were great sections of San Diego, but like Los Angeles, there was tremendous poverty, especially among the Mexican immigrants. The kids got an education but the parents were poor and undereducated and the high crime and poverty was a reflection of the high unemployment rate for Hispanics in the city. This gave rise to criminal gang activities which rose right up from the Mexican side of the border, only a few miles away. The gang violence in Mexico was spreading like wildfire to San Diego.

Maria and Bill thought about moving to Fort Lauderdale, near Mark, but Ana, the mother, was not interested in moving, which made it a difficult choice for Maria and her family. Jen Silva got out at an early age and made both a career and a good life for herself in Los Angeles in the movie business. Jen was single, lived in LA, and worked in the production end of the movies. Her degree in cinematography from UCLA opened the door for her with internship projects. Being gorgeous didn't hurt either.

Sean had his tongue hanging out, being the single Irish bullshit artist that he was. His Boston accent, pushed to the limits for effect, for pick up purposes, was alive and well. Joe stared at him, shook his head for an invisible moment, not unlike their moments breaking down doors during drug busts. He got Joe's drift, smirked only as Sean could smirk, and then realized he would be a dead man if Mark picked up on his intentions. To the group, that would be akin to being a kin. *Clever*, he thought, *but very real. You don't mess with your best friend's sister without approval*. He wouldn't get it.

It was getting close to seven p.m., so they moved to the back room that was going to be their private party for Louise, Mark, and the kids. Joe spoke to Mark's mother and sisters at great length in Spanish. Believe it or not, he had never met them before even though he felt that they were his own mother and sisters, especially, after Joe's mother died so young. Other friends of Mark arrived. Joe didn't know everyone. They were mostly friends from their neighborhood and new Coast Guard people that Mark met after Joe left Miami. He really didn't want to talk to any more Coast Guard members, other than his immediate close friends because he got tired of answering the same old questions, "Why did you leave? You were doing great, you could have gotten anything you wanted if you were unhappy. They loved you." He just wanted to get out and he did not want to talk about it again. His friends knew this and left him alone.

Joe reconnected with Louise's mother and father.

They were quite a couple. Ken Harding grew up 120 kilometers, about seventy-five miles, north of London, England. At twenty-one years old, he went to Miami with a few of his friends, after his schooling was over. He met his future wife, Louise's mother, Antoinette "Tony" in a bar in South Beach. Tony was half Irish and half Cuban. Ken spent a week with her and he fell head over heels in love. He had to return to England with his friends. That was the deal. He got home, repacked his bags, took a loan from his father, took his sheepskin, and flew back to Miami, one month later. Six months later, they were married at St. Augustine's Church in Coral Gables.

He took a job in the maintenance and engineering department at the University of Miami on Ponce de Leon, in Coral Gables, and he had been there ever since. His degree from England was the same as an Associate in Applied Science in the States. They have been married for thirty-eight years. Louise, now at thirty-five was their only child, and they doted over their two grandchildren. Both kids were bilingual. You really have to be, to live in South Florida.

It was close to seven-thirty p.m., everyone was in place, and the lights were off. You could hear Mark grumbling under his breath, "Why are we here? We could have gone out anytime. The kids were tired, jeez." The door opened, the lights went on like an explosion and all you could hear as soon as Mark walked in was "Happy birthday!"

The look on Mark's face was priceless. He was in shock. The kids were literally rolling on the floor laughing. He looked around and all you could see was a grin from ear to ear. He turned to Louise. "I will get you for this," he said softly. "How the hell did you pull this off?"

"Wouldn't you like to know, sweetheart?" She laughed. "Perhaps now that you're an old man, I can give you a hand to your seat. Don't lose your breath blowing out all your candles," she said. "Remember, if you burn the place down with all those candles, I'll lose my job, sweetheart."

"What's with the sweetheart stuff? The last time you called me that, you said I do," he said.

"Well, if you don't make it through the party, old timer, I just wanted to make it special for you, old man."

"Thanks a lot, sweetheart," he said with an emphasis on the "sweetheart."

He greeted everyone with a hug and a kiss. That was his way. Everything was first class including the food, the bar set up, and the piped in music. All the nighttime head bosses and crewmembers, who worked with Louise, showed up and gave Mark several courtesy gift certificates that they give to the high rollers. He got free room, board, and tuition at the Hard Rock for next Friday and Saturday night. It was a good deal. Joe was flying out on next Sunday, so he volunteered to watch the kids overnight, since he was going to stay there Monday through Saturday anyway. He knew that Louise's parents were only down the road. He couldn't think of a better gift for Mark than a few nights alone with his wife at a resort hotel, only a few miles away. What else did he need? He had the life that he would never have had if he hadn't walked into the Coast Guard recruiting station so many years ago. Forced to join or not, it was the best decision of his life. Mark meant the world to Joe.

Mark's mother and sisters would be there Monday and Tuesday, flying out on Wednesday. Mark's sister, Jen, was in full movie production mode back in Hollywood and had to get back as soon as possible. Maria couldn't leave her daughter alone with her husband for more than a few days. His parenting skills were less than perfect so she thought. The guys had to leave soon as well. Joe also wanted to see if he could spend the day with Tom before he drove back to Orlando in the afternoon on Monday. They made plans to go into downtown Miami, have lunch, and get back so he could leave by three p.m. It was a done deal.

Tomorrow was Joe's day to see Jen, or not see Jen, as the case may be. After that, he would rent a car for a day and visit Tillie in Key Largo. He would stay overnight and be back to babysit the kids for the weekend. He didn't want to call Jen so she could hang up on him. He really wanted to see her. He just wanted to know if it was really over. It had been a while between school and his job being what it was. She was busy at the hospital, so she said. She was dating, but he didn't know how involved she was with anyone. She certainly had no problem getting a date anytime she wanted. She was that attractive. If you really thought about it, there were a million reasons why you couldn't do something—I have a headache, I have to work, I have to wash my dog—yes, an unnamed female had said that to Joe when turning him down for a date. Ouch.

No one ever said, "I don't want to."

There was only one reason why you wanted to. It was because you really wanted to. That advice Joe learned from his mother, along with the potato incident. Excuses were just that. All the rest was a cover. He missed his mother's wisdom every day. He couldn't eat potatoes without thinking about how much he loved and missed her.

The party ended at eleven p.m. The kids were exhausted and hung from both grandmothers' necks. Pictures were taken. Friendships were renewed and new friends made. Joe almost forgot about his life in upstate New York. He was still trying to figure that out. Someday, maybe someday, he might just come back to Miami.

Joe remembered that everyone at the Coalition looked at him like he was crazed, especially during the winter months. December couldn't be replaced in upstate New York. You could not replace the Christmas lights reflecting off the snow covered ground, the carols, church, all the little things, dinner at home, big dinner at home, watching football on the couch, and even leftovers. Leftovers were the best including turkey, his Mom's bread dressing, cranberries, and rolls from the Italian bakery. The next day was heaven. Then came the heart of winter and all that went away and then you misremembered what a wonderful time winter was in upstate New York and what it was like as a kid growing up. *Sorry, now at age thirty-two, it now officially sucks.*

One of Joe's main issues was his photographic memory. The problem was that you remembered the bad in as much detail as the good. It depended on what side of the ledger you were on, if it was a good thing or not. The jury was still out. It helped Joe when he had to analyze a situation but the details became overwhelming at times. He had to get Luis out of his head for now or it would drive him crazy.

The guys went back to the lounge for a few more beers and to catch up. Mike, Sean, and Jack were leaving at different times the next day. They knew Joe was going to see Jen if possible and they all wanted to know what his game plan was. They knew her as well as anyone could know a best friend's girlfriend. He told them his plans and then on Monday how he would be meeting with Tom.

Tom went to bed as soon as the party broke up. "I can't hang with the big dogs." He laughed. He meant pond scum rookies who didn't know their ass from their elbow as he recalled.

He reminded Joe of his original conversation when

he turned nineteen and how to get along without smart-mouthing every second. Joe remembered the conversation well. The guys heard about Joe's "million-dollar grant club membership" and he did the "Oh, gosh, thanks, fellows" routine. They mocked him well into the night. Mark and Jack, and even Sean and Mike kept quite because they knew what would be coming down in the near future. The million-dollar club would be bankrupt by the time they were done.

The others, including Tom, were happy for Joe.

Joe shook his head. "You know about my apprehensions about Luis, moving too quickly, getting quick responses. Getting funded is one thing, meeting all the goals and objectives we outlined…well, that's something else. Where the money went is something that I need to keep close to the vest, meaning you guys only."

Thinking about it, again, after several beers with the boys, Joe was a little maudlin. With or without Luis, he really didn't know how they could mobilize as quickly as they needed to meet the timeline submitted and the deliverables under the grants they won, let alone get 300 jobs for unemployed young people in their teens and early twenties, especially when so many other, older adults who worked for years, were being laid off left and right. Maybe, this was the only way to get people jobs. Get them certified in new technology, for the new world order at an early age. Certifications seemed to be more valued than degrees in this new economy. They wanted people who could hit the ground running. There was no money for training. Degrees meant retraining from the college campus to the real world. That was why Joe questioned Luis's experience compared to his own. His connections and degrees were something but not everything. Job training for at-risk kids was the only way they would ever be successful and leave the downward spiral of poverty.

Joe really was passionate about this. He didn't want what he believed was happening to taint a very strong program.

Joe remembered when Luis told him, on his way out that night, when he was on his way to Miami the next day, "Don't worry about it. I got this covered. That's where my vice president of operations title comes in handy. I'll clear the way."

He was that confident. Usually, Joe was "wait and see," but this was moving real fast, and no one was in Luis's path. At the time, Ted Simmons and the board gave him the green light. Luis said he knew how to sub-contract everything they needed that they themselves couldn't provide.

"As we built up our capacity, we would hire more people for those counseling jobs, creating even more jobs, which would serve them well in this down econo-my," Luis told them. "New York State wants new in-demand jobs as was listed on their Labor Department web site. These jobs seem to fit the bill, especially in the area of nanotech and associated businesses that fed that industry. Hell, they already put close to five billion dol-lars into the Capital Region nanotech industry, which gave the region the 'Tech Valley' nomenclature. It is worth the bet according to those in the know."

Joe could see through this bullshit but now he had to get his relationship with Jennifer behind him and then ask Mary out. He needed to focus on his own mental health that he had neglected over so many years in the service. He'd deferred his own feelings, but now, he needed more from life.

☙❧

Joe, once again, remembered the story that his father had told him to make a point when he was living at home while in high school. His father said that he had left for vacation one time, many years ago, and didn't come back to a job. He was laid off the minute he showed up at the door that morning. He got no benefits, no severance pay, and no vacation, nothing. That's why he started his own construction company. Joe really couldn't blame his father for that attitude. He had no degree, no future, kids and a wife, and he was damned and determined that nothing was going to get in his way. It left him with a less-than-perfect personality but no one thought they could ever take advantage of him. At least Joe's father, brother, and a few of his key craftsmen, would stay employed.

Joe's father was now in his early sixties, still working, and had nothing better to do since his mom died. He was also very good at his job. He was the bluntest man Joe ever met. Joe knew where he got that particular gene. Joe remembered pissing him off about nothing one summer day, hot as hell, and then compounding it by making fun of him. Christ, he wasn't even eighteen yet. His father chased his rear all over the building that they had been working on. Joe laughed and thought that he wasn't as pissed as he let on. His father had several contracts for inside remodeling jobs that winter. They specialize in energy efficiency upgrades and many of the contracts were funded through low interest loans and outright grants for those low and moderate income. His father saw the writing on the wall and became a New York State certified home energy contractor. Homeowners and businesses had to use these certified companies to get their loans and grants. He was paid directly through the New York State Energy Division. *God is good.*

For all his faults, in the fathering and nurturing department, Joe thought his father was really smart and had a sixth sense and always stayed ahead of the curve. In the contracting business that was essential or you were out of business in a flash. You can't be a little bit pregnant. You were either in business or you were not. It was that simple. Joe came back to reality. Those life lessons gave him his backbone. He knew what he had to do and how he had to do it when he flew back to Albany.

All in all, the party went great. Everyone had a wonderful time. Joe forgot Troy and Albany New York, even for a short time. Why the hell did he leave Florida? he wondered. He just wanted a change, especially after he left the Coast Guard and then with Jen and with his mother's passing, he had to move on. But did he really? Now with Luis, he wasn't so sure. He can wait and see what happens or head back to Florida. With his degrees and skills, he was sure he could get a pretty good job. Why did he ever move back to the coldest region in the country?

He just felt at home in upstate New York. He missed his traditions, not so much his father and brother, but he did miss his old friends. Going to RPI meant a lot to him and getting his MBA from there meant everything to him. He remembered dropping out of MIT after only one semester so many years ago. Now he had two degrees, a job, actually a career if he wanted it, but more than that, he was in charge of his own life for the first time in a long time. Joe said goodbye to everyone. He went to his room and went to bed, finally around two a.m. There was a long day coming.

CHAPTER 24

Joe was headed down to Miami by way of the Tri-rail, hoping to catch Jen at home, later in the morning. He left at nine-fifteen a.m. from Fort Lauderdale, and it took about an hour to get to the Miami International Airport, all for five bucks. From there he would walk the short distance to his old apartment, which he wanted to do anyway to rid his body of all the toxic liquid he poured down his throat last night. He should be there a little after eleven a.m. Perhaps, he and Jen could go to lunch if she didn't punch him in the face, or was not otherwise tied up. If she weren't there, he would leave a note with his new cell number, telling her he was at the Hard Rock in Hollywood if she wanted to contact him. He had already made up a note on Hard Rock stationary, just in case. There was no sense looking around for paper and pen at her front door.

Joe needed this time to himself on the Tri-rail, to think of where he had been and where he was going, especially in light of the Coalition situation. Ted was dead and Jim was in the hospital. Nothing seemed to be the same. Joe was out of sorts and he knew it. Nevertheless, all in all, his life had worked out better than he had imagined. He could still be a high school graduate working construction like Pete, who wasn't going anywhere soon. His life consisted of the local Burgh Grill, home, work, and an occasional date. If they weren't taken by now, they didn't want to be taken, had other issues, or just plain settled in for life—just like Pete was doing.

Joe had no idea why he came back to Troy to stay, other than to get his degree from RPI. He came back to get past the Coast Guard. He came back to see his mother when she got sick so he could make up time lost which never happened. The things he could have said or done to make a difference, probably wouldn't have made a difference, but was nice to think so. What the hell does institutional research and grant writing have anything to do with what he did for ten years in the Coast Guard, being with his best friend every day? *Nothing.*

Seeing or even talking on the phone to his other friends on a regular basis, no matter where they were stationed, always took a priority because they were his true friends for life. What did the years spent in a room at the COMMSTA center breaking down highly classified intelligence documents on cartels, terrorists, or just plain thieves have anything to do with where he was today? He was going to ask his buddy, Jim Clark, downstairs at the Coalition if it was worth coming back from Hawaii to take care of his aging parents. He and his wife seemed happy. Who knew Jim would wind up being mugged in his own parking lot?

As Joe sat on the train going into Miami, he started to remember his involvement in various historical events over his ten years in the Coast Guard. He had just graduated in early summer 2000 from intelligence school. He spent a short time at headquarters in Virginia, and Mark and he moved into their assignment in late August, at the COMMSTA Center in Miami. He just got settled into a routine when on Thursday, October 12th, terrorists in

Aden Harbor, Yemen hit the *USS Cole*. Al-Qaeda in the Arabian Peninsula "AQAP," the Yemen branch of al-Qaeda, claimed responsibility. Seventeen sailors were killed and thirty-nine injured. That woke Joe up fast. The attack was the deadliest against a U.S. naval vessel since the Iraqi attack in 1987 on the USS *Stark*. A small craft approached the port side of the *USS Cole*, a destroyer, and an explosion occurred, creating a forty-by-forty-foot gash in the ship's port side, killing and injuring all those men.

The Coast Guard was not included as a formal member of the Intelligence Community until December 2002. Because of their hands-on work with the USS *Cole* and assistance with the ongoing intelligence issues, the political changes in Congress, internal Coast Guard actions, and the tragic attacks of September 11th, provided context to the passage of a Congressional provision that formally included the Coast Guard as a full member. Derived from a thesis completed in 2003, it illustrates the importance of Coast Guard's ability to gather electronic data immediately. Thus, Joe's understanding of the Coast Guard changed almost immediately.

They all had to do double-duty in Miami as well as at all the other intelligence facilities on the Atlantic Coast. Their people were pulled and Mark and he were pushed in to the deep end of the espionage pool. They had to pick up exactly where the departing men and women left off, as they moved into key positions concerning the *USS Cole* investigation. No one probably realized that those USS patrol boats with mounted machine guns protecting the now sitting duck *USS Cole* were Coast Guard vessels.

As he passed the Hollywood Tri-rail station, he tried to remember as best he could, in chronological order, all the events that seemed to have happened only yesterday. Obviously one of the biggest tragedies in the history of the United States was the attack on the Twin Towers in New York City on September 11, 2001. How that happened boggled the mind. They were pulled immediately from Miami and sent to Washington DC Intelligence headquarters and they were fully involved in the investigation, mainly for the Pentagon tragedy. They were in Washington, living out of a suitcase for months, and then those in Command thought that it would be more important to continue to monitor the Ports of Miami. The most logical way al-Qaeda could totally disrupt the commerce of the United States was through its port systems. Miami was one of the largest and probably most porous. If one shipping container held any kind of nuclear device, it could take out the heart of South Florida in an instant. Terrorism replaced drugs as the number one priority from then on.

For the next several years, Joe had a steady position in Miami. They were called into action for the first Haiti earthquake in 2002 but after their initial *Help the People First* initiatives, the navy took over the larger shipments of humanitarian aid. There was very little trouble during this earthquake. Yes, people were hurt, looting took place, and many lost their homes and way of life, but the devastation as measured by recent years and more disastrous earthquakes was minimal. Deaths compared to their latest tragedy were also minimal in 2002.

Until the hurricanes came, Joe's chief duties were intercepting foreign electronic transmissions, interpreting data and breaking codes, while also assisting in the takedown of cartel drug interventions in South Florida, when their fellow Coast Guard members were short-handed. They were always short-handed. From West Palm Beach to Key West, into the upper Caribbean, they had almost daily seizures of contraband and drugs.

In 2004, Joe's investigation and subsequent intelligence plan led to one of the largest cocaine seizure in its history to that date. He and Mark were working with the U.S. Customs and Border Protection in patrolling parts of the northern Caribbean. They, together, heard chatter in Spanish, intercepted the electronic data and knew that a major shipment was coming in to Key West the following day. Mark and Joe hitched a ride on the Miami Patrol Boat that was to be used for the interception. They had a Coast Guard helicopter fly over the vessel for a closer look, the suspects on the boat began throwing bales overboard and then tried to speed away in the boat. They caught up with them and intercepted the shipment. It was not easy. Bullets were flying. It was one of Joe's first takedowns and he was very nervous, but it worked out. Their Coast Guard cutter crew stopped over in Key West with a special delivery: 4,355 pounds of cocaine they seized off a go-fast boat. They—like he would know, he thought—estimated the drugs to be worth $58 million, if sold on the street. They had a pretty good time in Key West that night. It didn't happen very often.

They got back to Islamorada, their Florida Keys headquarters, and Joe met Julie and Tillie and took them to dinner. Julie was growing like a weed and in high school. He told her that they should start looking into colleges and universities the next time he got back. She was doing great in school and in track, especially in cross-country. She was all Monroe County that year and was writing up a storm for the school newspaper and in her literature classes. She'd wanted to be a writer for the longest time. Both Tillie and Joe encouraged her to be the best she could be. When Joe showed up in his brand new, rented, red Mustang convertible, dressed in full uniform, to be her driver for the prom, he thought Tillie, Julie, and her date would lose it. She said it was the best time she ever had.

The turning point in his life began in late August 2005. Hurricane Katrina formed over the Bahamas on August 23, 2005, and crossed southern Florida as a moderate category one hurricane, causing some deaths and flooding there, before strengthening rapidly in the Gulf of Mexico. He was at home before going to work. He called Jen to see if she was okay. She worked the late shift at the hospital. When the winds began and reached almost ninety miles an hour, it felt like a freight train going through his apartment. The rain was coming in sideways and several trees started coming down. Fortunately, when he looked out later, two trees just missed his car. *Thank you, Lord.*

He called in to COMMSTA and they told him to come in ASAP and be fully prepared to mobilize. FEMA worked feverishly on planning and evacuation and they were their first responders in Miami and secondary on the Gulf Coast. He got in a little later, slow going, couldn't see his hand in front of him. Evidently, the category one went all the way up to West Palm Beach and then turned right around back at them, in Miami, and headed toward the Gulf of Mexico.

Joe got in by then and felt a lot safer in his headquarters, which was built precisely for those conditions. He called Jen. She was safe but the emergency room started to get crowded. Electricity was off everywhere and their generators were now on. The old, the infirmed, pregnant women, and accident victims were line up at the door. Joe told her he was about to be deployed and he would call her as soon as he knew.

The hurricane strengthened to a category five hurricane over the warm Gulf water, but weakened before it made its second landfall as a category three hurricane on the morning of Monday, August twenty-ninth in southeast Louisiana. It caused severe destruction along the

Gulf coast from central Florida to Texas, much of it due to the storm surge. The most significant number of deaths occurred in New Orleans, which flooded as the levee system failed, in many cases hours after the storm had moved inland. Eventually, eighty percent of the city and large tracts of neighboring parishes became flooded, and the floodwaters lingered for weeks. However, the worst property damage occurred in coastal areas, such as all the Mississippi beach towns, which were flooded over ninety percent in hours, as boats and casino barges rammed buildings, pushing cars and houses inland, with waters reaching twelve miles inland. It looked like Joe was headed to New Orleans.

As soon as he got to New Orleans, all hands were on deck. It didn't matter what your job category was, you were there simply to save lives at first, and then try to keep the peace, especially near the ports. There was an over exaggeration concerning multiple murders and anarchy. Nevertheless, he had never seen such devastation in his entire life including the earthquake in Haiti in 2002. They worked sixteen hour days, seven days a week, for thirty days at a stretch and then came back home to rest in Miami for one week before returning to New Orleans, and starting all over again. They did this tour of double shifts for six months before they were furloughed back to their home base.

As soon as Katrina hit New Orleans, the Coast Guard responded immediately by moving as many helicopters as it could to the affected areas, calling in aircraft from as far away as Cape Cod in Massachusetts. Five hundred United States Coast Guard reservists were called to duty immediately, and many of the hundreds of small boats in the Coast Guard fleet were sent to help. Coast Guard helicopters flew around-the-clock rescue missions. The Coast Guard was saving lives before any other federal agency, despite the fact that almost half the local Coast Guard personnel, living on the coast, lost their own homes in the hurricane.

As President Bush said, "You're doing a great job, Brownie." Coast Guard personnel were in the process of evacuating more than thirty thousand people, six times as many as they saved in all of 2004 put together. According to an article in a national weekly magazine, in the famously decimated St. Bernard Parish, east of New Orleans, the local Sheriff said that the Coast Guard was the only federal agency to provide any significant assistance for a full week after the storm. With 40,000 active-duty personnel, the Coast Guard was tiny, but, as Joe thought, *we are very effective.*

During the six-month tour of duty, Joe worked with his own Search and Rescue teams. The devastation was beyond anything he had ever seen. They couldn't save everyone. The police and fire departments were gone. There was basically not the anarchy that was overblown in the daily news but the devastation made New Orleans look like a poor third-world country. Most of the problems were created by the private security companies. They treated the poor left behind like animals.

At the start of the flooding and soon after, the looting would stay with Joe, forever. They were shot at coming out of the helicopters. He guessed the gangs in New Orleans didn't want boots on the ground, even to save their grandmothers. FEMA workers, trying to do an impossible job, were shot at in the streets. They couldn't wear their identification or blue shirts with FEMA on the pockets. They had to buy New Orleans basketball team hats and jackets to fit in, just to go to their trailers to get something to eat after sixteen-hour days. Hey, not everyone was like that but it felt like a state of siege.

Joe could have been in Fallujah Iraq for all he knew,

especially with *Blackwater*, the private security company, in town. The inhumanity changed his life. It took him a long time to feel good about anything. When he got back to Miami, Jen looked at him differently probably because he looked differently at himself.

In many ways, he didn't blame the citizens of New Orleans for any conduct that was exhibited during those very trying times. Joe did believe that racism was there in full force but not exhibited by the efforts of every man and women wearing a Coast Guard uniform. But there's an even harsher truth, which some New Orleans residents learned in the very first days but which was only beginning to become clear to Joe, now thinking about his time there. It seemed like a lifetime ago but it will always stay with him. What took place in that devastated American city was no less than a war, in which victims, whose only crimes were poverty and blackness, were treated as enemies of the state.

The problems started immediately after the storm and flood hit, when civilian aid was scarce and private security forces already had boots on the ground. Some, like *Blackwater* were under federal contract, while a host of others answered to wealthy residents and businessmen who had departed well before Katrina and needed help protecting their property from the suffering masses left behind. According to reports, *Blackwater* set up their headquarters in downtown New Orleans.

Armed, as they would be in Iraq, with automatic rifles, guns strapped to legs, and pockets overflowing with ammo, Blackwater contractors drove around in SUVs, unmarked cars, and SUVs with no license plates. When asked what authority they were operating under, they supposedly said that they were under government contract with the Department of Homeland Security. Evidently, they also said that they could make arrests and use lethal force if they deem it necessary. The operators described their mission in New Orleans as securing neighborhoods, as if they were working in the Middle East.

These were United States citizens being treated this way with no one stopping the operators, except the Coast Guard immediately and then the National Guard later on after they figured out who was in charge. This was an indictment of the Bush administration and its government officials. Not being prepared was not an excuse for treating these citizens like dirt. Even the National Guard spokesperson said that this would be a combat operation to get New Orleans under control. This happened in the United States of America. Joe lost faith in his government.

When he returned to Miami, although he was extremely proud of the job they as Coasties did, he was fed up with his own government. It was time for him to move on, after what he thought was the worse treatment he had ever seen of his own fellow citizens in his own country, by those who were in charge and should have had compassion for those who'd lost everything.

The year he left in 2008, he at least got to be in Washington for President Obama's election night speech. They were working at the Coast Guard headquarter in Washington, DC. The Headquarters Building, located at 2100 Second Street in Washington is the administrative and operational command and control center for the United States Coast Guard. Mark and he met the Commander of the Coast Guard for the first time. *You might know it took him ten years to shake hands with the top Commander,* he thought. Their Commandant directed the policy and administration of the Coast Guard under the general supervision of the Secretary of the Department of Transportation "SECDOT." The Commandant prescribed broad policies for the government of the service and generally directed, supervised, and coordinated service endeavor and performance. The building housed 1,500 active Coast Guard members and 1,200 civilian employees. Joe and Mark were temporarily housed in Fort Belvoir, Virginia, consisting of forty-four units that housed families of Coast Guard enlisted men. There were several units open so they, who were on temporary assignment, stayed bunked together. They were shuttled into town for several weeks before and after the election results.

Joe and Mark's jobs were to develop intelligence from chatter in Spanish over the lines. Mark and he worked again as a two-man team passing along their findings to the higher command. The Coast Guard's only full, four-star Admiral, the Commandant served as the principal advisor to the Secretary, regarding service matters. The Commandant established and maintained effective liaison and relations with other agencies of the Federal government and with the public in general. The Commandant served on interdepartmental or international bodies concerned with other matters in which the Department and Coast Guard had a substantial interest. That was Mark and Joe's interest as well since they lived in the middle of that interest. The Commandant kept his men and women informed to insure Departmental uniformity of decision and continuity of action.

It was cold and bitter and they were at Coast Guard Headquarters reviewing intelligence concerning the election. Joe and Mark later strolled down the street and saw where President Obama would stand as the first African American President of the United States for his upcoming inaugural address. On election night, after the results came in, people of all colors were out on the streets celebrating a new world order of change, or so they hoped.

CHAPTER 25

As Joe was nearing the last stop on the Tri-rail, at the Miami International Airport, his final thoughts were about Jen, how they met, how their relationship evolved, and finally ended. He just had to see her one more time. It was the right thing to do. Joe went back to his thoughts on his long journey, leading up to today, and what was to come. After he joined the Coast Guard, it was clear that it would be a long time before he ever, if ever, got back to college.

At the time, he had hoped that the Coast Guard would see him as a good investment and help him get his degree while still in Miami. If he got transferred, he would have to start all over again. It was his understanding that he could transfer only so many credits to his final college from which he would graduate. At the time, he only had eighteen credits with all C's, but it was from MIT, so he had hoped for some consideration. Losing credits meant losing money. So, with permission from his commander, he resumed his quest for a degree going nights to Miami Dade College. He thought he had wasted enough time. He was older, now at twenty-four, and he knew what he wanted. He didn't think he would make a career out of the Coast Guard but he sure wanted a paid education for his troubles. He enrolled in two classes at Miami Dade College. They gave him his eighteen credit hours from MIT toward an associate's degree. He also knew that if he could do well and take all general courses, that those courses would be transferrable to another college or university, and he would be much better off. So, he needed fourteen courses to graduate, over seven semesters, all year around, when possible. He had to miss in the fall of 2005 because of Hurricane Katrina, but he made it up quickly when he came back. He finished his required courses for his Associate's Degree in Liberal Arts in May of 2006. He was fortunate at that point because the Coast Guard let him take courses, online, at the Coast Guard Academy in New London Connecticut as well as take summer courses at the Academy, a full load, so he could finish by the end of 2008. He graduated in December 2008. He took his diploma and went home.

What the hell does that have to do with Jen? He forgot he was supposed to be thinking about Jen. He met her at Miami Dade College in early 2005, before he deployed to New Orleans for the fall. He got back just in time to start the spring semester. He had six courses transferred, eight courses down, needing six more courses to graduate. His professors understood his situation. They liked the steady influence of military personnel in their classrooms, students who took their courses seriously, which balanced out the normal brain-dead eighteen year olds, just starting.

Jen and he were in the same class, a Contemporary Literature course, together on a Tuesday and Thursday nights from six to eight p.m., on the MDC campus in downtown Miami. Jen was twenty-two at the time. Joe was twenty-four going on twenty-five in April. She needed some liberal arts courses for her Associate's Degree in Nursing. She went to work directly from high school and worked as a medical assistant in a doctor's office in downtown. She started taking night courses at age twenty to become a nurse. She would graduate in the spring and start at Baptist Hospital in Miami as soon as she passed her state exam. Nursing was tough, depending on your specialty. After several classes, they started talking during the fifteen-minute break. Toward the midterms, Joe asked her out for a cup of coffee. They talked for a while at a coffee shop around the corner that catered to students, *even older students with canes,* he thought. She said she was second generation Cuban, lived at home, and would move out after she graduated and passed her nursing boards for the State of Florida. Joe spoke to her in Spanish. She was shocked and pleasantly surprised. She also picked up that his language was not just textbook Spanish, but it was very clear that he had street Spanish, Spanglish, down pat.

She wanted to know how an Irish Catholic boy from upstate New York knew what he knew. Joe said that he was in the Coast Guard Intelligence Division, but he really couldn't tell her much about what he did in Miami. He also explained that Mark was his best friend and he only spoke to him in Spanish unless he was pissed and then had a litany of English swear words he used on him all the time. She said she was smart enough to guess and left it at that.

After several more classes, he asked her out on a real date. She accepted and he had to meet her at her parent's house. He remembered that he had not really had a date since his Senior Prom in high school in Troy. That did not go well. He hoped this would go better. His love life had always been suspect at best.

God, he hoped that this would go better than his normal encounters. She said to pick her up Saturday night at seven-ish. The seven-ish meant meeting her parents alone downstairs while she was fussing upstairs. Her parents were nice enough, pleasant, and not unkind. After all, Jen and Joe were in their twenties, not teenagers. Joe didn't feel any great warmth or any great hostility. Someone once said, "In business if everyone is mad at you just a little, it means you're doing okay. Too much one side or the other and your management balancing skills went out the window."

After that, they dated pretty much full time until she graduated. The summer was fun, and then he got called up for Katrina.

Meeting Rose and John Alvarez gave him a different perspective culturally of what it was like being Cuban and living in South Florida, especially for those who made it to American shores from Cuba by any means possible. Becoming an American citizen, through naturalization, meant everything to them. Jen was second-generation American. Unlike the majority of Latinos, who tended to lean liberal and vote Democratic, Cuban-Americans seemed to move in the opposite direction, politically.

He really wanted to understand what made Jen's parents tick, the father more than the mother. He did some research so he would not make any clear blunders whenever they met. According to the Miami Herald, only thirty percent of the Cuban Americans polled, said they were Democrats. Evidently, Cuban-American conservatism was strongly rooted in the anti-Castro sentiments stemming from the 1959 revolution, the botched Bay of Pigs invasion during the Kennedy administration and Republican support for the U.S. embargo against trade with Cuba. The sentiments only strengthened as Fidel Castro kept power for decades and an influential group of Cuban-American politicians, especially in Miami, as they became entrenched in the Republican Party.

Joe really didn't understand the Elian Gonzalez effect on the Cuban-Americans living in Miami, but as he read about it, it became very clear that the Democrats shot themselves in the foot with this voting constituency. At the time, Attorney General Janet Reno decided to forcibly remove Elian Gonzalez from his family's Miami home. It only exacerbated Cubans' distrust of the Democratic Party.

Cubans were largely against returning Elian, who was found clinging to an inner tube along the shores of Miami, was returned to his father in Communist Cuba. Besides their very strong anti-Castro feelings, Cuban-Americans had also tended to side with the Republican Party on fiscal and social matters. Immigration was another issue that was a greater concerned for other Latinos, especially those with Mexican, Central or South American roots, than for Cuban Americans. Cuban immigrants were protected from deportation under the "wet foot, dry foot policy," which meant once they reached American shore they could not forcibly be returned to Cuba. The others were not.

So, being an Irish Democrat from upstate New York, with Vermont roots, probably didn't make Rose and John feel very comfortable with Joe dating their very Cuban daughter. Speaking Spanish was a benefit, but he did not have the Cuban accent. What he learned was influenced by Mark's Mexican roots. The Catholic part was fine. Not being overly Catholic probably didn't help on his part. He had a lot of work to do, if he wanted to be on good terms with Jen's parents. She was, after all, very close to them and listened to them, let alone lived with them.

Their two years together was fine—until it was not. There was a tug of war between Jen and her parents and she gave in to them. Joe could not understand why. When he was up in Troy attending RPI and his mother died, she didn't even attend the funeral. They were polite and sent flowers from her and her family, but that effectively ended their relationship. She would never move to New York. He never asked her to. If they were together, after his graduation, he would have gladly moved back. With an RPI degree, he could have gone anywhere. Many of his calls were left unreturned. The ones she picked up were less than pleasant. Joe simply wanted a good ending if that was possible. That's why he was headed to the old apartment.

With his thoughts swirling in his mind, he got off the Tri-rail at the Miami International Airport, the last exit. He walked to her apartment. It was South Florida in winter. It was seventy degrees, low humidity, sun shining. It was perfect. He walked fast but looked around every step to remember the days when this was his old stomping ground. He saw the sports bar where they got Yankee games on satellite and the Cuban restaurant where he and Jen ate, seemed like every other night. It was cheap and good and couldn't be beat.

He got to Jen's block, walked up her steps, and rang the bell. There was no sound at first, so he knocked and rang the bell again. Finally, the door opened and there was Jen.

"Hi, Jen, how are you?" Joe said. He thought he startled her.

"Good, Joe. How are you?" she said. " I'm sorry, but I'm on my way out for an appointment."

"Will you be back soon? I can wait for you," he said. "I have the whole day free."

"I have a bunch of errands before work today," she said, "and I won't be coming home. I'm going straight to work."

"You still work at four p.m., don't you?" he asked.

"If you want, I could ride along with you and we can talk. I have the whole day," he said again.

"I would prefer not, Joe," she said.

"Okay." He turned around, walked down her steps, and out of her life forever. He never looked back. He had no idea if she looked at him or even cared.

Now he remembered that he was really pissed. *Boy I was pissed. I don't know what I did to deserve that.* Actually, he was glad that he now knew how she felt. It was like he didn't even exist. His stomach was in knots and sadness came over him like an ocean swell. He thought that he should have known when she couldn't even come to his mother's funeral. This, after all they had been to each other. She knew he was leaving the Coast Guard and wanted to complete his MBA. She never said a word. It was time to move on.

For his mother's funeral, she couldn't take time off of work, so she said, and appeared to be uncomfortable leaving South Florida, even for a few days. Like it was the end of the universe. After the funeral, he called one of her nurse friends at Baptist to see if she knew what her real issues were. The nurse confided in Joe that her parents gave her a lot of pressure to dump him for a Cuban boyfriend who would stay in Miami and raise little perfect Cuban kids. God, after all that time, he thought they were over that, but he guessed not. It was one thing to be close to your parents, but another to have them live your life for you. She allowed them to do that and ruined his and her relationship. He guessed that compared to her family, he was raised by wolves. He was on his own at eighteen. At twenty-six, she was still a daddy's girl.

He asked Mark about it.

"It's a cultural thing," Mark said. "That's why I married Louise. I didn't want that situation for myself. Joe, I tried to warn you a few times but I guess it never stuck."

Joe walked back to the Tri-rail and debated transferring to South Beach station or head to the Hard Rock. The Hard Rock and a few beers with his friends was still a possibility before they split. The Hard Rock won. Instead of spending the entire afternoon with Jen, he spent approximately two minutes at her front door. That was two minutes he would never get back. He remembered that he was going to call Mary but decided to wait until he got back to ask her out.

He had to meet Tom Jones tomorrow for lunch and then rent a car and head down to Key Largo to visit Tillie. He had to be back to babysit the kids and then he would head home to deal with another pain-in-the-ass situation. It was more than that. It would probably be deadly.

CHAPTER 26

Joe got back from Miami on late Sunday. He planned on going in early Monday morning. He couldn't wait to see Mary and ask her to lunch. That was all he thought about for the entire week in Miami. How was he going ask her out? What was he going to say to her? Would she accept his invitation? *Christ*, he was a wreck. He decided to go over to McGuire's and have a few beers before heading to bed. It was only around the corner. Back in lovely Troy, New York. Troy was the hotbed of activity for upstate New York, not.

"Hi, guys," Joe said as he walked into the bar, the first time in quite a while.

"Hey," Lee McGuire, the owner and today's bartender said.

"Didn't Mike come in today?" Joe asked.

"No, I gave him the day off because I love working from ten a.m. until two a.m. in the morning. What do you think?" he said.

I feel like I'm walking into Cheers, Joe thought. His life revolved around work and this place and, if this was the sum total of his life *take me now, Lord, take me now,* as Red Fox said on all the reruns of *Sanford and Son,* on cable.

Joe ran into Cathy Wells sitting in the booth by the door. At one time, he liked her enough, just not that enough. She was local, twenty-nine, single, and had been around, but had an okay reputation. She was with Molly, her girlfriend. Hell, she was always with Molly. That was one of the problems. Double dating with Molly didn't happen. Molly dating didn't happen. She held on to Cathy for dear life. Joe let the relationship slide without confirming it. It was the best he could do without creating a scene.

"Hi, Cathy, hi, Molly, how are you guys?" he said.

Right away, Molly started up. "Where the hell have you been? Cathy missed you."

Oh shit.

Cathy looked pissed at Molly or probably him. "How are you, Joe?" she said.

"Fine, busy with work," he said. "Got a new boss, had to spend a lot of time getting him acclimated. Probably won't be around as much."

"Are you still going to bartend here?" she asked.

"Not for a while." *At least not until you get another boyfriend or dump Molly.*

Joe sat at the bar and carried on a conversation with Lee. Joe had a few beers and a corned beef on rye, the best in the area. Sunday night was his favorite, with a full corned beef and cabbage dinner for eight dollars. *Corned beef and Irish, what a concept.* Overstuffed plate, plenty of rye bread and butter. Prediger's rye was the best out of Green Island across the bridge from Troy. It closed up when the owners retired and rye bread had never been the same. This bread was good but not great. He thought, maybe he should call Lee the next time, before he came in just to see if Cathy and Molly were there. But then, Joe could starve to death. It was his only full meal every week.

He walked home. It was only around the corner to his apartment on Third Street, near Congress. He still lived in a back apartment in a brownstone, across the street, kitty-corner to the president of Russell Sage College. His back entrance apartment was just the right size, living room, kitchen, bath, and two bedrooms, one bigger than the other. He used the smaller bedroom as his office, when working at home. He found this place by accident after he got out of RPI in 2010. For the first two years coming home, he stayed with his father until he graduated. After his Mom died, he thought it would help the situation by staying with his father. It was okay, but he fell back in to being his son. It wasn't going to work out in the long haul. Both had tempers and both had very large independent streaks.

Joe had started bartending at McGuire's while he went for his MBA. It fit his schedule. After graduation, he looked around downtown, before going to McGuire's for his shift, and saw this educational consulting firm, the Troy Education Consulting Group, a non-profit, as he was walking around the area. He walked in with his resume to see if they were hiring, before he got the job with the Albany Coalition for Families.

They were not hiring, but he spoke to several people in the office, including the executive director, Johnathon Mills.

Johnathan said he really didn't have enough work for a fulltime analyst but he was just about to put a notice in the paper about the small apartment in the back. He said if Joe wanted to, he could trade off some of his time and knock off the monthly rent. Instead of $1,200.00 a month, which Joe could not afford—even if it was worth it—the rent would $700.00 a month, which included utilities. Trading twenty-five hours a month at twenty dollars an hour, under the table, seemed fine with him. He smiled at the time. "Johnathon, you have a deal. When can I move in?"

What a great deal, he'd thought, but he kept it to himself. He moved from the Burgh with friends' help, and he had been there ever since.

☙❧

He had been there a couple of years now and it had really worked out well for him. Not only was he downtown and close to "what was happening" in the city of Troy—not really much—but also he was close enough yet far enough from his family in the Burgh in the north end. His brother would stay over every now and then when they decided to go bar hopping together.

Joe believed that if something happened to his job at the Coalition, and it took a turn for the worse with the economy, he could still keep his place there and probably work in some additional consulting work. His student loans at RPI were now below $10,000.00 and on schedule to be fully paid off in two more years. He had the research background that they needed, and he was a good enough of a writer that he could take what they had, and turn it around quickly for their State Education Department publications, that they published monthly. Five hours a week, twenty feet from his front door, didn't make a dent in his schedule and he actually liked working there. It was fun and interesting. To top it off, he was able to slide his car into the back driveway, without blocking the alley, just inches from the end of their property. Parking was a bitch in downtown Troy, especially near the Sage College complex. Johnathon Mills, the Director, must have been sent by God to get him restarted in life.

☙❧

Joe got up, same as always, and headed to downtown Albany, getting there around seven a.m. Today was a little different. He had a headache from last night. He didn't leave the bar until after one a.m. He wanted to ask out Mary for lunch, and he was sure that Luis would be waiting for him to discuss everything and anything. He was really starting to hate it there, except for the Mary part.

Luis didn't get in until after nine a.m. Evidently, the honeymoon with the first floor was over for Luis. He was back in his office upstairs and told Joe he wanted to see him after he got settled. Joe asked him to give him an hour to straighten out his desk. Instead, he went down to accounting to visit with Mary.

She was so good to him in filing his grants that he wanted to get her something appropriate. He bought her a necklace in the Florida Keys when he went to visit Tillie. Tillie had helped him pick out an appropriate necklace made from coral from right in Key Largo. It was expensive, but he really wanted to get Mary something nice.

He walked into the accounting department, said hello to everyone, and walked up to Mary's desk. "Mary, could I take you to lunch today? I want to thank you for all your help in getting my budgets completed for our grants."

"Sure, Joe, what time?" she asked. "Oh, welcome back. How was your trip?"

"I had a great time, Mary, just what I needed. Thanks for asking." He told her he had to meet with Luis, all morning, but he would free around twelve-thirty p.m. "Can you make it then?"

"Sure, Joe, I'll look forward to it," she said. "I have to be back by one-thirty p.m. for an accounting meeting. Okay?"

"Sure, I'll see you then," he said.

At twelve-thirty, they walked out together and went across the street to a little hole-in-the-wall Italian restaurant. "Mary, I really have another motive," he said, blushing. "Yes, I really did want to thank you for all your help, but I have wanted to ask you out for some time, ever since you started last May. I didn't want to hit on you at work, and I didn't want you to think I was a stalker."

"Well, it's about time. I was wondering what took you so long?" she said.

"Now, you're really embarrassing me," he said. "I'm not really good at this. You would think I would be by now, but I'm such a novice."

"I'm glad you're a novice," she said.

"I've really been busy, Mary," he said.

She laughed. "I know, Joe, you've made me twice as busy as before."

He looked into her eyes and handed her the present he bought her in the Keys. She thanked him and opened the tightly wrapped box.

Her eyes lit up. "Oh, Joe, it's beautiful. What's it was made of?"

"Coral, from Key Largo." He told her that Tillie, and he explained who she was, as well as Julie, helped him pick it out.

Mary reached over and gave him a kiss on the cheek. He started to blush and she laughed.

They ate lunch. He was so relieved he hardly ate anything. She smiled at him and he found some courage. "Will you go to dinner with me tonight?"

Mary nodded. "Yes. You can pick me up at my apartment at seven p.m."

She gave him the directions to her place in Latham, not really that far from his own place in Troy. She had lived on her own for some time and really liked the solitude. She graduated from the University at Albany with a BA in Accounting, worked at two non-profits before the Coalition, but was offered more opportunity with the Coalition and she accepted. She was also a certified public accountant and could probably have gone anywhere she wanted. She said she really liked working there.

Mary smiled then. "I might never have met you if I didn't work there."

Joe was quite shocked. "I'm glad you came to the Coalition."

"Me, too."

At twenty-seven, she was very confident in her own abilities and it showed. She was pleasant, good looking, but more than that, she was fun to be with. She was someone he could really have deep feelings for, if offered the opportunity. He didn't ask her if she was seeing any-one, but he was sure she would have said something if she was. She just struck him as being very honest and straightforward. Maybe it was true of all accountants, who knew? Nonetheless, he was very pleased that she accepted his invitation.

They got back to the office and Joe continued his meeting with Luis. They were ready to hand in the Hud-son Foundation grant at the end of the week. They re-viewed their status reports, and Luis told Joe that every-thing was taken care of on the first floor.

"Do you want to go see Jim in the hospital togeth-er?" Luis asked Joe.

"I can't," Joe said, "but I'll probably go in a few days when I get settled. I'll call Marie and find out how he's doing."

Joe hoped he'd gotten away with not going with Luis. He certainly did not want to be seen side by side with Luis. Not now, not ever.

ღოღ

That night, Joe picked up Mary and they stayed close

to her place, going to an Italian restaurant, south of the Latham Circle on Route 9, toward Siena College. It was expensive but nice and quiet for a Monday night. Very few independent restaurants were opened on Monday in the Capital Region, other than those on Wolf Road that were national chains. He liked Red Lobster. Mary did as well, and the Olive Garden, but not tonight. They talked for some time, had a wonderful dinner, and it was almost eleven p.m. by the time they left the restaurant. It was worth every penny. They exchange life stories, not everything of course, no need for that. They got along fine, had a bottle of wine, and nursed it through the evening. He took her home, gave her a kiss on the cheek,

"Thank you for a wonderful night," Joe said. "Can we do it again?"

"Of course, I had a great time, Joe. See you at work tomorrow."

He thought about asking her to go to McGuire's that weekend but he didn't want to complicate his life there. Last weekend was a zoo with people coming in late from shopping or just catching up with friends. They had a band going all night. It was a hopping joint. He was sure they would bust his ass and give ammunition to Cathy and, especially, Molly. He would probably never hear the end of it. It wasn't going to happen. Maybe he could cook for her Saturday night. That sounded like a plan. They would have steak, salad, and fresh Italian bread from the Italian bakery down the street. He would ask her tomorrow. He pulled in behind his apartment with just enough room for a gnat to park behind him. He couldn't wait to get to work tomorrow. *Sweet dreams, Joe,* he thought. It was a good night. Jen was behind him, and now he had someone in his life, once again.

That wouldn't stop the trouble that was coming, however.

Chapter 27

While Joe was away, Luis didn't waste any time in building up his little empire in Albany. He brought in Dave Perez from the Hartford Career Center and Alicia Torres from the Hudson Foundation in New York City. He brought them both in under the guise that the Hudson Foundation wanted a tour of the Albany Coalition for Families facility and that Luis was Dave's mentor for the association's program. Luis introduced both of them to key board members. They were the same ones who asked him to become the interim president after Ted died. Luis thought that he had them in the palm of his hand.

Planning around Joe's vacation was pure genius, Luis thought. When he got back, Joe would walk into a situation that included the board's full backing for whatever Luis wanted. He thought Joe was a good grant writer but not much else. He was able to do all the paperwork and fill out all the forms correctly, but Luis thought anyone could do it. He had to be careful, though. He did know that Dave failed with his grants because he didn't have someone like Joe following up and making sure everything went in properly. He might interview a few others in Albany as associate grant writers to "help" Joe and Missy, but would move them up after he no longer needed either one of them. If he left after his commitment, he would keep Joe as the fall guy if everything came crashing down. Hell, Luis never signed anything of significance, so he was not responsible, financially or otherwise. He was only a loaned executive helping out the organization. Luis believed that this was the perfect plan.

Because Dave was a graduate from the Hispanic Management Outreach program, Luis could also send Joe to Hartford to help Dave with his paperwork. Joe wouldn't have a clue that he was being manipulated. Luis would tell the board that if he built partnerships across state lines, they could get more national funding as a national model for replication for youth work programs. Hell, with these foundations providing matching funds, he could go after the United States Department of Labor and Health and Human Resources grants that would keep them busy forever. He might even be willing to stay after the two-year commitment. In only six plus months, Luis was able to transfer well over a million dollars to the Mexican Mafia owned vendors without raising an eyebrow. Luis knew that Jim Clark had gotten suspicious but he wasn't really sure what Joe knew or didn't know. Taking care of Jim Clark gave him that much more leverage, now that he filled two jobs to help the Coalition. The board thanked him profusely for caring about their organization.

After Dave and Alicia met with the board, Luis brought them both on a tour of Albany, winding up at the Orange Street Boys clubhouse. When he walked in, he handed their leader twenty five thousand dollars in cash as a bonus for getting rid of Jim Clark and as their cut for the month for helping him on the first floor Career Center. The five "students" sold over one hundred thousand dollars in drugs in less than a month, right out of the Coalition, with no one the wiser. Luis sent almost seventy-five thousand dollars in cash, by FedEx, to the gang, addressed to Frank at the law firm. Frank wasn't happy about it coming directly to him, but he took his cut, and split the rest between the gangs officer' families. Five thousand here and ten thousand dollars there added up and kept everyone happy. If every one of the ten members at the ten non-profits did the same, the families would be happy just with the cash from the drug sales. The twenty million plus dollars that flowed through the gang-owned vendor companies went directly into real estate ventures and other projects including money lending activities right on the streets of Los Angeles.

Luis met Joe that morning and gave him implicit instructions on the foundations that would follow. Joe was also told, by Luis, that he, himself, would handle all the Career Center operations for now on until Jim Clark returned. Luis was very specific in telling Joe that the board fully approved his actions. Joe didn't believe that Jim would ever return to the Coalition. Jim was almost fifty-five years old at this point and it looked like it would take him at least nine months to recover, if he could *ever* fully recover.

At least Jim had long-term disability coverage through the Coalition that would pay him almost sixty percent of his normal pay. That coupled with New York State disability payments of another four hundred dollars a week would just about make him whole. In fact, he could probably collect this amount right up until he turned sixty-two years old and then would collect social security. Jim's family health insurance plan was fully paid by the Coalition, so whatever medical treatments were needed, he was covered. It didn't take the place of good health, but so many times families had gone under for lesser problems. Joe saw him at least once a week as he was convalescing at home.

"Two of my fellow Hispanic Management Outreach program participants came to visit me while you were in Florida, Joe. It didn't hurt that one of them actually worked for the Hudson Foundation. That application just went out. The foundation was impressed by our application and they wanted to see the Career Center before they approved the application."

Joe wondered how that worked. Wasn't there a conflict of interest in having a foundation employee inspect the Coalition's facilities? At the same time, the employee was a close friend of Luis's and a graduate of the same program. Joe kept that thought to himself.

CHAPTER 28

Joe had always wondered why he thought differently about things than most people. As he met friends and business associates throughout his lifetime, and even those in the service, he noticed that left-handed people were, in fact, different. Most were good at math, and they were creative. They also ran into a lot of right-handed doors and couldn't use a pair of scissors to save their lives. Joe was left-handed. He found it interesting on how he interacted with others throughout his life, especially in dealing with right-handers. Joe was always aware if someone was left-handed.

One time while attending a New York State finance meeting, about budgets for grants, with other finance people, nine out of the ten at the meeting were left-handed. Just for the hell of it, he asked what month each individual was born in, and a majority said they were born in April. Joe found that fascinating but he was not at all surprised. He kept that nugget in the back of his brain. Whenever he knew there was to be a difficult situation, he would find out if the individual with whom he was dealing with were left-handed or right-handed. Luis was right-handed.

Joe remembered going through grammar school with

the nuns. He had to write like a right-hander by turning his paper sideways to the left and then writing backhanded over the line that he was writing on. He had to write upside down as it were. Thank God they could use ball-point pens by that time. Joe tried one of his father's fountain pens with a quill-like point that dispensed ink in a very liquid form. As a left-hander, he would smear the ink going from left to write because his left palm would hit the ink. It was also, from observation, only that a great disproportionate number of left-handers were born in the month of April. He remembered asking that question from an early age. It held true as an adult in the finance meeting that he just attended.

It was also true, from Joe's observations, that a majority of left-handers were very good in math but not in some other non-technical subjects. Left-handers used the right side of the brain for thinking, and just the opposite for right-handers. The joke was that left-handers were the only ones in their right minds. Joe was at a math fair in high school and eight out of ten of the finalists were left-handed. He had kept track during the years and his theory seemed to hold water. The downside was that he was unable to open most doors. Most obvious was that he couldn't open the refrigerator without hitting himself with the door. Throughout the years, he opened many doors and walked right into them. It was more than he cared to remember. He now remembered that during drug takedowns, he could not be first in line simply because they knew his left-handed condition for walking into doors. The only advantage ever developed for left-handers was the typewriter and computer keyboard since the vowels, which were used most of the time, were on the left side of the keyboard. He always used a Mac instead of a PC because a Mac opened its windows from left to right and the PC opened just the opposite. He pointed out to non-believers that Steve Jobs was left-handed, the inventor of the Mac.

The biggest benefit to being left-handed was in sports. A friend of Joe's lost only three tennis matches in four years, all because the opponent thought he had the best backhand they ever saw. Unfortunately for the opponent, they thought they were volleying to his backhand but it was, in fact, to his left side power drive right down the line. They were in awe until he explained to them after they lost that he was left-handed. He smiled. They were pissed.

Joe's favorite sport was baseball. Until he was in high school, Joe was a left-handed second baseman and catcher. He had to buy a left-handed catcher's mitt, which was not easy to find. Since most of the batters were right-handed, his throw to second base, from behind home plate, was always near the head of the batter, hitting several in too many games. However, his move to third, swinging to his left, behind the batter, directly to third base, was a thing of beauty. He loved catching until a right-handed batter brought his bat back to swing as Joe reached in to catch the ball. It caught him right on the back of the head, knocking him unconscious. After that, his coach convinced him to be a left-handed pitcher.

Left-handed pitchers were few and far between. If you could throw it over the plate, every coach in America wanted you. Unfortunately the stories of left-handers being wild were not a myth. In fact, those stories were very accurate. Since most of the hitters were right-handed, the left-handed pitcher had no target to throw to, except to the catcher, right down the middle of the plate. Most kids couldn't do that so they wound up walking too many batters.

This was where Joe's left-handed thinking and photographic memory had informed many of his decisions, including pitching predicaments. He love the New York Yankees, always had. Andy Pettitte was his favorite pitcher. Why? Because he was left-handed and every time he walked a batter, he usually picked him off at first base. A left-hander has an enormous advantage leaning from the left. It took less time to throw over to first base, and you could usually catch a runner daydreaming or not paying attention. He watched Andy for years and copied his moves down pat. When he was on the mound, Joe was Andy Pettitte. Why? Because he would walk six or seven batters every game.

In high school they played seven-inning games, so he would walk one an inning. But because of his photographic memory, and since they played the same teams and players, living in the same town, he knew every at bat and what each player did against him. If they got a hit against him, he would walk them, the next time they came to bat. It made them cocky as they say. They would stroll around first base, take a lead, and he would gun them down almost seventy-five percent of the time. First pitch went to first base.

Only one coach in four years ever figured him out. When he went to first, the next pitch would come home to the batter. This coach knew that and would give the sign to steal to his runner, immediately after he went to first. It was disheartening until the following year, the coach of the opposing team asked him to come play for him. He taught him how to mix up his pick-off moves. Joe could always hit for average, so the coach wanted him in the game anyway.

He remembered his senior year in high school. His record was six-three on a team that only won eight games all year. Being left-handed, he was offered partial scholarships to play baseball at the Division II level. Only Division I and Division II colleges were allowed to offer scholarships. Joe was already offered a math scholarship to MIT, a full ride, a Division III school, and he only played baseball for fun. So, he didn't want to compete on a scholarship basis.

Joe told his coach in high school that on the days that he didn't pitch, and if he was still in the game, if the game was close, he would come in to pitch, to hold a lead or a tie. He never went in to pitch to the batter, but the coach sent him in with one or two outs in the top of the seventh, to pick off the runner that was on first base. Joe never pitched to the batter. First pitch over to the base surprised the crap out of the runner. He was now a non-pitching-to-home pitching-specialist. They won the other two games that way.

The point of his argument was that he really did think that left-handers do think differently than right-handers. Manuals meant nothing to Joe. He couldn't follow the instructions. Lefties were truly differently abled. When he went to MIT in the fall that year, the only thing that kept him in class, before signing up for the Coast Guard, was fall baseball. He told his coach that, as a pitcher, he would be wild but he could pick off anyone. He told him to either start him or sit him because he was walking people. He still threw out three out of every four that he walked. He won three out of four games that fall.

As he thought about his MIT baseball career, he remembered they played nine- inning games but double headers were only for seven innings, so they could get the games in before the snow started flying in early November. If he pitched the first game, as he told his coach, put him in the second game if a runner got on first in the last inning and they were tied or ahead. It was a thing of beauty. Joe had no pitching record for the second game but he had an assist on the putout at first base, as he picked off the runner daydreaming. This was his only regret leaving MIT. At least he had three years left of eligibility. He was wondering, to himself, if he could ever play for the Coast Guard Academy, later in his career, especially since they played MIT every year and they still had his old coach. He probably would have blown his pickoff move cover.

Joe loved numbers, hence the MIT math scholarship, and that was why he did well writing grants for the Coalition. Most lefties loved numbers. All his budgets were flawless and matched the narrative perfectly in every case. Joe still loved baseball statistics and read about players every day—now online, not like before, opening the local paper every day and going to the sports pages to see how Andy Pettitte and the Yankees made out the night before. If he was bartending, Joe could watch the games on cable, right behind the bar. It was a hard habit to break. Win or lose, Joe still knew every statistics available. Made some money with his photographic memory, especially for sports stats.

CHAPTER 29

Little did Joe know that Luis had been checking up on him over the last month. Luis wanted to know who he was dealing with. He knew that Joe was reasonably smart, but what the hell could he know from ten years in the Coast Guard that Luis couldn't figure out in a relative short period of time? He knew Joe had been stationed in Miami, but the man talked very little about it. Joe had spoken of several rescue missions, including a tour in Haiti during the earthquake, and in several hurricanes, including Katrina, and Joe had been was in New Orleans for several months. Luis was sure Joe had training as a combatant, knew ships, and something about drug raids. But what could he know as the guy breaking down the doors? He was cannon fodder in the war on drugs. *Hell, he probably wouldn't know a terrorist from a peapod*, Luis thought.

Luis figured Joe got hired for this job because of his MBA. Everyone residing in the Albany area would be impressed with his degree. It wasn't like Luis's Ivy-League degree, but it carried some weight. Luis thought the rest of the senior management team was a bunch of clowns on their way to a happy retirement. He really wasn't there for the long run. In two more years, the Albany Coalition would get a second and even third wave coming from the NCWA intern program, if Luis didn't want to stay. It all depended on what his father wanted. He was the general. Hell, they could do this indefinitely as they continued to establish new legitimate businesses that would invoice the non-profit, forever. If Luis pulled the plug, the Coalition wouldn't have a clue. However, Luis was, and would continue to be, very careful. He learned from his father that you didn't plan for what you expected, you planned for anything that could happen. That was why he wasn't surprised when he got a message from his cohort at the NCWA.

Elena Perez, the new director of the Hispanic Management Outreach program at the NCWA, sent Luis an encrypted email to call her on her burner cell phone. Elena was Dave Perez's cousin. She also knew that Dave would have difficulty in the position that he was in, but he was family, and she didn't want anything to happen to him. She told Luis that she found out that someone was looking at the association's internal records of the interns from her program. Someone broke in and read all their files online. She followed the trail and it led her to an address in Troy, New York. She was well versed in computer IP address protocol and knew something was amiss. She followed, as best she could, and discovered at two-oh-two a.m. earlier that morning, the electronic intern folders, which had their digital fingerprint information, was disturbed. She couldn't tell exactly what happened but she was concerned. She called Luis immediately.

Luis then sent encrypted messages to all his other non-profit and foundation contacts to let them know to be careful and to have all their records checked very carefully. He didn't want to raise any suspicions so he down-played the request and told them to be on their toes. Anyone not on board would be dealt with severely. They all knew the reputation of the Mexican Mafia, that it was known for its violent acts toward anyone who was perceived to have crossed them. This was a breach, but he didn't want anyone to know about it and told Elena to keep it to herself, for now.

Luis had already placed his California gang members on the streets of Albany, living out of the motel on lower Broadway. He also placed five of the Orange Street Boys in the youth training programs at the Career Center. They were recruited as "local" youths who only needed a chance to turn their lives around. These individuals participated fully in the every-day activities, including GED, life skills, and certification programs. They would, in turn, recruit other local small-time gang members to participate and, at each of the ten locations across the country, they would do the same. The drug sales alone put plenty of cash back into the hands of the family.

Each of the Hispanic vice presidents, now at the other nine non-profits, would sell these local youth as fresh-faced kids who were striving for a better future. Originally, Luis had his group of five from California, who went by bus from LA to New York City and then transferred to the Albany bus and got off in downtown Albany. These five were his local recruiters for the drug trade in Albany, and they would work with the OSB and, eventually, would fill the seats in classes at the Coalition. He also recruited several members of Los Vegos from East Harlem. They too were moved into the motel, a few rooms down. They came to Albany from New York City by bus. They stayed by themselves and took orders only from Luis. They knew that the others were there but they were to be fully involved in the drug trade only.

All of this travel by bus, and having the gang members hidden in out-of-the-way rooms, was done so none of their movements could be traced. It was perfect. Luis had already moved up to a condo on Albany Shaker Road, only a few miles from downtown, but it said "respectability" to the community. He kept everyone oblivious to what the other recruits were doing. The California crew only knew what the OSB was doing and the New York City crew only handled the local drug trade. They might have been at the same motel, but Luis cautioned them not to talk to each other. He told them that it would protect them if anything happened and there was a bust. What he didn't tell them was that they would take the fall for anything that happened, and he would be long gone. They all had different jobs to do if they were to be successful, and they *would* be successful. Luis knew that he could be caught if any of his gang talked, so he took a bite of every transaction that came his way. He already had close to $250,000.00 in cash in small bills at his condo in a go-bag, in case he had to leave quickly. He was prepared for anything.

Luis laughed to himself. They didn't have a clue, any of them.

He wasn't put here to run a non-profit. It was very clear that he was the top dog among the new-age group of twenty well-educated gangbangers that were left out of the original thirty. This was going to be a billion-dollar money laundering enterprise, with many subsidiary drug rings, running out of every non-profit brought on board. The prize was not in taking over the non-profits, but in running an untouchable enterprise where no one in any city would ever have any idea of what was going on and who was involved.

Luis never trusted anyone, especially Joe Traynor. It was the way he was raised. It wasn't anything Joe did or said. It was his way of keeping his thoughts close to the vest that troubled Luis. He didn't have a good read on Joe and that was dangerous. Perhaps Joe could have an accident just like Ted Simmons. Hell, accidents happened all the time. Perhaps he would be mugging victim number two. It was in a really bad section of Albany, right next to the slums of Orange Street. The phone call from the association had put Joe on Luis's radar, big time.

Luis thought he needed to, once again, talk to his boys and take care of business. So far, that had worked pretty well. He would wait and hold a quick meeting at the Express Motel as soon as everyone could come together. He had a list of several new things he wanted to do, and a short list of who he wanted taken care of. Joe was on that short list.

Luis was in charge of reporting back to his father and the other generals. They were due a call, through Frank Ramone. Luis knew it would be fatal to screw up at this point. He wasn't going to let some "Troy Boy" or anyone else get in his way. It just wasn't going to happen.

CHAPTER 30

Joe was ready to go to the Albany FBI to take Luis down. He believed that he had all he needed for a warrant. Under the Patriot Act, he didn't even need that. He had all the proof he thought he needed to be presented to the local FBI office and coordinated with his friends Paul and Terry from the FBI in Miami. They had coordinated with Tom Matthews, and he was prepared to speak to Joe about the game plan. In fact, they were ready to take every one of them out across the country. Based on Joe's information, a major sting was to take place soon. Mark and Jack got Joe all the evidence he asked for, as well as the data he had acquired through his own investigation.

He believed the local FBI office would think that they had a case for a criminal financial conspiracy to defraud, or at least money laundering, on a huge scale. They might have caught it early enough. They had to wait and see. Joe would be meeting with Tom Matthews shortly, and he would bring Dan Simmons along, in case he needed an attorney. *You never knew,* he thought. If he was wrong, it could be the biggest screw up of his life. He didn't think so, but with the government, who knew?

Joe didn't want anyone to get away with it. Not now.

They were too close. Sean showed up right before Tom Matthews arrived. He drove over from Connecticut from the Coast Guard Academy.

Joe called Tom at the FBI office in Albany. "I'll be right over," Tom said.

Tom got the call from Paul Philips in Miami, and he was ready for them. He was given the go ahead from his boss at Homeland Security, and from FBI headquarters in Washington. Tom got to Troy in a half an hour. Joe told him to park in front of the consulting group's front door, and he would let him in.

They sat down and fully reviewed everything they had.

"I believe that we have enough to move ahead under the Patriot Act," Tom said.

The USA PATRIOT Act—commonly known as the Patriot Act—was an Act of Congress that was signed into law on October 26, 2001 in response to Nine/Eleven. Joe knew that much from his time in Miami and so did the others sitting around the table. They all wanted to be clear. They knew they didn't need the RICO Act, so Tom went ahead and read what they thought they understood.

"The title of the act is a ten letter acronym—USA PATRIOT—that stands for Uniting and Strengthening America by Providing Appropriate Tools Required to Intercept and Obstruct Terrorism Act of 2001." He paused and looked everyone in the eyes to make sure they understood. "The act significantly reduced restrictions in law enforcement agencies' gathering of intelligence within the United States and expanded the secretary of the treasury's authority to regulate financial transactions, particularly those involving foreign individuals and entities. The act also expanded the definition of terrorism to domestic terrorism, thus enlarging the number of activities to

which the USA PATRIOT Act's expanded law enforcement powers could be applied."

As they had gathered, from other previous interventions, the Mexican Mafia now fell under this jurisdiction.
Without it, Joe and his team would have had a great deal
of trouble proving their circumstantial case against the
gang and some very prominent California professionals,
who were going down as well. Tom got the okay to pro-
ceed ahead and set up, not only the Albany sting, but a
national sting as well. They were ready.

For Joe to continue his involvement, he had to sign a
few papers, very reluctantly. In order to carry a service
weapon and to work with the FBI and Homeland Security, he had to sign papers placing him back in the Coast
Guard, as a Coast Guard Special Agent for Investigative
Services—for thirty days, only. His last rank was that of a
chief petty officer or E-9. The new title gave him the rank
of chief warrant officer 4. He signed. He would report to
the Coast Guard with a direct line, on loan to the FBI and
Homeland Security. He was now official. He checked the
paperwork to make sure that his official last day was in
thirty days, and there was no funny business.

Dan closely checked the language as an attorney and
friend, but especially as Joe's attorney. If he was killed in
action, he had certain benefits that would accrue to his
designee/designees, which included his father and brother, Mark and his family, Sean, Jack, and Mike, and Tillie
and Julie in Key Largo. Not that he didn't trust the government after ten years. *Yeah, right.* What they had tried
to do to keep him, before he left the Coast Guard, was
incredible. The document was signed by the attorney
general of the United States, under the Patriot Act, super-
seding all other orders. Mark and Sean were already part
of Homeland Security.

They gave Joe the latest version of his former service

weapon that he gave up when he left the Coast Guard. The weapon was a P229R DAK, which was the standard pistol of the Department of Homeland Security and the US Coast Guard. They selected this state-of-the art version after a three million round grueling torture test. The P229R was compact in size, with a choice in firepower of 9mm, .357 SIG or .40 S&W. Joe got the .40 Smith and Wesson version. The new DAK trigger system delivered a safe, reliable and consistent six-point-five-pound double-action only trigger pull. This weapon was extremely accurate, very durable and very reliable. It was an overall exceptional duty weapon. It held twelve rounds. Joe also received the Coast Guard concealed body armor vest to wear under his suit for on-land takedowns. The armor didn't work on a ship because it would have weighed them down if they wound up in the water. He wouldn't have to worry about that on the Albany hill.

Their game plan was that Joe was going in first, wired, to see if he could get Luis talking. But Joe had no expectations of Luis telling him anything. He really had no idea what to expect. Luis believed he was smarter than everyone else at the Coalition. However, his arrogance and over-the-top self-assurance would be his downfall. He was Ivy-league. He was smart, and no one could touch him—so Luis thought. He formed his own posse in Albany in only a few months. He brought the gangbangers in as good kids, young adults, needing a GED and a job. They just needed a chance. Half of them were trying to sell drugs out of the Career Center, for God sake. Jim Clark had finally awoken and told Joe what he believed Luis was doing with the Career Center. Joe had Mark take his deposition the day before as the representative of Homeland Security, since he was the only one around at the time.

Joe became a notary when he started at the Coalition

because he could then notarize the forms signed by Ted and even the board chairman. It still came in handy for this. Jim had found out that Luis laundered their cash, trading Coalition checks for post office checks. Joe thought that Luis couldn't help himself. He was a God-damn criminal.

Joe was to go in the next day and stay late. Luis always thought Joe was a hard worker, staying late, helping to right the ship. He also thought Joe wasn't all that bright. Little did Joe know, until he witnessed it for himself and after he spoke to Jim Clark, the gangbangers walked into Luis's office, that same day, calling him *jefe*, like Luis was king of the world. *Well* jefe, *your time has come*.

The takedown would be set up for eight-thirty p.m. the next night. It was going down. The feds were involved. They would not notify the police until the operation was completed. The Patriot Act did not involve the local police. Luis would rendition to Guantanamo Bay detention camp by the time the office opened the following day. If Luis were found guilty in a court of law, they would simply place him in a federal prison where he would start a new chapter of the Mexican Mafia.

He would immediately become a general and start all over again. He could be killed, since he failed, but who would take his place? He knew how to work the system outside the prison better than those running the gang inside. He could prove too valuable to the Mexican Mafia to be removed. Then there would be his father Jorge to contend with, if Luis was harmed. Rendition was the way to go, Joe believed. He hoped it went as planned. God willing.

Chapter 31

Tonight was the night. Joe hung out in his office after everyone, except Luis, had left. He checked his gun and he had on his vest. He thought the vest would not be too noticeable as it fit snuggly and he could move freely. He checked his wires on his small recorder that would be placed in his coat pocket. He was ready to go.

He'd kept his suit jacket on all day, just to keep the vest concealed. It wasn't noticeable. Joe told Mary to stay away and take a mental health day. She would need it when she arrived the next day, after the takedown, if all went well. She knew something was coming down, just not what.

About eight p.m. Joe started to saunter down the hall. He saw Luis talking to three "students" from downstairs. He was being quite loud. He was speaking in Spanish to them, so Joe knew that these were not their everyday Albany youth pulled from the streets.

Joe had heard a while ago that Luis recruited street kids for the job placement and training service. Joe wasn't following it because he was not involved. He was now. He also heard that some of Luis's recruits were selling drugs in between classes downstairs. Jim confirmed it in his deposition. Joe was sure that Luis was using the Albany Coalition for Families as his own piggy bank. But proving it, at this time, was different. Joe had memorized what he was going to say to Luis when he confronted him. He especially wanted to know if Luis had anything to do with Ted Simmons's "accident."

It seemed like too much of a coincidence to have Luis rise to the top of the Coalition, after such a short time. Joe knew that the senior management team and the board were enamored by Luis, but this infatuation might have caused the downfall of an organization that served the poorest of the poor, and that would completely devastate such a dedicated staff. Once you had ever seen social workers performing their duties in the most adverse conditions, going in and out of the most horrible conditions, in and out of dilapidated homes that you wouldn't put your worst enemy in, you realized they were not in it for the money. In fact, many counselors and social workers were themselves abused as children, coming from a world of poverty. They were the most dedicated people that Joe had ever met.

After listening to the conversation from the hall, Joe knew these three individuals were imported from Los Angeles. Their Spanish was of Mexican dialect and had a specific accent, not unlike Mark's accent. Joe knew dialects because he had such a hard time with Jen's parents, Rose and John. He thought, at the time, they would at least be a little impressed that he spoke Spanish fluently. Being judged for having the wrong accent and dialect was too much. Joe also discovered, only a short while ago, that Luis kept his room at the Albany Express Motel, even though he'd moved to the condo up the hill on Albany Shaker Road. Joe wondered why? He'd followed him one night back to the motel after becoming more suspicious of Luis's methods and actions. Luis walked across to the bus station and met a few young Latinos. All had tattoos and looked very different from Albany youth, regardless of their ethnic background. They were getting off the bus that had just arrived from New York City. If you hung around enough on the street, especially in Miami, you could tell the difference.

Joe knew what gang members looked like. He'd taken down enough of them in his ten years in the Coast Guard. It was not profiling. He had been involved in too many takedowns and was considered an expert witness. He had been on the stand, when a few of their busts went to court. It was not really subtle. Gym bags in hand, they sauntered over to the back door of the motel, only a few yards from the bus terminal. How convenient could it get? Luis was a full service provider.

Joe knew, since he had been writing grants for two years, how hard it was to win. The odds of winning were slim. Luis made it too easy. They won too quickly, even in spite of Joe's leaving off a signature and skipping a few questions deliberately. They never lost a point, and they were once again informed that the grants submitted, the last two times, were said to be one of the top applications submitted. Luis was too smooth. Joe didn't think Luis even read any of the material submitted. He hardly ever signed anything, even after Ted's death when he became interim president of the Coalition. Joe knew he was on the right track.

After getting confirmation, or as much confirmation as he needed about Luis's tattoo, Joe was firmly convinced about what the man was doing in Albany, and what the Mexican Mafia was doing to launder money in a whole new way. When Joe saw the pictures from the reception after the wake, of Luis scratching his uncovered ankle, he knew it had to be gang related. The confirmation from Jack that it was the same *eMe*, with an orange

background, that Jack picked up from the gang tattoo database, located on the secure FBI website, was the ammunition he needed.

From the actual picture, it was very clear that Luis
never even thought twice about where he was, what he
was doing, and how it was photographed for posterity.
That coupled with the pictures of Luis walking with the
gang, who all had the obvious tattoos, from the bus station to the motel, confirmed Joe's suspicions, along with
everything else they had discovered in such a short time.
It was no longer just a bullshit observation on Joe's part,
spurred on by any thoughts of jealousy.

Now, as he stood in the hallway unseen, he heard
Luis explain to the three, in Spanish, that he had his
group meeting down at the motel, and he had to take Joe
out, that Joe was a problem.

Evidently, Luis knew about Joe's investigation at the
NCWA and he was pissed.

Damn, he found out, thought Joe. Luis had also
found out that invoices were electronically reviewed, and
he was going ballistic. He said they were to meet later to
plan out Joe's departure.

"Make sure the others don't get involved with any of
the girls in these programs," Luis told his men. "You
guys tend to think with your little heads. Don't do it, or
you won't have one to think with. Now get out of here
and do your collections. I'll see you at ten p.m. Then we
need to take care of this problem."

The three guys left Luis's office, and it was now
eight-thirty p.m. Joe had Tom Matthews, backed up by
Mark, Sean, and several FBI agents, hanging outside in
the shadows. All he had to do was press the number one
on his cell. That was the signal to rock and roll. He had
his .40 caliber S&W hidden close to his leg, toward his
back left pocket, out of sight, just in case.

This was no different than any other operation, except now he was completely alone, and in charge.

"Hi, Luis, working late?" Joe asked.

"Hi, Joe, come on in. Glad you're here. I wanted to talk to you before you go home."

Joe went to sit in front of him. He had his gun down below the seat line of the chair. Luis reached into his drawer for what looked like paperwork about the next grant. As he turned, Joe saw the gun in Luis's hand, pointing at him, and a smile on the man's face.

"Joe, Joe, Joe, thought you were smart, huh? Didn't think we could figure out that some asshole was checking out our Hispanic Management Outreach program and our program graduates? You really thought you were clever using the Troy Education Consulting Group to do your dirty work. We checked the email and found out that they had the same address as your home. We know how to do that too, you know?"

Although Mark and Jack had done the original hacking at the association in San Diego, Joe went back in to recheck social security numbers and to find out the names of the most recent graduates, just to prove that this was not a one-time deal. He knew that it would continue, if not stopped. Joe also knew that he'd screwed up. His anal-retentive nature put him in jeopardy. He promised himself that it wouldn't happen again, but he was sure it would.

Joe was nervous but focused and tried to appear even more nervous, to put Luis at ease, so he would talk. Joe was wired, had his recorder turned on, and he had his gun hidden down by his left side. And since Luis turned to get his gun, he never noticed that Joe had one. He may have been a "gangbanger want-to-be" but he really didn't have the street experience, Joe thought.

The first thing Joe would always do was to have the

suspect raise his arms. Oh, Luis was smart enough, great academic degrees, but simply being smart didn't trump experience. You never turned your back on anyone that you didn't trust. Luis simply didn't know that, or was obviously not trained enough. After ten years, Joe was well trained and ready. *Always be prepared for anything, not just what you'll think will happen.* The good nun, who taught Joe the times tables so many years ago, taught him to focus, concentrate, and be ready. He had muscle memory and could always tell when to be on high alert. Luis did not appear to have that skill. He thought his own self-importance was all he needed. He was sadly mistaken.

"Luis, I know everything," Joe said to him in Spanish. "You're going down."

Luis was still aiming the gun at him but Joe could tell he'd shocked the shit out of the man.

Luis smiled. "So you speak Spanish, wow, didn't see that coming," he said, also in Spanish. "I thought you were just another dumb fuck, like then rest of the people here. How did you know?"

"You know you could have risen to the top without all this crap, Luis," Joe said. "But, then again, since you were part of the gang, I suppose you would've never made it out alive, or even been here without them."

"You know, I wish you had been in the same fucking car with Ted, when we got rid of his ass," Luis said.

"You had Ted killed?" Joe asked.

"Of course, you moron, what the hell did you think?"

I hope you picked that up and recorded it, guys. I got it on my recorder, hopefully.

"He was a pain in the ass and I got tired of his same old questions about actually performing the work and meeting all the goals of job training," Luis said. "Jim Clark did the same thing, and he got his ass beat on, too."

Joe wanted him to keep talking for the benefit of his wired audience. "How did you do it, Luis? How did you make it look like an accident?"

"Ted had sleep-apnea, everyone knew that. He came in half the time with his eyelids half closed with an hour's sleep. I knew he was getting a C-Pap machine because he went to the sleep center to be tested. He said he was getting it the following week. How hard was it to crush up a few over-the-counter sleeping pills into his favorite Diet Pepsi? I went to a late meeting that afternoon with an opened can of Diet Pepsi with the crushed pills in it," Luis said. "He said thanks and drank the entire can. Bet he didn't think it would be his last one. I'll bet he was falling asleep on I-90 right about where I would have suspected. Rolling over six times across the median to the other side and crushing his chest was quite effective."

He smiled, still pointing the gun at Joe. "If he didn't die in the crash, my boys were already following him to make sure something happened, maybe a hit and run, what do you think, Joe?"

Man, I have seen evil in New Orleans in the middle of Katrina, but never evil like this, Joe thought. *He must have been trained by the Devil himself.*

"We were never going to train three hundred kids, for Christ sake. We would just move them in and out and send the payment to our own company. Do you think the foundations run by our own people were going to do an audit? I can't believe Ted and the board thought anyone could train these kids for high tech jobs in six months," Luis said. "Really, did you ever believe it?"

Unfortunately, Joe had really hoped that they could.

"I had the Orange Street Boys take out Jim, too."

"Wow, Luis, you really had this well planned out, didn't you?" Joe said.

"What do you think? You think we're a bunch of amateurs, for Christ sake?"

Joe certainly hoped that his guys were ready downstairs.

"I'm tired of screwing with you, Joe. It doesn't really matter what you know or think, because you won't make it to tomorrow." Luis hit a button on his phone. "Get back here now. You're going to be busy tonight."

Joe didn't need an explanation of what that meant. He didn't have time to hit the button on his cell. He simply dropped to the floor, and, as he did, Luis pulled the trigger, creasing Joe's right arm. Joe rolled to the left, like always.

No one really thought about someone being left-handed in the heat of the moment, and they really didn't expect anyone to act any differently than a right-hander. Ninety percent of the world was right-handed. They would be wrong to expect left-handers to act the same. Three of the last four presidents of the United States were left-handed. It might not be an aberration.

Luis dove over the desk ready to fire again, and Joe shot him right between the eyes with his left hand. Dumb ass never even suspected that Joe had a gun, or even once looked to his left. When he dove over the desk to the wrong side, Joe knew he had a chance. He could still, in the split second that Luis looked at him, see the look on his face. Luis had a look of total disbelief.

Joe heard the front door slam and people running up the stairs. It had to be the gangbangers coming back. The FBI crew was in the shadows and had to wait for his call, which had not yet come. Joe knew that Mark and Sean would be getting antsy. They probably heard the shots as well and were ready for action. As soon as Joe heard the noise on the stairs, he turned off the lights and went behind the open door, to the left side.

The first banger came charging through the door after saying "Luis, you okay?"

Joe shot him in the chest. The other two tried to bull
their way through with their guns blazing away. Again,
by Joe going to his left, they were surprised. He shot
them both dead. He then hit the button on his phone. He
didn't have to. His guys were already running up the
stairs, yelling, "FBI."

Joe still had eight bullets left. *Great new handgun*, he
thought. He'd hoped he could keep it, but now it became
evidence for the United States government.

"FBI," Tom Matthews yelled at the top of his lungs.
"Joe, where are you? Are you okay?"

"I'm fine," Joe shouted. He *was* fine but the adrena-
lin was still pumping through his body. He could barely
contain his emotions. As they hit the second landing, Joe
shouted, "In here, hold your fire."

Mark and Sean came in right after Tom. Joe didn't
know what they thought. Four dead people on the floor of
Luis's office. Both Mark and Sean knew what Joe could
do, and Mark had seen him in action in Miami when they
took down a few drug crews. Sean heard about it.

Tom looked at Joe in shock. " Are you okay, Joe?

"I'll live," he said. "More than I can say for these
guys. I got hit on the right arm but it looks superficial."

They had been trained that if you brought your service weapon, use it. If someone pulled a gun on you, you
shot first and asked questions later. No questions asked.
No answers required. Joe's arm hurt like hell but it was
just a scratch. He'd had worse in a few takedowns in Miami. Falling down those stairs years ago, running after
their suspects hurt a lot worse. At least he didn't get a
concussion this time. The falling down the stairs and
banging his head on the cement knocked him out completely. He was glad his back was covered this time.

However, this time, he was one hell of a lot more experienced that the first take down in his early twenties.

Joe saw the bullets coming. Luis had not.

The Albany Police car sirens were going full blast up Central Avenue then parked sideways in front of the building. Tom left two of his men in front of the building, expecting this to happen. It always did. They had their full gear on, including vests, FBI hats, and windbreakers.

Two cops got out of the first car with full riot gear. "What the hell happened?" one of them said.

"Can't tell you," said the agent. "Homeland Security operation under the Patriot Act. Please get back from the door."

The chief came next, same explanation. Then Tom came out and spoke to the police chief. "We need this bundled up quickly. It's an ongoing investigation that's going down in many other cities across the country. No news to the local paper, please," he said. "I will give you a full report tomorrow, late morning."

"Fine," said the chief.

As soon as they got down to the street, Joe called Mary. "Mary, it went down, and everyone is all right."

It was touch and go, and could have gone either way. He didn't want her to know that. He told her he would meet her tomorrow during the day. The place would be swarming with Homeland Security, FBI, and others doing a complete forensic accounting audit of the Albany Coalition for Families.

After he called Mary, Joe saw Dan standing to the side waiting for him. "Joe, are you all right?" he asked.

"Yes, Dan, I'm fine, just a scratch," Joe said.

"Do you have enough on the tape to use in court, Joe?" Dan asked.

Joe handed Dan his own recorder. "We won't be needing the tape for Luis. He's far past the tape session.

Get it back to me tomorrow. You can sue just about everyone over your father's murder, if you want. We have all the evidence."

"What do you mean, Joe?" Dan asked.

"Luis and his three gangbanger friends are all dead. I killed all four of them upstairs."

Dan looked at Joe a whole lot differently than he ever did before. "Did he say anything about my father's murder?" he asked.

"He confessed to spiking your father's Diet Pepsi with sleeping pills, knowing that, with the sleep apnea, it could be fatal. Luis also said, if he didn't go off the road, he was being followed by his men, and they would have pulled a hit and run anyway. Having your father fall asleep in the bad weather made their day," Joe said. "They paid for it though, Dan. I told you they would. I know that there is little satisfaction in knowing your father's murderer is dead. I only hope that you and your family can move past this and know that Ted is watching over you at all times. I truly believe that, Dan."

"Joe, you have no idea how appreciative my family and I are having you as our friend. I better leave now and go see my mother and sister and give them the news. I know they will be in shock, but knowing that you got Luis to confess, and on tape, will mean a lot to them. Thanks again, Joe. Go get your arm checked out, please."

"Thanks Dan. I will," Joe said.

The Albany Police were given the task of rounding up the local Orange Street Boys, who were Coalition "students." Joe gave them their names and they shook their heads. Jim had given Joe the names after he just called him and let him know that they were safe and that Luis was dead. The Albany Police knew a lot of them, where they lived, and had full files on them.

"Drugs and money laundering in one of our own

non-profits? Great. The mayor's going to love hearing about this," one officer said.

"Would you rather hear about it when your entire city was organized as a chapter of the Mexican Mafia?" Joe said. *I don't think it has fully sunk in ye*t. This was one of the most brilliant, well-planned operations that the FBI had ever seen from a gang that was completely run from prison.

໙໓໙

After going to Albany Med for his wounded right arm, Joe had to spend the rest of the night writing up all the documentation, and his version of the take down of Luis Hernandez, interim president of the Albany Coalition for Families, and three gangbangers, all killed within three minutes of each other. Of course, Joe's version was the only version, since Luis and the gangbangers couldn't give theirs. The FBI would back Joe all the way.

Mark and Tom pulled up discretely in their un-marked FBI car at the Albany Medical Center emergency room door. Mark shook his head. "Why do you even have an unmarked FBI cars?" he asked Tom. "They're so ob-vious, you might as well have a sign on the side door that says, 'Do not touch, FBI inside.'"

Tom only snorted.

The nurse looked at them as they came rushing through the emergency room side door. Christ, they were lucky to even find the emergency room with all the con-struction going on at Albany Med. It had taken over sev-eral square blocks in the last ten years, making it a city unto itself. The emergency room exit had been moved five times, in five years. Tom flashed his credentials and asked to speak to the doctor in charge of the emergency room. The doctor came out, and Joe was taken into a side room. The doctor was asked to look at his arm, now. He did. It wasn't bad. He put in three stitches, cleaned it, and put a cover over the wound, securing it tightly. He said it would start throbbing soon, and gave Joe some pills to relieve the pain and a prescription for antibiotics to prevent infection.

Tom turned to the staff. "Send the bill to my office in the Federal Building in Albany. We have to leave now and that includes, Joe."

All of this was moving so quickly that Joe didn't have time to think about it. It was now time for his official write-up to the FBI. He had better write it down quickly before the medicine started to take effect. He was glad that the FBI and his boys were right behind him all the way. *Can you imagine trying to explain shooting the interim president of a local non-profit, and three other young men from Albany? Thank God, they had the tats from the Mexican Mafia, even if they were all covered up by their long-sleeved shirts and high collars.*

Luis had a very discrete tattoo on the inside of his left ankle, same tattoo as the gangbangers but miniature in size. It certainly proved that they were together. Who said bigger was better? Evidently, these new age gangbangers in charge wanted unnoticeably smaller identification with their affiliation. No one would have ever guessed about Luis's dual identity—Ivy-league MBA/gangbanger from California.

Joe was sure it would hit him soon. He was also sure that the board of directors would be changed. A full audit would be needed to determine the extent of the fraud, laundering operation, and drug sales operation, all from a twelve million dollar non-profit—now including an additional three million after Ettinger just got announced—operation. All in less than a year. Multiply that by the other nine operations, the foundations, the NCWA in San

Diego, and all the supposed legal for-profit businesses, and it added up to quite a tidy sum. Tomorrow should be even more interesting as the hits took place on each and every operation in the conspiracy. Joe guessed the operation would be called the "Mexican Mafia Conspiracy." He still thought of it as "Montezuma's Revenge."

CHAPTER 32

The next afternoon, after Joe slept for ten hours—Mark too—they went back to the Coalition office. It looked like Grand Central Station. Boxes were being packed, FBI agents in their hats and windbreakers were moving about. Last night, Joe told Tom that, as soon as Mary came in, he wanted her fully protected and for her to be part of the discovery operation. Their controller, Doug Jacobs, didn't seem to want to come in the front door. As soon as he started to come in, he turned around and left. He had a lot of explaining to do. Why had he been pushed around and why did he let Luis sign off on every invoice without checking to see if the work was done, or even if it was legitimate? He was as enamored and enthralled as all the rest of the senior management team. There was a lot of egg on a lot of faces today.

As the Coalition's regular employees came into the building, they were led into the large conference area, and each one, individually, was grilled about what they knew, what they suspected, and how it all came about. Everyone, but Mary and Joe. *God was good.* Mary was appointed by Homeland Security as the Coalition's director of finance, and she would be quite busy for some time. Joe had assured her that when it was over, she could name her own ticket with the feds or with any organization she wanted, with the full backing of the United States Government. It might take close to a year. She could restart the Coalition as well. It didn't change the need in Albany. In fact, these assholes took food out of the mouths of the most needy. The need had not gone away. Now, with the Coalition having to close down for the audit, the need would only increase.

Joe knew that he was done at the Coalition. You really couldn't shoot the interim president and a few of his friends and expect to continue there. He learned at RPI that, in corporate takeover situations, the agent of change could never manage the business on an every-day basis after the change had taken place. It just didn't work that way. Joe could have guessed that without an MBA or even a GED. The calls started coming in—Tyler, Texas, done; Bethlehem, Pennsylvania, done; Racine, Wisconsin, broke down the front door; Gary, Indiana, waiting for them at seven-thirty a.m. this morning; Boca Raton, done. They were waiting at the front doors in Oregon and Washington, running three hours behind Albany. Gilbert, Arizona, starting in one hour; Hartford, Connecticut, done.

All the foundations went the same way. Mike was at the front door with his Coast Guard commander and three FBI agents to take down the two Mexican Mafia graduates, who were ensuring that the next group of Los Angeles high school students would be moved right along at the command of the Mexican Mafia heads. Those interns would also be rounded up along with the high school officials who were turned in by the new kids who didn't want to get in trouble.

The house of cards fell quickly. The nice thing was that the founders of the conspiracy were already in jail. Joe was sure that, by the end of the day, Jorge Hernandez and his lower-ranking Mafia officers would be getting their punishment.

Joe would have loved to see the faces of the attorneys and accountants as they showed up for work in their two thousand dollar suits, in their very fashionable office suites, with their coffee and Danish waiting for them, served by their very shapely assistants. Never in their wildest imaginations did they ever dream that they would be considered terrorists under the Patriot Act. Being on the "No Fly" list would probably really screw up their vacation plans. Joe started to chuckle. *Well, Mr. Traynor, I think you have caused enough trouble for today.*

ഏഇഏ

Later that day, Jorge was escorted from his cell to the warden's office at the Duel Vocational Institute in Tracy, California. He was chained by the arms and legs and the chains were fully secured with a very thick padlock. He was placed in an adjacent room to the left of the warden's office and fastened to both the table and the floor. Two correction officers stood on both sides of Jorge as the warden came in to the room with two other individuals. Warden James Washington barely fit through the door at six foot, six inches tall and 275 pounds. He was an intimidating personality and the first African American warden at the Tracy facility.

"Mr. Hernandez, the reason you were brought in to this room today was to unfortunately tell you that your son, Luis, was killed last night in Albany, New York." The warden did not say he was sorry for Jorge's loss because he wasn't, and it was not in his character to lie.

"Luis is dead? How is that possible?" Jorge said.

"Well, I believe you know why he was in Albany, Mr. Hernandez," Warden Washington said. "He was killed in a shootout with three of his Mexican Mafia friends at the Albany Coalition for Families."

Jorge hesitated. "I don't know anything about that."

"No problem, Jorge, but your attorney now says differently."

"What do you mean?" he asked.

"Mr. Hernandez, you are now being released from this State of California facility and transferred to the custody of these two gentlemen standing beside me," the warden said.

"Who are they?" Jorge asked.

"Doesn't matter who they are, Jorge. You're going with them."

The two gentlemen stepped forward "Mr. Hernandez you are being released to our custody under the United States Patriot Act for domestic terrorism," the senior agent said.

"Domestic terrorism? What the hell is that?" Jorge inquired. "I want my lawyer now. It is my right under the Constitution of the United States. I want my attorney, Frank Ramone, right now. I know my rights."

"You *did* have rights, Jorge," the warden said. "You don't anymore."

"I don't believe that will be happening, Mr. Hernandez," the agent said. "No attorney. As a matter of fact, the Patriot Act doesn't even allow you to have an attorney and, where you will be going, you really won't need one." He smiled. "In fact, I think Frank Ramone will be joining you under this rendition program, Mr. Hernandez. I think you may like Romania. It's not as muggy as Los Angeles. In fact, you may be joining your son Luis in a very short time, if you don't fully cooperate with us."

"Jorge, you are now officially in the hands of the CIA, and so is your attorney," Warden Washington said. "The rest of your Mexican Mafia gang will go right after you, one by one, until the FBI knows everything about your operation and then some. All your assets have already been confiscated. Your attorney was very helpful in that matter. Your progeny has been cut off at the knees. There will be no retaliation on those who brought you down, Jorge, because there will be none of you at the top left to order anything. You are officially excused, Mr. Hernandez, and may you rot in hell," the warden said. "Say hello to your son for me when you see him again. Take him, gentlemen. He is all yours. Goodbye, Jorge."

EPILOGUE

"Christ, Mark, I really can't believe all this just came down," Joe said.

"Well, what the hell did you expect? You got in their face, you wouldn't back down, and they shot at you and almost blew you away."

"What's your point?" Joe said.

"It was goddamned heroic and really stupid at the same time," Mark said. "And, you were quite annoying to all your friends as well. Oh, I'm sorry, I guess I am your only friend. Right, Sean?"

"He isn't my friend," Sean said, smiling from ear to ear. "And you have the balls to tell me I have a line of Irish bullshit? Wow, just wow."

"I told the guys that I got into writing grants to be independent, and eventually try to write a book. Do you think I have enough to write about?"

"What the hell would you call it?" Mark asked.

"Well, I worked for a non-profit, up to a day ago," Joe said.

"Who the hell would think that would be exciting?" Sean said.

"Is killing your interim president and several gang-banger associates in your job description?" Mark said.

"No," Joe said. "But, as my father said, 'The only things in life you can be sure of are death and taxes.'"

"No," Mark said. "In this case you can only be assured of death and no taxes, being a non-profit and all." He chuckled. "Pretty clever, huh?"

"Well, you got the death part right. I really don't know if they are going to keep their non-profit status with all that laundered drug money," Joe said. "What do you report that as on this year's 990 federal form, 'miscellaneous income'?"

"I really don't know," Mark said. "You're the math genius. Did you keep enough for a few beers for your friends?" He smiled and swore at Joe in Spanglish. "Let's get the hell out of here!"

"I second that motion," Sean said.

Mark went back to Miami and back to his family and the Coast Guard. Sean reported back to New London, ending his "shore leave." Mark, at age forty, had seven years to go and then out. Joe really hoped that, for his sake, he made it.

Joe left the Albany Coalition for Families, officially handing in his resignation to Mary, shortly after his mini-vacation to Fort Lauderdale. This time, it was relaxing. While he was there, he called Jen one last time, and she apologized to him for her behavior the last time he was there. He accepted her apology. She said she was really sorry. Evidently, she was in total shock in seeing him at her front door. She said she responded badly but didn't expect him to just say "Okay," turn around, and walk away, which he did.

Joe went to visit Jen, one last time. The visit was pleasant. She once again apologized and he accepted and gave her a kiss on the cheek. They went to lunch, reminisced about the good times only. He told her about Mary and his feelings about her. He also told Jen that he would never forget her and he was really sorry that it didn't work out. She said she should have never let her parents interfere in her life, and it was a lesson learned. It was a very sore point in her ongoing relationship with both of her parents.

"If I ever decide to develop another relationship, they are to keep their feelings to themselves or they will be out in the cold."

For Joe it was a day late and a dollar short. But he felt grateful for this opportunity to close the door and open a new chapter in his life.

He got back to Albany. He took the late flight and got to the Albany Airport at eleven p.m., got to his car, and headed home. The next morning, he walked around the side of his building to the front door, of the Troy Education Consulting Group office.

Johnathon Mills greeted him at the door. "Hi, Joe, how the hell are you? Been reading quite a bit about your little adventure in Albany."

"Yes, well it's over. I really can't go back. A lot will be coming down in the very near future and I will expect to be testifying," he said.

"Joe, I know this might be premature, but could you use a full time job? We can match what you were making with benefits and keep the same deal for the apartment," he said. "We really like you. We want you here, and we know you will work as hard for us as you did for the Coalition."

"Can I take time to think about it?' Joe asked. He then smiled. "Okay, that's enough time. I'll take it. Thank you."

⋅⋅⋅

After everything went down and he got back from

Miami—and now that he seemed to have a job again—Joe was really curious about the entire conspiracy started by the Mexican Mafia. He started to review everything in his own mind, start to finish. It started through their attorneys, and then through Luis, and his other cohorts, who worked at the various non-profits and foundations throughout the country.

Joe called Dan Simmons at around eleven a.m., after speaking to Johnathon, and accepting the new job. Dan said he would be right over to his place.

They both sat down that day so they would understand, as best they could, what they were dealing with in this entire scheme. They would both be testifying about their own personal circumstances. Dan would also be there as Joe's personal attorney, if anything blew up in his face. They didn't believe that would happen. But now was the time to talk about it, not while testifying. They went online to see specifically what statutes had been violated, themselves included, not that it mattered since this would be settled under the Patriot Act anyway. They both just wanted to know for future references.

They looked up "criminal conspiracy."

Joe read to Dan, "'A criminal conspiracy takes place when two or more people get together and plan to commit a crime and then take some action toward carrying out that plan. The action taken does not have to be a crime, in itself, to further the conspiracy.'"

Well, they guess they proved that.

Dan concurred.

"According to the website," Joe said, "the crime of conspiracy could be charged whether or not the crime was ever actually carried out. Also, in some jurisdictions, no action toward carrying out the crime had to be proven for a conspiracy to exist. It went on further to state as an example 'if two people planned to rob a bank and they went out to buy ski masks to wear during the robbery, they could be charged with conspiracy to commit bank robbery, even if they never actually robbed the bank or even attempted to rob the bank. Buying ski masks was not a crime, but it furthered the conspiracy to commit a crime.'"

Luis and his boys didn't have ski masks but they did have a dead president of the Coalition, Joe thought. He was sure Dan thought the same thing.

It further stated that, in most states, persons who helped plan the crime, but did not participate in the actual criminal act, could also be given the same punishment as the person who carried out the crime itself. The person who committed the crime could be charged with both the crime and conspiracy to commit the crime.

Joe and Dan went on to look for other criminal activities and found that the process behind "money laundering" was fairly simple in practice.

"A criminal makes money from some illegal activity, whether it's extortion, gambling, drugs or other illegal activity," Dan said. "That money is subsequently transferred to a bank, often under false pretenses. Once in the bank, there are a number of different possibilities. The money may be transferred again and again through a series of banks, often to offshore banks in countries with lax regulations, or to accounts held by different entities—but with connections to the criminals. Payments may be made to phony businesses or even actual businesses that act as fronts for the criminal organization. Once the money has been through a number of those steps, it becomes very difficult to trace it back to the original crime, and it can then be spent without fear of prosecution.

"In this case involving all the non-profits taken down, the money-laundering scheme also included out-and-out "fraud" by securing funds from a foundation un-

der false pretenses by a legal 501C3 non-profit organization and then paid fraudulent invoices to vendors for
work not performed. This is actually contract fraud. The
site stated that a contract was a legally binding document
that described the specific details of a mutual agreement
made between two or more parties. Contract fraud occurs
when at least one party intentionally misrepresents the
terms listed in the contract, inflicting damage on the other
party," Dan continued. "Misrepresentation occurs when a
statement is presented as fact when it is actually false. In
order for this to be considered fraud, the guilty party has
to know the statement is indeed false and the statement
must qualify as a substantial fact that creates damages to
the other party. Luis knew that the original applications to
the foundations were untrue and that the work would
never performed as stated in the application."

They both read that there was also contract fraud and
misrepresentation by the vendors that stated that work
would be done, under contract, with no intention of doing
any work as subscribed under the contract. The entire
"fraud" from beginning to end was wrapped around a
money-laundering scheme where the Mexican Mafia used
their illegally gotten gains to start these supposedly legitimate vendor businesses. Those vendors were, in fact,
fronts for the Mexican Mafia that were incorporated and
started for the sole intention of invoicing specific non-
profits for work never to be performed. The Mexican Mafia's original illegal funds were laundered into these supposed "legitimate' businesses that were supposed to train
and educate at-risk young adults for jobs that did not exist.

After they completed their research, Joe sent an
email to Mark, Tom Matthews at the FBI in Albany, to
Paul Philips in Miami—as if the FBI didn't know, but Joe
wanted them to know that he also knew what they were

dealing with—and to Mike, Sean, Tom Jones, and Jack in Virginia. They all knew what went down, but in summary on paper, it looked a hell of a lot trickier to prove. Thank God, they didn't have to prove anything else. The Mexican Mafia criminal conspiracy was officially over. Dan and Joe went to lunch. A liquid lunch proved most worthy as their reward.

While at lunch, Joe asked Dan, "Would you be interested in taking over your father's position as president at the Albany Coalition for Families?"

"You know, Joe, I never really thought about taking over the Coalition until right now," Dan said.

"Well, I couldn't think of anyone better," Joe smiled. "You are young, but you aren't crooked."

Dan laughed. "Thanks for the vote of confidence."

"No seriously, Dan, I think you would do a remarkable job. You are smart, an attorney, and especially, you could do this to support your father's legacy," Joe said. "I can't stay under the circumstances, but I can recommend to the attorney general's office that you would be my first choice. However, you need a new board of directors, and you obviously need to replace Doug Jacobs as controller. He was completely derelict in his duties as controller and, when the crap hit the fan, he turned around and left through the front door instead of staying and helping. I will help you out when you need grants done. I will do the proposals through Troy Education and Johnathon Mills, and I don't think you would be billed much more than if I was full time. I can't really testify against the previous staff and then go work at the Coalition on a daily basis. If I were you, if you got offered and accepted the position, I would also appoint Mary Lynch as your new controller. She is a certified public accountant, a good friend to you and your family, and a tireless watchdog. Otherwise, I'm afraid she will be made an offer by the

FBI's financial division here in Albany. What do you think?"

"Let me think about it," Dan said.

He really didn't have much to lose. The pay would be equivalent to what he was making at his law firm. The work he would be doing at the Coalition would be so much more rewarding. He was on the partnership track at his firm, but quite frankly, he was bored, and he could slide right into his father's position, and bring in the law firm to clean up all the legal issues.

They would be thrilled and he would only be down the street. He could work for a few years straightening out the organization and find the right fit for good employees who would be much more cautious about their non-profit status and positions. The board of directors, at the end of this misadventure, didn't have a clue and ran the Coalition as if it was their private club.

"I know my father fell in to a trap of complacency, and, quite frankly, I do blame him for bringing in Luis and not standing up to the board after he found that he didn't like Luis's attitude and pushiness," Dan said. "You know, I might just like to do this. I'll talk to my mother and my girlfriend, and I will let you know as soon as possible."

"Great, Dan," Joe said.

They parted ways. He went to his office for a few goodbyes, and then he walked back to his car after cleaning out his desk at the Coalition. He headed home. *Maybe I'll stop for a few beers at McGuire's.* All the staff at the Coalition felt terrible the way everything ended but they were thrilled that the Albany Coalition for Families would continue. Immediately after the takedown, all the Coalition bank accounts were separated to isolate grant funds from normal operations, which were needed to continue to serve the poor on a daily basis. Their lives still went on and they still needed the Coalition's assistance. The Career Center closed temporarily so that it could be reviewed as to what could continue and what was nothing but smoke and mirrors.

When all was said and done, it really was a great idea to train those young adults who had little hope for jobs that paid more than minimum wage. Everyone believed that supporting those who needed their help began with the proper education, training, mentoring, and certifications so they didn't continue on that downward spiral to poverty that had plagued their families for so long. Joe knew that Dan could straighten out the program in a heartbeat and, with his political pull in the capitol, he might be able to get funding to continue the programs that were never started, but should have been.

Joe headed home with his stuff on the back seat of his car. He stopped and saw Johnathon Mills at his office. "Could I start tomorrow?"

"Certainly. The staff is looking forward to you working full time, here. By the way," Johnathon said. "Rookie, from now on, you make the coffee every morning."

Mary came over after work and stayed the night. Joe had made his peace with Jen on his last trip. It ended well, and he had moved on. Mary wanted the same things that he did, and quite frankly, he thought that Mary and he might be a better match. Joe thought he might be in love with her. There was a knock on the door.

"Just a minute," he said.

Joe opened the door as far as the chain would allow and two older men were standing at the door. "Can I help you," Joe said.

"Yes, you can, if you are Joe Traynor," the older man said.

"I am," Joe said.

"My name is John Jefferson and this is Fred Tucker.

We are agents with the FBI. May we come in?" They showed him their identification.

He opened the door and showed them to the kitchen table. Mary came out and he introduced her to the two agents.

"Joe, we would like to discuss something with you in private," Agent Jefferson said.

"Mary, can you excuse us for a few minutes," Joe asked.

"Sure," she said, and moved into the bedroom, closed the door, and turned on the television.

"Joe, your investigation and bringing about the downfall of one of the most amazing laundering schemes in history has not gone unnoticed," said Agent Jefferson. "We have been asked by the director of the FBI and the attorney general of the United States to come and meet with you to see if you would help us with a few situations for which we know you are more than qualified," he said. "We know you quit the Albany Coalition for Families and went to Miami for a short time."

You were watching me?" Joe asked.

"In a way. Nothing to invade your privacy. We checked with the Coast Guard and we know that you and your *Coastie* friends were closer than brothers and that's a good thing. We know that you and Mark are insepara-ble. Can you ask Mary to come back in to the room, we have something to present to you," Agent Jefferson said.

Agent Tucker concurred.

"Mary, can you come in here for a second?" Joe asked.

"Sure," she said.

"We are also here on behalf of the President of the United States, on behalf of the Coast Guard, and on be-half of the United States of America," Agent Jefferson said. "Warrant Officer Traynor, we would like to present to you the Coast Guard Commendation Medal with a Ribbon. It is the highest award issued for heroism, not involving combat with an enemy outside the country, by the United States Coast Guard. Joe, congratulations, it is well deserved."

"Wow, thank you very much, I don't know what to say," Joe said. "Mary, look at this. Wow," he said again.

She kissed him and told him how proud she was of him. The agents also said that they had to give it to him in a private ceremony because they wanted him to continue in the service as a special agent on an as-needed basis, and it was still considered as a clandestine operation and could not be revealed. A written acknowledgement would follow by the president of the United States.

"By the way, Joe," Agent Tucker said, "You don't have to worry about any retaliation from the Mexican Mafia."

"How so?" Joe said.

"Luis's father, Jorge Hernandez, was taken by two CIA officers from the Duel Vocational Institute in Tracy, California, and will be under rendition under the Patriot Act for domestic violence. If he cooperates, just as his attorney, Frank Ramone, did, he will be enjoying a very long vacation as an ex-patriot, out of the country. If not, he will be joining his son, Luis, sooner than he expected," he said. "All the others responsible for this will be going down one by one until the entire Mexican Mafia is closed down. Hopefully, it won't happen again, because of you and your friends, Joe. Thank you. We also know how much you like discipline and orders," he said, laughing. "We would like Mark to join you as well on loan from the Coast Guard whenever a problem comes up, so he can keep his years toward retirement," he stated. "He needs seven more years, right?"

"How the hell do you know that?" Joe asked.

"We're the FBI, you know?" both agents said at the same time

Joe laughed. "Yeah, yeah, big deal. Can you at least let me sleep on it? I just took a job at the Troy Education Consulting Group out front. I'm starting tomorrow. I need the money."

"You know, if you don't mind, we can talk to them and pay your salary if they would allow it. It certainly would be a good cover." He laughed. "You know about good covers, don't you?"

"Fine, I'll let you know after I talk to Mary," Joe said.

"I'm standing right here, you know?" she said, smiling.

"Yes, I know I can't tell her everything. Right, Mary? But, if I can't tell her anything, it won't be happening." She smiled at that. "Good night, gentlemen," Joe said and closed and chained the door.

You never knew what lurked around the corner. It was going to be a long night talking to Mary.

The phone rang. *Christ who the hell is calling now?* he thought.

"Is this Joe Traynor?" the voice asked.

"Yes. May I ask who's calling," he said.

"Yes, Mr. Traynor, this is Samaritan Hospital Emergency Room calling," the voice said. "Is your father John Traynor, residing at 527 Fifth Avenue in Troy, telephone number 237-0034?"

"Yes," he said, "that's my father."

"Mr. Traynor, your father was just brought into the emergency room at Samaritan. He hit nine-one-one and the police went to his house. They had to break down the door and found him unconscious on the floor. It looked like a home invasion."

"I'm on my way," Joe said. *Christ when will it stop,*

ever? "Mary, I've got an emergency, do you want to go with me?"

"What happened?" she asked.

"I'll explain it to you in the car. My father is hurt. He's in the hospital unconscious. I'll call my brother when I get there." *I wonder where the hell he is? He's never around when he's needed. He's probably at some bar as usual. It's never ending, you know?*

The End

About the Author

Daniel J. Barrett was born in Rutland, Vermont and has lived his entire life in Troy, New York, ten miles north of Albany. He is a graduate of both Siena College in Loudonville, NY, with a BS in Finance, and Rensselaer Polytechnic Institute in Troy, NY, with an MBA in Management. He has had a varied career, first as a commercial banker, then as the chief accountant and manager of financial and strategic planning for a large division of a major international corporation. He has extensive international experience, traveling worldwide.

Currently, he serves as a grant writing and development and strategic planning consultant for a major non-profit organization in the Capital Region of New York State. Barrett continues to live in Troy and has been married to his wife, Sandy, for 47 years. They have three children, Sean, Eileen, and Ryan, and four grandchildren.

An avid reader, and inspired by numerous authors, Barrett has read over 2,100 books in the last eight years in preparation to write his Conch Town series.